Smith's
MONTHLY

Every Month Original
Novels, Stories, and Articles

USA Today Bestselling Writer
Dean Wesley Smith

TABLE OF CONTENTS

SHORT STORIES

FULL NOVEL

SERIAL STORIES

NONFICTION

POEMS

SMITH'S MONTHLY ISSUE #6

Introduction:
The Origin of a Novel

IN A LAND LONG AGO and far, far away (actually right here in this house, but about ten years ago), I wrote a novel.

If I stop and think about it, in the twenty years I have lived in this house, I wrote a lot of novels here. Maybe over a hundred. More than likely over a hundred, now that I really stop and think about it.

I think I need a nap.

So back to the one novel I wrote ten years ago. After I finished it, the novel took on a sort of mythology all its own. The title of the novel was *Dead Money*.

I had gotten tired of writing media books (*Star Trek, Men in Black, Spider-Man,* you know… all those tough jobs) and I wanted to get back to writing more of my own work. So I had written a few fun books just for me, such as *The Slots of Saturn: A Poker Boy Novel.* (I never

published that either. I just went over it and then wrote a sequel, so *The Slots of Saturn* will be in next month's issue.)

But back then I had an agent and I told her about the Poker Boy novel and she ignored me and asked me why I didn't just write a major poker thriller. (She didn't want to market a poker puzzle mystery novel it seemed. I should have fired her right there in hindsight.)

So I wrote the political poker thriller she suggested.

Through a lot of painful lessons, and after a full year and three agents who thought they could sell *Dead Money* for a lot of money, the book was sent out to publishing houses by agent #3, a top thriller agent.

A quick lesson in traditional publishing: In a major publishing house, the editors are the low person in the corporate ladder. But since it is a corporate structure, all vice-presidents and publishers had worked up from editors through the

Thanks for the Support

Dean Wesley Smith

3

corporate ranks. They all still bought books and approved what the editors wanted to buy.

They could write big checks.

So *Dead Money* went directly to eight top vice-presidents of companies that published thrillers.

And to a person, they loved the book. Glowing letters. Two of them saying the book kept them up all night reading.

And to a person they declined to publish it because, as they all said in one way or another, poker didn't sell. At least at the numbers we were asking for in money.

So disgusted at the stupidity of the entire publishing industry, I tossed the book into a file cabinet and went and played professional poker.

Slowly, over the next year or so, I came back to writing, but mostly I was done with novels. I was writing short stories until the indie publishing movement came about.

Then one fine day, Kris and the publisher of WMG Publishing decided that the mythological *Dead Money* needed to finally see print. They asked me and I wanted nothing to do with it, but said I didn't care.

The next thing I knew, *Dead Money* came out in a beautiful trade paper and electronic edition last fall. (You can buy copies at any of your favorite bookstores and booksellers. See the ad on the next page. The ad below is for short stories associated with *Dead Money* and *Kill Game*.)

I'm very happy *Dead Money* is finally out and readers are getting a chance to prove those vice-presidents wrong.

DEAD MONEY could be the start of a new thriller genre— the political poker thriller.

—Sheldon McArthur,
former owner of
Mysterious Books in Los Angeles

Available Now
from all your favorite booksellers in trade paper and electronic editions.

So why am I saying all this? Well, back when I wrote *Dead Money*, at one point in the book I had this nifty group of retired Las Vegas detectives. They solved cold cases and played poker together. I called them the Cold Poker Gang.

It became clear that for a thriller, the Cold Poker Gang was going to slow things down, so I cut them out. After all, they are retired detectives who don't move at a thriller pace.

But one of the detectives had a daughter who became a major character in *Dead Money*.

For a decade, I kept thinking about the Cold Poker Gang sitting down there in Las Vegas playing cards and solving cold cases.

So finally, in January of this year, I sat down and wrote their first novel.

The full novel is in this issue and it's called *Kill Game: A Cold Poker Gang Novel*.

I'm really happy with how it turned out and you meet the main character of *Dead Money* in passing at one point. So the books are tied together with more than just Las Vegas.

But *Dead Money* is a political thriller. *Kill Game* is a twisted puzzle mystery.

I hope you enjoy the puzzle and the read.

And thanks once again for supporting this crazy project. I'm having a blast.

Dean Wesley Smith
February 6th, 2014,
Lincoln City, Oregon

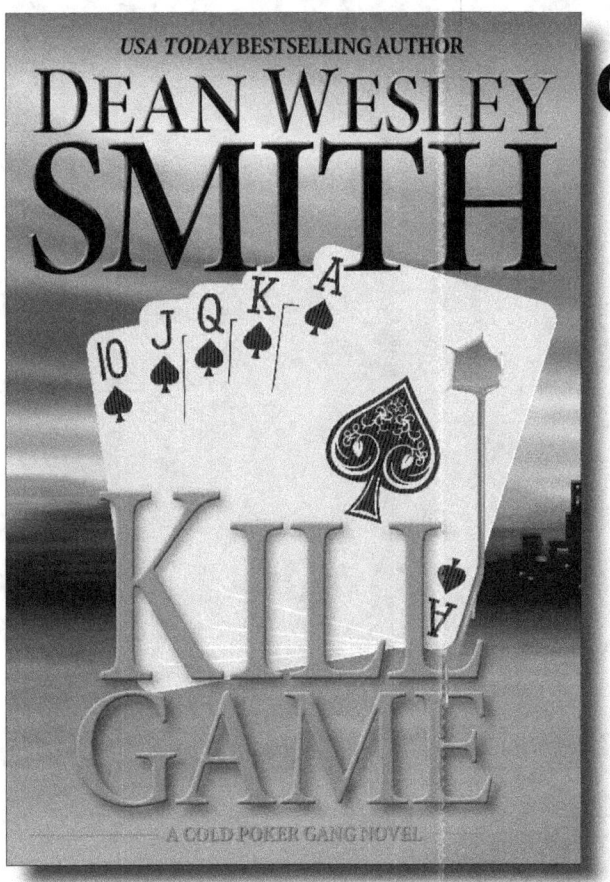

COMING IN MAY
from all your favorite booksellers
in trade paper and electronic editions.

Also in this issue!!!

**FROM THE
SAME WORLD AS**

USA Today *bestselling writer, Dean Wesley Smith, returns once again to his most popular series, Poker Boy.*

This time Poker Boy awakes to a blood-curdling scream that only he hears. Some of his team think the scream a sign he faces death.

But Poker Boy plays professional poker. He faced worse over a no-limit poker game numbers of times.

A funny and touching story of redemption and cold feet.

YOU FORGIVE THE NIGHT'S SCREAM
A Poker Boy Story

ONE

I WOKE WITH THE SOUND of a woman's scream echoing in my head.

High-pitched.

Full of terror.

I sat bolt upright in bed.

My heart pounded like it wanted to get out of my chest and run for the closet and every Poker Boy superpower sense I had was amped up to full power.

Beside me, my girlfriend and sidekick, Patty Ledgerwood, aka Front Desk Girl, lay sleeping soundly, her wonderful long brown hair like a shadow over her pillow in the dim light coming from cracks around the side of the drapes.

Outside, the city of Las Vegas never slept and certainly never turned off its lights. The strip was only a few blocks from Patty's apartment building and my invisible office floated just to the west of her apartment and directly over the MGM Grand Hotel and Casino complex.

I held my breath, waiting for another scream, trying to listen over the pounding of my heart.

Nothing.

A little noise from a truck on the street below Patty's apartment. Then a couple quick beeps as it backed up.

Nothing else.

Yet every danger Poker Boy sense I had was shouting, making me want to get out of there.

That scream had been close, as if it was inside this very apartment. Yet Patty was still sound asleep.

Something was very wrong.

Very wrong.

I've had bad dreams before, but when that scream let go, I have no memory of actually being in a dream.

The scream was real. Outside of my possible dream.

At least real in one fashion or another.

I gently touched Patty's shoulder.

She stirred and rolled to look up at me. "What —"

I put my finger to my lips and shook my head. Then I eased out of bed. I was wearing sweat pants and nothing else. I slipped on my thin brown slippers.

Patty came awake at once, saying nothing and moving silently out of the other side of the bed, slipping on her white bathrobe over her nightgown and her slippers as well.

I stood near the door to the bedroom that led out into the living room, listening for any noise coming from either the living room or kitchen area.

Silently, Patty came over and touched my arm, using her powers to calm me down some. The pounding of my racing heart subsided and I mouthed the word, "Thanks." One of her superpowers was the ability to keep people calm and focused.

I loved it in stressful situations when we worked together. We had discovered that as a team we were far stronger together than apart.

Plus I was head-over-my-slippers in love with her.

She pointed to her ear and shook her head, meaning she was hearing nothing.

I wasn't either, so silently I went out into the living room.

And as I walked ten steps, the temperature of the room dropped a good thirty degrees until suddenly I could see my breath in the dim light.

Patty grabbed my arm and pulled me back into the bedroom, a panicked look on her face.

I'm glad she did. I would need a lot more clothes to go back into that living room.

"Out of time," she whispered and I did, slipping us between instants of time. It felt like I stopped time when I did that, but in reality, time never stopped. I just moved me and Patty inside an instant of time.

Normally, in a busy casino or outside, I could tell instantly when I did that, but in the silent and dark apartment, nothing seemed to change.

"You know what caused that chill?" I asked, shivering as I tried to warm up a little. All my senses were still screaming that there was danger close by and the memory of that scream seemed to echo in my mind.

I moved over and grabbed a sweatshirt that said "The Golden Nugget Poker Room" and pulled it over my head, easing the chill some.

"Did you hear something?" Patty asked.

I nodded. "A woman's scream. That's what woke me up."

"Oh, no," she said.

Even in the dim light I could tell her face went white.

I glanced up at the ceiling. "Stan. Help!"

Patty nodded and a moment later Stan appeared.

The God of Poker had on what he always seemed to have on. Tan slacks, button down sweater, and loafers. In all the years I had worked for him, I had seldom caught him out of that outfit, day or night.

"Wow," he said, instantly spinning around, looking for the danger. I could feel him strengthen the time bubble and put a shield around us, which helped my screaming warning senses some.

"What is causing that?" he asked.

I shrugged, since I honestly had no idea.

"He heard a scream," Patty said. "In his sleep."

"Oh, shit!" Stan said and instantly vanished, leaving the screen and the stronger time bubble.

I looked at Patty who clearly wasn't in the mood for any of my one-line jokes, so I wisely said nothing. Not a skill I often had, but at the moment with every warning sense I had still going off, it seemed prudent.

Besides, the way they were acting was starting to scare me to death.

The longest five seconds later, Laverne, Lady Luck herself, appeared in our bedroom with Stan and Ben beside her.

Lady Luck didn't have on her normal power business suit, but instead wore a pair of jeans and an old sweatshirt. She looked downright normal for one of the most powerful beings in all the universe.

Ben was a god in the book world that was a member of our team. He looked like a little old librarian and had a perfect memory of everything he had ever read and the history of all the gods.

Lady Luck instantly strengthened the shields around them even more and the sense of warning and fear again decreased but didn't vanish by any means.

"Who heard the scream?" Lady Luck asked.

I sort of half raised my hand.

"Damn it," she said.

Now when Lady Luck swears, you know things can't be good. And I wasn't sure if I wanted to know just how bad things actually were, since all the bad seemed to be focused at me.

TWO

PATTY HELD ONTO MY ARM, keeping me as calm as her superpower could manage. But I was feeling anything but calm.

"So what's out there in that cold?" I asked.

"A banshee," Lady Luck said.

Ben nodded, confirming what Lady Luck said but not adding to it.

I almost said that I thought those were myths, but then realized who I was and who was standing around me. I just hadn't been in this superhero business long enough to know what was a myth and what actually had some reality attached to it.

"So tell me exactly what you are worried about," I said.

"The banshee is a fairy that is known to mourn the coming loss of a life," Ben said.

"By screaming?" I asked. "More like it would scare a person to death."

"By screaming," Stan said, nodding. "And the person who hears them is supposed to be the one who will die very shortly. It's both a warning and a sad cry that the person is dying."

Well, I had to admit, I didn't much like the sound of that.

I took a deep breath and could feel Patty's calming influence flow through me. Honestly, over the last few years, I had faced death and the end of the world a few times. And a lot of really tough players in no-limit poker games. So if some being was giving me a warning, I needed to thank her and just flat ask her what was going to happen.

And when.

Never hurt to know when a fella was going to die, I figured.

Seemed so simple. I'm sure there were a dozen reasons it was a stupid idea, but my friends around me just seemed determined to stand next to me when I died and do nothing, so I needed to do something.

And my terrified mind couldn't come up with one other idea. I knew death could follow me anywhere, since I had met two gods of death so far, and sort of liked them both, honestly. So running was out of the question.

I moved over to the closet and pulled out my heaviest Oregon coat. Since I was originally from Oregon and my home casino was in the mountains of Oregon, I at least had a few heavy coats, one of which I had brought to Vegas and stashed in Patty's apartment because at times I had been damned cold here as well.

"What are you doing?" Patty asked, again taking my arm as I came back to her zipping up my parka.

"Going out to talk with the banshee," I said, giving her a quick kiss and heading for the door into the dark living room.

"Not a great idea," Lady Luck said.

I stopped and looked at her. "Has a banshee killed anyone?"

"No, she just warns people," Lady Luck said, her voice sounding sad and tired.

"Then it seems I'll be fine. When was the last time anyone just talked with the banshee?"

Ben shook his head. "There are no records of anyone doing such a thing."

"Five hundred years," Lady Luck said softly.

Ben glanced at her and said nothing. He knew something he wasn't saying.

"Well, if this kills me," I said, doing my best to screw up every ounce of courage I had, "someone tell the next person to not try it."

"I'm coming with you," Patty said.

"No, I heard the scream, I'm the one the banshee is trying to warn."

I glanced at Lady Luck and nodded. I almost said, "Wish me luck" and then stopped as I realized how stupid that really would have sounded to Lady Luck.

Her expression didn't change from extreme seriousness combined with sadness, something I had never seen on her face.

"While I'm gone," I said, standing near the door of the living room, "someone might want to check with Death, see if I really am on a list at the moment. We did save his ass and help his daughter."

Lady Luck nodded. "I'll do it," she said, and vanished.

I took a deep breath and turned and went into the living room.

The intense cold slapped me and I staggered, but managed to move forward.

"My name is Poker Boy," I said to the cold air, my breath freezing in front of my face. "I heard your scream and came to see if I could help."

Being brash seemed to be the most logical thing I could do.

And that's what people who rescue other people do, after all, go toward the sound of a scream.

"Thank you," a soft female voice said from the other side of the couch.

"Can you stand a little light?" I asked.

"It is not a problem," the voice said.

An instant later the table light beside the couch clicked on. A beautiful and mostly nude small woman sat on the couch under the light. Her skin was a light blue and she had two fragile-looking silver wings tucked behind her.

Her beautiful, long, silver hair cascaded around her and covered most of the important parts.

But there was no two ways about it, she was stunning.

I moved over to a large chair facing her across a frost-covered coffee table and sat down, my hands in my pockets of the heavy ski parka. Somewhere between the door and the chair I had lost touch with my feet, since they were only in thin slippers and I was sure they were already frozen.

"So I assume you were calling me for help?" I asked, doing my best to not push any power toward her for fear she might think I was trying to meddle.

"I was," she said, nodding, moving her silver hair around in such a fashion that any good strip club would hire her in a moment.

"Not warning me like you normally do."

"No, calling you for help," she said.

Relief flooded through me but did nothing to warm me up. You would think it would have.

"I have been stuck in this frigid-state for almost five hundred years now," she said, her voice taking on a little more power. "I have done my job as instructed for five hundred years."

I nodded, a little worried about what was coming next.

Being brash seemed to be the most logical thing I could do.

"I would like you to help me become free of this punishment."

Oh, great, she's asking the newest member of all the superheroes in God's world for help with something that happened five hundred years ago, as if I should know what that was.

"Why do you think I can help with this?" I asked.

"I have watched you and your team save many, many lives," she said. "I hope you can now save mine."

I nodded. "We can try. But can I bring a few members of my team in here to help me?"

"You can," she said, nodding.

Being afraid to stand on my frozen feet, I shouted to the door. "Patty, Stan, Ben, could you join us?"

She nodded, making her hair dance around the important parts of her body. "I am honored you are willing to try to help me."

Stan had bundled all three of them up in parkas and gloves and they came in slowly like an expedition to the South

Pole lost in Patty's apartment. No dog sleds, luckily.

Patty came over and sat on the arm of the chair beside me, calming me some with a touch. Stan and Ben both nodded to the banshee and remained standing.

She nodded back.

I turned back to the banshee and said, "We are ready. Could you tell us what caused this punishment five hundred years ago?"

"It is not punishment for a crime," she said. "It is punishment for love. I loved the wrong woman."

Well, I was as liberal as the next person, but honestly, that answer surprised me, right down to my frozen feet.

THREE

I NEEDED TO GET THIS GOING before I froze completely to the chair. "May I ask first who put this punishment on you?"

I glanced over at Ben who was shaking his head from side-to-side. "You don't want to know," he said softly.

"I did," Lady Luck said, entering the room right after Ben said that.

She did not have a ski parka on and seemed oblivious to the intense cold.

If I got many more surprises like that, the blood actually might reach my feet again.

Patty squeezed my arm to keep me calm.

"How are you, Laverne?" the banshee asked, smiling.

"I am well," Lady Luck said, moving to the end of the couch and sitting down and facing the banshee. "You are as beautiful as ever."

The banshee nodded her head thank you, again doing wonderful and alluring things with her hair over her perfect blue body.

Who knew a blue body could be perfect?

Then the banshee said something that got me even more confused, which in this frozen state, was going some.

"Thank you for saving my life."

Laverne smiled and nodded. "I am sorry that it had to be in this fashion. It was what your husband would accept as a punishment short of death."

"I have survived," the banshee said. "Loving you was worth it. Is my husband still angry at me?"

"He is not," Lady Luck said. "He is retired, his daughter has taken over his month of duties as Death just last year, and he spends most of his time surfing in Hawaii with his new wife."

I just about choked. This banshee had been married to Death himself. And she had been in love with Lady Luck. Wow, I really needed to spend time with Ben and learn about some of the history of the Gods.

"Then is it possible to return me to the normal world?" the banshee asked.

"I just spoke with your ex-husband," Lady Luck said. "Poker Boy and his team helped his daughter make the transition last year, and I told him that Poker Boy was trying to help you now after five hundred years of punishment."

"Thank you," the banshee said. "He never knew you were the one?"

"He knew," Laverne said. "Right from the start. And he knew it broke my heart, as wells as yours to do what I did. That's why he allowed the punishment."

"I have been wailing over death and broken hearts now for five hundred

Now Available
from all your favorite booksellers in trade paper and electronic editions.

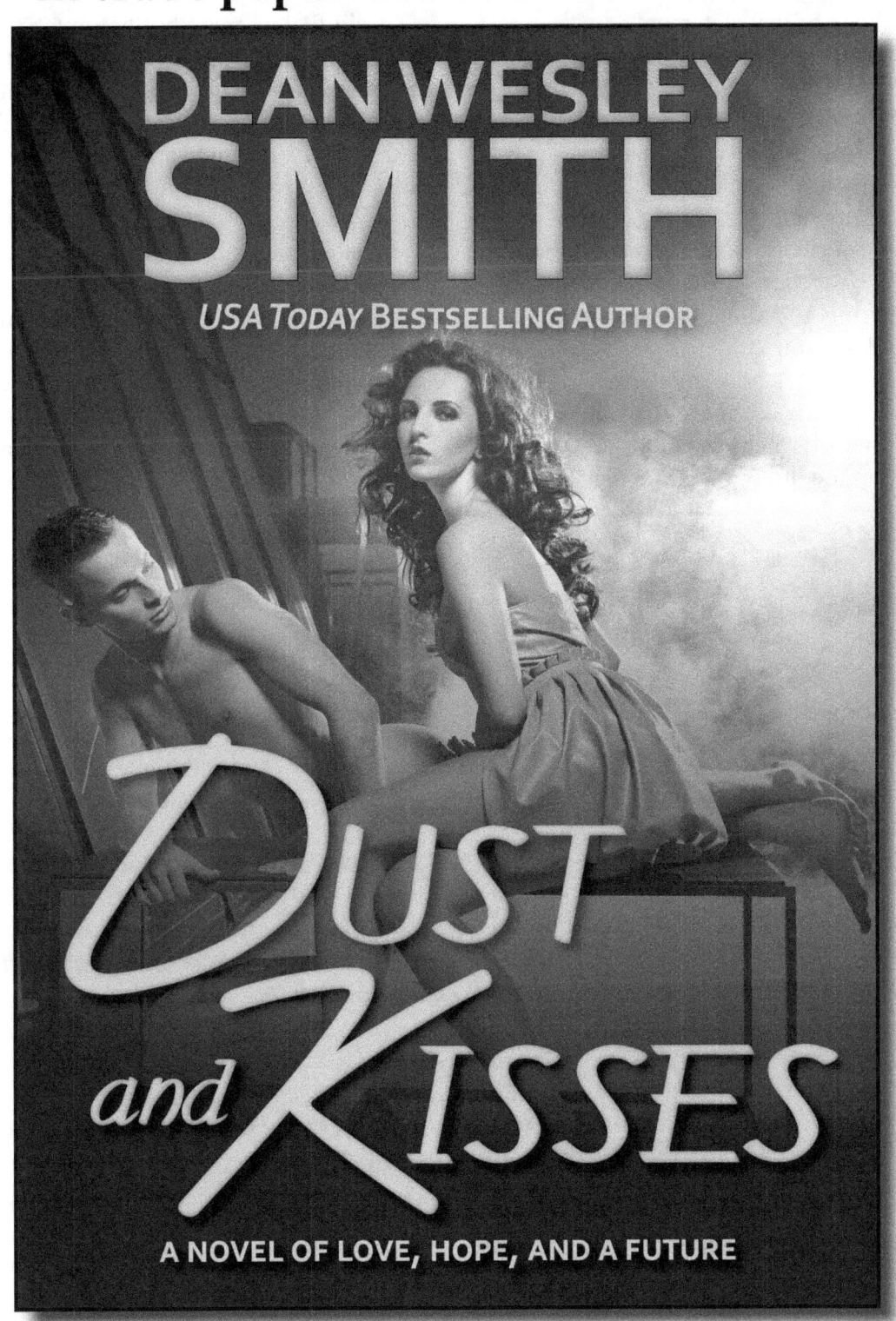

DEAN WESLEY
SMITH

USA Today BESTSELLING AUTHOR

Dust
and *Kisses*

A NOVEL OF LOVE, HOPE, AND A FUTURE

years," the banshee said. "And with every one I mourned the loss of your love."

"You never lost it," Laverne said.

Once again my toes felt warmer from the shock of that statement.

"You are married, have four grown daughters?" the banshee asked, staring at Laverne in clear surprise.

"My husband and I have," Laverne said, smiling, "shall we say, an open arrangement."

I just about said, "More information than I needed." But my teeth were chattering too much luckily to get that stupid joke out.

Laverne stood and with a "thank you" into the air, more than likely to the banshee's former husband, she waved her hand in the direction of the banshee.

Intense heat filled the room and the banshee sat there, smiling, soaking it all in.

And then finally, after a few seconds, it was over.

I did feel warmer, but not much.

Water was dripping all around Patty's apartment from the melting frost and I could feel the temperature on my face returning to normal, although it would not surprise me to have frostbite on my nose.

The banshee now was no longer blue, but a tanned golden brown all over. And I do mean all over. And her hair was now just as long but a rich brown. And her wings shimmered in a rainbow of colors.

Laverne reached out her hand to the banshee and then said, "Jayne, welcome back."

Jayne took her hand and stood, smiling, her long hair doing little to cover some pretty amazing assets.

"It's a pleasure to be back."

Then Jayne turned to me and said, "Thank you, Poker Boy, and your entire team, for being willing to take a chance on talking to me."

I just nodded, not trusting myself to say anything sane.

"We have some catching up to do," Laverne said, smiling.

"Now that's something I've been looking forward to for five hundred years."

Then, like two teenage girls, they both giggled, and vanished.

Lady Luck giggling was unsettling, to say the least.

Stan shook his head and said, "See you tomorrow." Then he and Ben vanished.

Patty stood and shivered, water dripping off her coat from the melting frost.

"Would you do me a favor," I asked as she offered to help me out of my chair.

"Anything, my frozen love."

"Would you start a warm shower running. I'm just going to teleport out of these clothes and into the shower from here. I don't think my feet will carry me."

She laughed. "I'll be there, naked, standing under the hot water, ready to catch you."

And she did.

And I got real warm, real quick. I'll leave it at that.

~

USA Today *bestselling writer Dean Wesley Smith returns with a second novel in the world of* Thunder Mountain *from the second issue of* Smith's Monthly.

Historical interior designer April Buckley and architect Ryan Knott are hired to design and furnish a huge lodge to the year 1900 standards. The two that hire them are Bonnie and Duster Kendal, two of the world's great mathmaticians.

Only problem: The lodge can't be built. It can't exist. Yet somehow it does because they built it. And fell in love in the process.

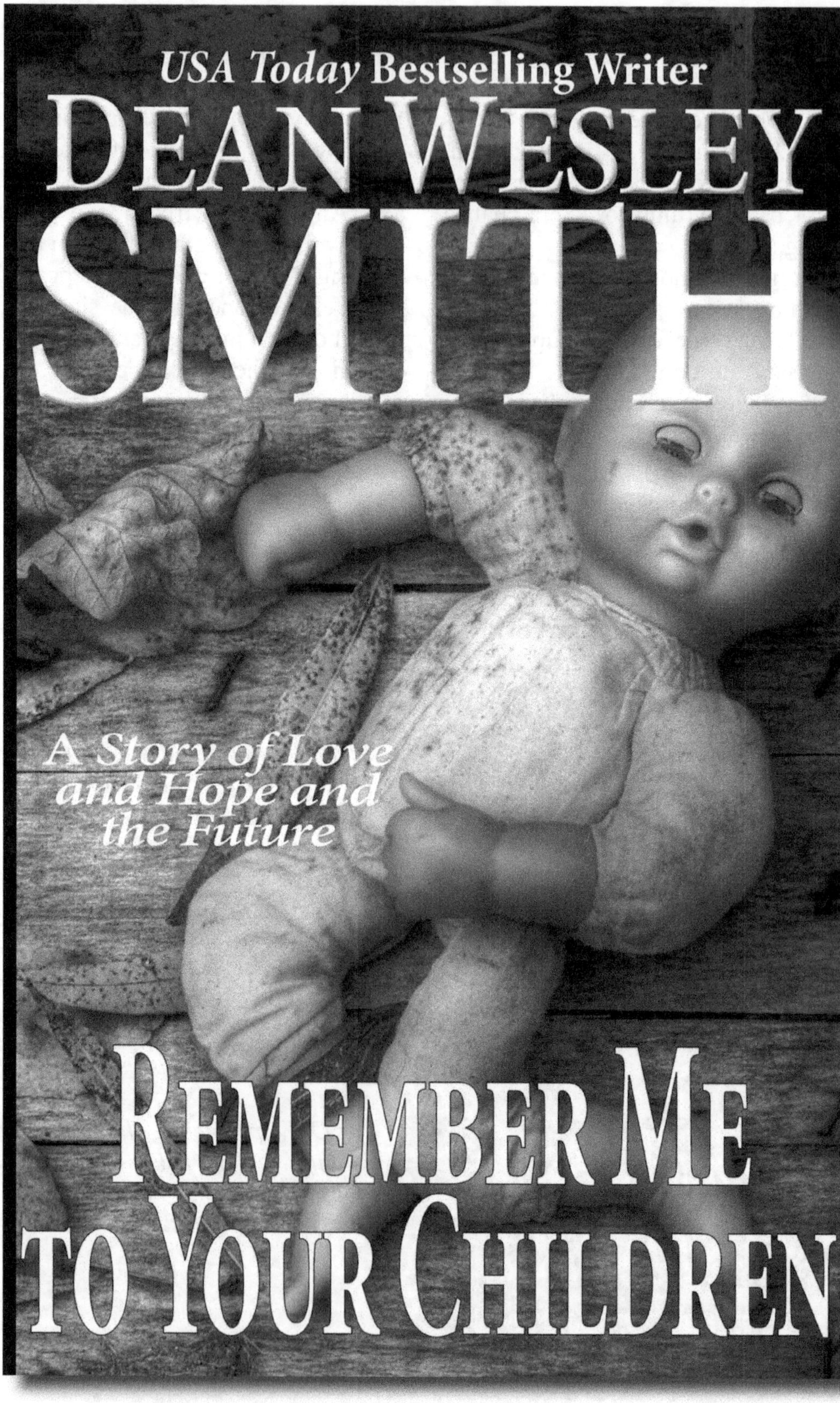
USA Today Bestselling Writer
DEAN WESLEY
SMITH
A Story of Love and Hope and the Future
REMEMBER ME TO YOUR CHILDREN

USA Today *bestselling writer returns to the world of his latest novel, Dust and Kisses, the first of many books that span time and space in his Seeders' Universe.*

In this heartfelt story, Tammy works with her best friend and love, Hal, to help in the formal discovery and burial of the dead lost in the Big Death. The survivors call the task The Respect Project.

On a Portland, Oregon, suburban street, Tammy discovers from the tragedy of a family that the future can be a hopeful place.

REMEMBER ME TO YOUR CHILDREN

"TAMMY, CAN'T YOU JUST RELAX A LITTLE?"

Tammy glanced around at her best friend and lover, Hal Lemmon, as he tried to follow her up the center of the suburban street. The day was hot and Hal was sweating, staining his white tee shirt around the brown straps of the backpack he carried. His longish brown hair was damp where it stuck out from under his Yankee's baseball cap.

His handsome face was flushed and he looked tired, even though they had only gone four blocks in distance.

She was hot as well, which was why she had been walking fast, trying to get them to their starting target before they stopped or the heat got them. It normally wasn't this hot in Portland, Oregon, or at least that's what some long-time residents of the area had told her earlier.

She was wearing jeans with tennis shoes, a sleeveless tank-top with a sports bra under it, and she had her short blonde hair under a Dodgers baseball cap. Sweat was running off her neck and down her chest and she desperately needed a drink of water.

She had her Smith and Wesson pistol in a holster on her hip and Hall had a small twenty-two saddle rifle tied to the side of his backpack. It had been years since they had gone anywhere without those guns, winter or summer. They both had admitted they would feel naked without them.

On both sides of the suburban street around them, the houses were like tombstones for the people who had been killed inside of them when the Big Death happened five years before. The once green grass lawns where children had played were brown and had long turned to tall, dry weeds. The house windows were dirty and almost every house had drapes pulled, at least on the lower floors.

Weeds and grass had started growing in patches of dirt along the street and up through cracks in the concrete. What had been perfect lines of lawns, driveways, sidewalks, and street were now blurred as Mother Nature slowly took back the neighborhood. Tammy had seen a projection on how in fifty years a neighborhood like this would be completely overgrown, in one hundred years it would be all plants and piles of rubble, and in five hundred years it would be almost impossible to tell what had been here.

Just as Mother Nature had killed most everyone on the planet one day with a burst of electromagnetic waves from space, she now was slowly reclaiming the planet.

The Big Death had hit at a little after eight in the morning here in Portland, so most people in this neighborhood were either at work or taking kids to school or some such thing. Tammy and Hal had been two of the million-plus lucky ones who had been either underground in subways, in vaults, or deep inside ships. She had been down in the vaults of her Boise newspaper, doing research through old papers not yet scanned, on a story that no longer mattered, other than being down there had saved her life.

Hal had been in a bank vault in downtown Boise getting something from his safe deposit box. She and Hal had stumbled upon each other on the second day of wandering around in the dead bodies. They hadn't known each before, but they stayed together and helped each other survive those first few years until they joined up with other survivors working to rebuild a civilization.

Over that first really hard year, they had fallen in love.

Now they lived together in the new city of Portland, Oregon, worked together both on the local newspaper, and searching for the dead, and she couldn't imagine being without Hal through any of it.

She looked around at all the empty houses. This neighborhood hadn't been cleared yet, which was the process they were sent to start.

They were to inventory the bodies in every home along the street and mark from the outside which homes had bodies so the removal crews could come and take them to the new cemeteries.

And in each home they were to look for information as to who lived there and double-check it with their database, even those without bodies in them.

The ultimate goal of the Respect Project was to give everyone who died in the Big Death a proper resting place and a record of their existence for the future, including where they had lived and what they had done for work.

It was almost an impossible task, but everyone in the five now-growing new cities around the country, which included Portland, and the new national government, were committed to the task.

"We can start anywhere, you know?" Hal said. "How about we start here, work back to the truck along both sides, then cool down and bring the truck to here and go the other direction?"

Tammy stopped and glanced at an address still visible on the side of one of the homes. From what she could tell, they were about halfway along the long subdivision street. Hal's idea was a good one. They had to get out of the sun. It was only ten in the morning and this day promised to be far too hot to stay out in the sun for very long.

She nodded. "Good plan."

"Thank you," Hal said, stopping and taking off his pack, letting it drop to the concert in the middle of the street.

They had been going out four mornings a week to catalog houses and bodies in the vast subdivisions that surrounded Portland. It had bothered her some at first, nosing into people's personal homes, but then she had grown numb to it. After all, the people they were investigating were all dead.

The thing she could never look at were the children's bodies, often in cribs. Every time they found a home with a child, Hal took that house on his own, even though they had clear orders to always stay together. Not that there was anything dangerous in these old subdivisions besides slowly rotting wood.

This subdivision had lots of signs that children lived in these homes, from swing sets visible in the back years, to small bikes and other toys left near the front doors.

She wanted a child someday, with Hal, but she felt the new world wasn't stable enough yet to commit to that, even though hundreds of healthy children were being born every month in the new Portland. Hal wanted children, he was

clear on that, but he was willing to wait until she was ready as well.

At the moment, she just wasn't ready and when searching homes, she just couldn't make herself deal with the dead children.

She took a long drink of semi-cold water that tasted wonderful and then handed the bottle to Hal, who took a drink and sighed. Around them a slight breeze kicked up filling the air with faint noises of houses creaking and dry brush rustling. The sounds did nothing to break the death silence of the subdivision.

"Let's go get snoopy into people's lives," he said, handing her back the bottle of water.

"That one first," she said, pointing to a light blue house on her right. "Let's do two on that side, then two on the other side, as we work back to the truck."

"Sounds perfect," he said, smiling at her and picking up his pack.

She loved everything about him, his dark eyes, his solid build, and his strong arms. But mostly she just loved that smile.

Somehow, over all the years of living in the middle of death, that smile of his had kept her sane.

They headed up the front sidewalk of the two-story home that must have been very nice in its day. The drapes were pulled and more than likely the front door was locked. Both of them had been trained before they started this job to pick a lock. Hal was slightly faster at it than she was, but only by a second or so. They hadn't found a lock so far that had stopped them.

The people in charge of the Respect Project wanted all the homes to be respected as well, if possible, even though eventually they would all just rot away. Tammy was fine with that as well.

Hal left his pack on the front step and took out his rifle, slinging it over his shoulder before bending down and picking the front door locks. Thirty seconds later he stood and pushed the door open.

The smell of mold and dust and something with a slight tang greeted them and they both stepped back out of the smell and pulled out their cloth masks and tied them over their mouths and noses. That smell with a bite meant there was a body in the building.

They always wore masks when a body was in the building.

The masks also helped them with the dust and they went through about a dozen of the masks a day, maybe more on a hot day like today.

Even though there was some light filtering through the drapes and from a back window in the kitchen beyond the living room, they both clicked on flashlights. When they first started out doing this job, they had both tripped over various things in homes that they just hadn't seen in dim light. So they took no chances now.

Tammy panned her flashlight around the living room. More of a formal room that didn't look much used. A layer of gray dust dulled down all colors in the room.

Moving slowly to not kick up too much dust from five years of no one moving around in here, they headed for the kitchen and the family room beyond.

Tammy was relieved to see no sign of children's toys around the family room.

Hal slowly opened some drawers near the family dining area. Often families left personal information in drawers near a kitchen table.

While he was doing that, she turned and opened the back door leading into a two-car garage. There was one car there. And a spot for a second one. Tools were in their places on the walls.

Nothing else of interest.

"One car left," she said as she went past Hal and toward the rooms to the right of the big living room. One looked like a guest bedroom and was as sterile as the living room. Whoever lived in this house believed in keeping everything in its place. Even after sitting abandoned for five years and layers of gray dust making everything pale, that feeling of "in its place" was clear in this home.

It made her wonder what the residents of this home had been like. Clearly different than she and Hal. Their large apartment in a building in the downtown area was always awash with clutter of various types, mostly books. They were both just comfortable in that.

She would not have been comfortable in this place. It felt sterile and even more dead than most homes she had been in, as if this home had been dead before the Big Death hit.

"Anything?" she asked.

Hal shook his head. "Nothing. Drawers in perfect order, but no bills, no letters, nothing. More than likely all that is in a study someplace from the looks of all this."

With Hal leading, they headed upstairs.

The light was brighter upstairs as most of the back windows in the home had the blinds open. They all looked out over a lush backyard that had held a

A layer of gray dust dulled down all colors in the room.

pool. Tammy had no doubt it had been beautiful in its day. And from the looks of the house, the lawn would have been mowed perfectly and the pool cleaned twice a week.

At the top of the stairs a hallway led the length of the house. It had a number of closed doors. Tammy had a hunch behind one of those doors would be the body they knew was in here from the faint musty smell. The smell had a slight tang to it after five years, but it wasn't a smell that was easy to miss.

And now that they were upstairs, the smell was thick.

And even though it was still fairly early, this upper area of the house was already heating up. Any body they did find would be well mummified in this kind of heat.

A mummified body was a lot better as far as Tammy was concerned than a body torn up from animals. Not all animals had survived the electromagnetic pulse. Dogs and rats and mice had been killed, but cats had survived. And with a cat trapped in a home with a dead human, they ate the dead human when they got hungry enough.

There were no signs this home had cats, so the body would be mummified and look moderately human even after five years.

The first two doors were to small bedrooms with no occupants. They had been furnished with small single beds and just left. One room was painted pink, one blue.

Clearly the rooms had been meant for future children that had not arrived yet.

And now never would.

The third door was to an empty bathroom and the next door was to a master bedroom and bath, also empty. The bed was made perfectly.

There was nothing out of place in this entire house. Tammy found that amazing and very closed up and creepy.

The next door on the other side of the hall was to a study with a big desk.

"Got it," Hal said, moving to the desk and file cabinet that would let them know who had lived here.

There was one more door at the end of the hall and that meant it had the body in it.

Tammy went to it and opened it slowly, making sure to not stir up any dust as she did so.

The blinds were open in the room and it was a fairly large family room that also did not look used in any way. This room had a large-screen television, a number of couches, a game table, and plush carpet.

It had been designed to be comfortable, but clearly not made comfortable.

Everything again was in perfect position. Nothing was used. It was as if the people living in this house had just existed in it and never really lived in it.

There was a door off the family room that was closed. More than likely that was where the body was. They had found many bodies, since they started this job, in various stages of bathroom routines.

Hal came in behind her. "This is the home of Ben and Cathy Freeman. He worked at a pharmacy downtown and she was an RN."

Hal held up his digital pad. "We already recovered his body when they cleaned the downtown area."

"This place sure looks like they were planning for kids," Tammy said. 'Clearly didn't get the chance."

Hal glanced around and nodded. Then he pointed to the door. "You want me to look and see who is in there?"

"We both will," she said.

Slowly she opened the bathroom door to keep the dust from swirling while both of them shined their flashlights into the small bathroom.

What she saw stunned her and took her a moment for her mind to wrap around.

What had been a fairly attractive, thin, brown-haired woman lay in the bathtub face up. She had mummified, but she still looked pretty good, with her long brown hair fanned out on the back of the tub over her.

And her face was calm in death. Very calm.

What had really surprised Tammy was that the tub water when it evaporated had left an ugly brown stain.

It took her a moment to see why. Both of the woman's wrists that were crossed over her chest had been slashed.

A razor blade lay on a napkin on the edge of the tub.

"Now that's a first," Hal said beside Tammy in the bathroom door. "More than likely she cut her wrists right before the Big Death hit."

On the counter was a note card standing up with the name "Ben" on it.

Tammy looked at it, then glanced at Hal. Clearly that was Cathy Freeman's suicide note.

Hal shrugged, meaning she could read it or not. Up to her.

Tammy wasn't sure if she wanted to read it, but at this point she felt she had no choice.

She picked up the note and opened it. Then read it aloud as Hal held his flashlight so she could see.

Dearest Ben,

I am so sorry for the mess I have left you. I have tried to keep this clean and simple and plan this in a bathroom we seldom use.

I am so sorry that I cannot bring the children into the world we so hoped to have. I could no longer look at the deadness in your eyes and the disappointment I felt every time we made love. My passing here will allow you to move on, to find a new wife, to be happy, and finally have and raise the children you so wanted.

Please don't be me mad at me, love. This is for the best. Remember me to your children when they are old enough to understand. Have a wonderful life.

Love Always,
Cath

Tammy carefully replaced the suicide note on the counter.

"Let's get out of here," Hal said, gently touching her elbow. "We got all we need from here."

Somehow Tammy nodded and turned and followed Hal out of the family room and down the hall past the future children's bedrooms, then down the stairs and out into the hot air of the dead subdivision.

Hal picked up his pack, stuck his rifle back in it, and led the way to the street.

She pulled off her mask and tucked it in her pocket, letting the warm air work to clear her mind.

They stopped in the middle of the street, both their backs to the house they had just been in.

After a moment, Hal gently touched her arm. "You all right?"

"Honestly," she said, turning to look into his worried dark eyes. "I think I'm done for the day."

"I agree," Hal said. "Too hot anyway. So what are you thinking?"

She looked into the eyes of the man she loved, the man that had helped her survive more death than she ever wanted to think about. "I am thinking about a long cold shower in our air-conditioned apartment."

"We are on the same track with that," Hal said, smiling.

"Then maybe a few hours in bed making love to you."

At that, his eyebrows went up and he looked at her puzzled.

"After all this death," she said, sweeping her arm around to indicate the dead neighborhood, "don't you think it's time we bring some new life into the world?"

He smiled bigger than she had remembered him smiling in a very long time. "I do. Very much."

She kissed him, then took his arm and together they headed up the hot street of the dead subdivision.

A hot breeze twisted through the dead houses around them, and maybe, just maybe, if they had listened, they would have imagined they heard the faint laughter of the children.

~

USA *Today* Bestselling Writer

DEAN WESLEY SMITH

THE LIFE AND TIMES OF BUFFALO JIMMY

Chapters 16-18

What Came Before...

Nineteen-year-old Boston native Jimmy Gray had been traveling with his parents and older brother, Luke, headed west to find a new home and new riches. Before even reaching Independence, they were attacked and robbed by Jake Benson and his gang. Jimmy's parents were killed, his brother wounded.

In one of the wildest towns in all of American history, Jimmy Gray, a sheltered, educated son of a banker from Boston suddenly finds himself very, very much alone. But then, through some luck, he finds other young men about his age and down on their luck who might be able to help him.

Together, the five of them head west after Benson. They end up hunting buffalo as he always dreamed of doing, but then they are hit with a massive flash flood and Jimmy is left alone, his friends more than likely dead.

They manage to get back together after days of searching, and continue on their journey west, picking up another member of their crew. There are now six of them, with Jimmy leading, heading west, trailing the man who killed Jimmy's parents.

THE LIFE AND TIMES OF BUFFALO JIMMY

Part Sixteen
THEY MAKE HARD PROGRESS

THE VASTNESS OF THE WEST was overwhelming to Jimmy, not in a bad way, but with a feeling that kept generating excitement. Every day he marveled at one sight or another, from small things like the sight of an animal he had never seen to stunning rock formations.

And the smells seemed to constantly change, from dry sagebrush to wetlands along the river.

They had traveled through the fifth leg up the river to the ford of the North Fork of the Platte River, making a steady pace for seven days. The trail was much, much rougher, and the wagon companies were clearly having more trouble with the pull.

They were doing fine, walking most of the time to rest the horses.

In a couple places, the trail was a full day's ride away from the river, so they had to watch their water more carefully.

At Independence Rock, all of them carved their names on the rock, along with thousands of other names. Jimmy couldn't believe so many people had gone past this place.

This was a rough trip for even someone in as good of shape as he was. And it was clear that if his brother had tried to make even these early legs, it would have killed him.

The seventh leg took them up to the top of the South Pass and over the Continental Divide. The air, the higher they climbed, got colder at nights, and twice over the four days up to the pass, it snowed on them during the night.

They walked the horses even more, and moved shorter distances because none of them were used to the higher altitude. Jimmy found it amazing that all the mountains around them were still covered in white.

He had never seen anything so beautiful in all his life. Pictures and paintings just didn't do it justice in any fashion.

And the smell of the pine in the crisp morning air just made his head spin in happiness.

The main trail then angled north to Fort Hall , then back south to the split in the Oregon and California Trails forty miles to the south of Fort Hall.

Fort Hall was small, with few salons or general stores. Considering that it was a major spot on the trip, it wasn't much to see.

There were a few Snake Indians camped near town, and very few wagons. It was the last place to really buy supplies on either the California or Oregon Trails, but most wagons didn't need anything here and just camped for a night, then pressed on.

"We're about halfway to California from Independence," C. J. said in the morning as they rode out of Fort Hall.

"The easy half," Josh said.

Jimmy didn't like the sound of that at all.

Forty miles later, they reached Raft River, where the Oregon Trail split from the California Trail.

The southern California trail went along the Raft River for a while, then went up and over a few ranges until finally dropping down on Goose Creek.

It was on June 14th, as they worked their way along a small stream called Goose Creek, just inside the eastern edge of Nevada, the union's newest state, that everything changed.

The trail ahead went around a low ridge and it was from that direction that the sounds of gunfire came.

Close, very close.

Then a woman screamed.

Jimmy froze, wondering if that was what his mother had sounded like when Benson killed his father.

Then there were more shots and another scream.

"Get down!" Zach shouted.

All the boys dove from their horses and scrambled for cover in a small grove of trees near the spring.

Jimmy had no idea what was happening, but it didn't sound good.

Again, the woman screamed loud and long.

All Jimmy could think about was that they had to do something to help her.

Anything.

His mother hadn't had anyone to help her.

The woman's next scream echoed over the hills and then died out in a horrible way with one more shot.

Too late to help her. That was all he could think.

Jimmy glanced around at his five friends. What had they gotten into this time?

Part Seventeen
DEATH COMES TO THE WEST

THE WOMAN'S SCREAMS were frightening in how sharp and clear they carried over the wide Goose Creek valley.

Jimmy jerked around in the saddle of his horse, trying to figure out where the shots and screams were coming from as Long, who had been leading the six of them at a steady pace, immediately dismounted and pulled his horse toward a grove of tall trees beside the stream.

Jimmy did the same, realizing just how big a target he was sitting up there on the horse.

So far, the vastness of the West had scared and overwhelmed him, a flash flood had almost killed him, and he had barely escaped being trampled by a buffalo herd. Yet that woman's scream sent more chills through his blood than anything he had heard since leaving Independence.

Around him, the Goose Creek valley looked like a peaceful place, a wonderful green strip of life in the otherwise brown hills. Large leafy trees bordered the creek, and kept the area cool from the heat of the day.

Keeping his head low, Jimmy followed Long deeper into the trees, finally stopping and tying up his horse on a large log.

All six them hunkered down together, listening. Not even a slight breeze broke the silence of the valley and the gentle sounds of the stream. Jimmy could hear his own heart pounding in his chest and he tried not to pant too loudly.

Two more shots rang out over the trees.

Jimmy could only think about what had happened to his mother, how she must have screamed when Jake Benson shot his father in the back. Jimmy wondered if his mother's screams sounded as chilling before she was shot as well.

The scream came again, then another few shots. Finally, the valley settled into an uneasy silence.

Like the silence at a funeral.

Jimmy pushed the thought away and turned to Long and the rest of his friends. Long knew the West and distances and seemingly everything else about survival out in the wilderness. Jimmy had come to count on him and his special talents.

"Indians?" Jimmy asked, his voice barely above a whisper.

He forced himself to breathe and try to keep calm, not let his total hate of guns and the sound of those screams get in his way.

"Bannocks in this area," Long said, nodding, his long black hair flowing around his shoulders. "They are a mean group."

Josh, their newest member, shook his head, his notebook and pen clutched tightly in his hand. "That doesn't sound like the type of guns the Bannocks would have."

All five of them turned to stare at their newest member. Clearly, besides writing stories, Josh knew guns. That was a talent that Jimmy would have to keep in mind in the future.

Long nodded, then whispered. "Josh is right. We need to take a look."

"Can you tell where the sounds are coming from?" Zach asked. His hands squeezed their only gun, a hunting rifle that used to belong to Jimmy' father.

Jimmy could tell that the sounds of the woman screaming had bothered Zach a lot as well. Usually Zach was the calm one. Now he was squeezing the butt of the rifle like it was a dishtowel he was trying to wring water out of.

"Just over the ridge to the right," Long said and Josh nodded in agreement.

Jimmy glanced at Josh. "Can you tell how many different guns were fired?"

"Three," Josh said. "One rifle, two revolvers."

Even Long looked impressed.

"Glad you're along with us," Truitt said, patting Josh's shoulder.

Josh smiled and nodded thanks.

Jimmy glanced around at his five friends and decided they needed to act. This was the west, after all.

"Truitt, you and C.J. stay with the horses. Be saddled up and ready to come riding fast with all of them if we shout for help."

Truitt nodded.

Zach checked quickly to make sure the rifle was fully loaded. Between blood-thirsty outlaws, stampeding buffalo, and deadly weather, the West was proving itself to be no parlor game.

"Go slow and stay quiet," Long said softly as he headed out for the small rise to the right of the stream.

To Jimmy, it seemed to take them forever to get to the top of that hill, picking their way first through the trees, then up the gentle incline through the sagebrush, moving slowly and carefully, staying in behind Long.

But in reality, it couldn't have been longer than a minute.

Just before they reached the top, the crackling of a large fire could be heard from the other side, then a man laughing.

The sound made Jimmy catch his breath.

It was the sound of evil. Pure evil.

Long motioned for them to spread out beside him, and then they crawled the last few feet on hands and knees to the top of the ridge as the hot sun beat down on their backs.

Beyond the top of the hill, Goose Creek doubled back into the sheltered alcove of a small valley. The main trail stayed in the larger valley. In the shelter between the two ridges, someone had built a small ranch with a slanted-roof barn and a cabin. A garden had been planted beyond the cabin, and behind the farm was a large grove of trees, so thick that Jimmy could barely see down through them. It looked like a wonderful oasis in the vast desert and rough lands of the Wyoming Territory

The house was starting to burn, black smoke billowing up into the clear morning sky. The crackling of the flames was getting louder as more and more of the house caught fire. Sparks flew into the air before vanishing.

And there were three bodies scattered around the burning building.

Jimmy was stunned and sick to his stomach at what he saw. Clearly the family that had lived in the house had been shot down.

Four horses were tied up near the barn right below them, and the sounds of men talking came from the barn.

Jimmy looked at the horses. He knew one of them.

Benson!

The man who had killed Jimmy' parents had now killed another family.

Part Eighteen
BENSON STRIKES AGAIN

JIMMY KEPT having trouble breathing as he stared at the scene below them. He forced himself to take slow, deep breaths and try to think.

He had to do something.

Beside him, on their stomachs as well, Long, Zach, and Josh just stared.

Josh kept making long swallowing motions, like he was trying to hold his breakfast down. Jimmy had no doubt Josh was taking in every detail. He seemed to have a real skill for seeing things that others didn't, and then putting those details in his stories. This wasn't going to make good campfire reading, that was for sure.

Four men came out of the barn, laughing, leading two horses.

Benson.

All Jimmy could do was stare at the man who had killed his parents.

Something had to be done.

But any movement that they made down the hill at the men would just get them all killed as well.

Zach muttered something Jimmy couldn't hear and then pulled the rifle to his shoulder. He took aim, then lowered his rifle, stared at the scene below, then took aim again at the four men.

Jimmy reached over and put a hand on the gun.

When Zach glanced at him, Jimmy shook his head. It wasn't the time, and even though Zach was a good enough shot that he might get one or two of the killers, the other two would kill all the rest of them. That wasn't the way to do it. They had to come up with something else.

Zach looked like he was going to object, then finally nodded and lowered the rifle, his face white, his breath coming in gasps.

Jimmy forced himself to turn back and stare at the homestead and death below them, trying to see anything that was possible to do.

"Ideas?" he whispered to the others.

All three shook their heads.

Jimmy studied the trees behind the house. They would allow someone to get close, but then what?

Those men deserved to be hanged.

The thought echoed through his mind and Jimmy knew what they had to try to do. One at a time, they needed to pick off these men, separate them, bring them to justice. Even though he had promised his brother he wouldn't do anything until they were together, he couldn't wait any longer. Too many people were getting killed.

He turned to Josh. "The rope on my saddle, and Truitt's rope. Run and get both of them as quickly as you can. And bring all the horses and the other two up here right behind us. The sounds from the fire should cover the noise."

Long nodded in agreement.

Josh looked puzzled, then without a word scampered away.

Zach whispered to Jimmy. "What are you thinking?"

"We have to stop those men before more people get killed," Jimmy said, his voice barely in control. In all his life, he couldn't remember being this angry. "And the only way we're going to stop them is one at a time."

He quickly outlined his plan to Zach and Long.

Long and C.J. were the best two riders, so they would be the decoys. And

C.J. had his special rock sling that might come in handy as well while he rode. It would be up to Jimmy and Truitt, with Zach standing guard with the rifle, to make the plan work.

Jimmy turned to Zach after he nodded agreement to the plan. "If you have to, can you really shoot a man?"

"I don't honestly know." Zach said, glancing down at the four men where they stood talking near the bodies of the family they had slaughtered. "But if I can't, I can at least give you cover."

Jimmy nodded. "Good enough. But it's going to be better to not fire a shot. The idea is to not let these men know what happened to one of them."

Zach nodded and went back to squeezing the stock of the rifle in nervousness.

Jimmy had no doubt they were way in over their heads with this plan. They were six basically green men taking on four deadly killers in the middle of the wilderness, with no chance of any help. More than likely, this was going to turn out badly.

But they had to try.

Jimmy just couldn't let more people be killed.

Zach and Jimmy went back over the hill to talk with the rest, leaving Long to stand guard.

"We have to move fast," Jimmy said after explaining the plan. "We will meet three miles off the trail in the trees just after dusk tonight, where we camped last night. Make sure none of the killers are following you."

Everyone nodded. Jimmy could tell they were all as afraid as he was, but all were willing to risk this.

Jimmy and Truitt each took a coil of rope. Jimmy put his over his shoulder so

he could drop it quickly if he had to run. Then heading along the top of the hill, he and Truitt worked their way over and down into the trees behind the homestead.

Jimmy could see that Zach took up a position behind a rock on the hillside where he could see both Jimmy and Truitt. He was such a good shot that from there he could easily knock a man off his horse if he needed to.

And if he could.

Jimmy just hoped he wouldn't have to.

Silently, Jimmy moved from tree to tree through the grove along the stream, until he found a good tree beside an animal trail, then quickly went up it with one end of the rope. He hadn't climbed a tree in years, but it was a skill he hadn't forgotten.

About ten feet up, he settled into the crook of a branch, then quickly got his end of the rope around the tree trunk. Then he made sure he was braced and the rope was in place.

Truitt, on the other end of the rope in the tree on the other side of the trail, nodded that he was ready. They had the rope up high enough that anyone riding under it wouldn't notice it.

Jimmy gave Zach up on the hill the ready sign, and Zach turned and gave it to Josh.

Jimmy knew that if this didn't work, they might be trapped in these trees, and if that happened, he and Truitt would soon be dead.

Through the trees, Jimmy could see the killers getting ready to mount up.

Less than ten seconds later, with a blood-curdling war cry, Long and C.J. came riding around the edge of the ridge, their heads down, their horses going at full speed. Long had untied his hair and it flew out behind him like a cape.

And C.J. had wrapped himself in one of Long's Indian blankets and put some dirt on his face to make himself look more Indian, even with his glasses. To the four killers, it must have looked like Long and C.J. just appeared out of thin air not more than fifty paces away.

C.J. lifted up in his saddle only long enough to twirl his rock sling and hit one man solidly in the side with a rock.

The guy swore as he went to the ground, trying to get his gun out of his holster.

C.J. and Long rode past the killers on the other side of the burning homestead and headed into the trees behind the house where Jimmy and Truitt waited.

Benson had his gun out the quickest and fired, but the shot missed both C.J. and Long as they pushed into the trees and flashed right under Johnny and Truitt and the rope they held between them.

All four killers quickly mounted up and rode after Long and C.J., just as Jimmy knew they would. They didn't dare let any witness, even Indians, live to tell what they had done to that poor family.

C.J. and Long, once they got out of the trees down the stream, would split up and circle out over the hills to the north. Jimmy had no doubt that they could get away. They were both fantastic riders and had fast horses. Jimmy was far more worried about what he and Truitt were about to try. If they missed, one or both of them would be more than likely dead.

The man that C.J. had hit with his sling was a little slower mounting up than

the other three and was trailing the other killers by a good twenty paces.

Benson and two of his men flashed past under Jimmy, the sounds of their swearing and horses' hoofs covering the sounds of the house burning.

> *Long had untied his hair and it flew out behind him like a cape.*

Both Jimmy and Truitt timed the rope drop perfectly as the fourth man rode under them. The idea was to knock him off his horse, tie him up, and take him away before the other three got back.

The rope caught the man squarely across the upper chest. Perfect!

Jimmy had braced himself in the tree and had the rope wound around the trunk once, but the impact of a man being pulled off a horse at full run yanked Jimmy shoulder-first into the trunk. The rope burned in his hands as he fought to hold on.

Somehow, he did.

The killer swung up high in the air as the horse kept going, then dropped back.

The killer did a half turn in mid-air and landed on his head and shoulders on the trail.

There was a loud crack that echoed through the trees as the man hit.

Jimmy dropped the rope and climbed quickly out of the tree. His hands were shaking so badly, he could barely hang onto anything. Truitt's face looked white and his eyes were wide as they both scrambled to tie up the killer.

But by the time they had his hands tied, it was clear to Jimmy that they didn't need to do more. Jimmy dropped the rope and backed away like he was backing away from a snake.

31

Truitt did the same, muttering softly, "We weren't supposed to kill him."

"Get moving!" Zach shouted softly from up the hill.

"Let's go," Jimmy said, glancing up at Zach. "They might be back at any moment."

"What are we going to do?" Truitt asked, a sound of panic in his voice.

"Hide him, just like we planned," Jimmy said. He felt like he was about to be sick, but they couldn't stop now. They had to stay on the plan, even though the killer was dead.

Truitt nodded, took a deep breath, and seemed to come back into his eyes.

Jimmy quickly slipped the rope under the killer's arms, then at full run they dragged the man's body away from the trail and the burning building, deeper into the trees, using the rope around his chest to pull him like a sled. Near a rock ledge and the edge of the thick forest, they dropped the killer's body into a depression beside a tree, then frantically tossed some branches and dead grass over him.

Jimmy walked ten steps away and looked back. He couldn't see the body at all.

Truitt was still standing over the body staring at the killer.

Jimmy moved back over to his friend and put a hand on his shoulder. Truitt clearly had no problems taking things, or playing tricks on people, but he had never been near death.

"It was an accident," Jimmy said, trying to convince himself as much as Truitt. "Let's go."

Truitt nodded, took a deep breath, and turned. "I'll get his horse." He ran back toward the trees where the man's horse had stopped and was grazing.

With one last look at where they had hidden the killer's body, Jimmy headed back through the trees. He grabbed the two horses that Benson had planned on taking from the homestead. Benson wouldn't get them. Not this time.

Jimmy glanced around at the dead family. Right now, he couldn't do anything for them. They would come back after the other killers had gone.

As fast as he could, Jimmy climbed back up the hill, pulling the two horses behind him.

A few moments later, Zach and Truitt joined him with Josh and their horses. There were four of them and they now had seven horses.

"The fall killed him?" Josh asked, his face white, his hands twisting the notebook.

Jimmy nodded. "Broke his neck."

He was having a lot of problems with the fact that they had killed someone. But right now, he couldn't think about it. He had to get himself and his friends out of there and to safety.

"Let's get riding."

"Yeah, I'd like to be a long ways from here when Benson gets back," Zach said, putting the rifle in his saddle and mounting up quickly.

C.J. and Long were riding at full speed north. Jimmy, Truitt, Zach, and Josh, with the extra horses, would ride at the same speed south, then wait until almost dusk to circle around back to where they had camped last night.

With luck, they would all be there.

Continued next month…

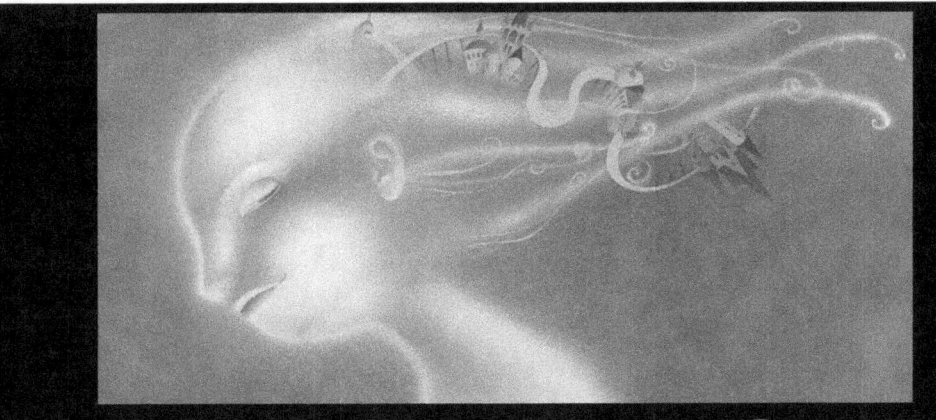

Poems by DEAN WESLEY SMITH

Wondering Through Time

I stop and wonder,
like an old man bent over a bowl of soup
in the basement of a church mission
studying his spoon like it was a mirror to his life.

I stop and wonder,
like a farmer studying the damage from a hail storm
on the crop that was supposed to pay his mortgage,
buy seed for next year, and milk for his children.

I stop and wonder,
staring at the days on my calander,
days that I didn't write,
days that nothing was produced.

I stop and wonder
and try to remember just what the hell I did
that was so important
during all the days I didn't write.

DEAN WESLEY SMITH

He Fought
the Aztecs
at the Alamo
to Save the Future

REMEMBER

Based On Fred Saberhagen's "Mask of the Sun"

Back in 2009, I got one of those letters you can only dream about as a writer. Robert E. Vardeman and Joan Spicci Saberhagen were editing a book of original stories based on a book by Joan's late husband, Fred Saberhagen. Fred was a great guy, and a great writer and his early death was a shock to us all.

And I was always a major fan of his work, so getting a chance to write in one of his worlds just had me jumping up and down. Then Bob told me what book of Fred's they wanted to extend new stories from and I got even more excited.

Fred had written a book called Mask of the Sun, *a short novel that was a stunner in world-building and storytelling. In essence, Fred came up with a world where the Spanish were defeated by the Incas and the Aztecs and now they were world powers, filling all of Central America and South America. And they were at war, of course.*

A war that stretched through time and alternate realities.

If you have not read Mask of the Sun, *you can find it along with this story and others in a book called* Golden Reflections. *Trust me, it will be worth your time to find and read. Plus in* Golden Reflections, *which came out in 2010, you can find the full novel, plus this story, plus six others, including stories by Harry Turtledove, David Weber, Walter John Williams and others.*

All set in the world of Mask of the Sun.

This story came about because in the Mask of the Sun *novel, I noticed that Fred had one paragraph where a character (shifted to this alternate universe) was happy to see that the United States was still in existence. I instantly thought, "Wow, that means they fought at the Alamo against the Aztecs. How cool!"*

And thus the following story.

I wanted to bring this story back here because I love this story and am proud of it and not many people ever saw it, and I loved Fred Saberhagen's work and wanted to point Fred's work out to fans in this new world.

REMEMBER

Based with permission
on the Fred Saberhagen novel,
Mask of the Sun

ONE

February 23, 1836
Bexar, Republic of Texas

"INCOMING!" a voice shouted from behind Dennis Holcomb as the muzzle flash from the Aztec cannon cut through the darkness, followed a moment later by the explosion of sound echoing over the mission. The cannon sat on a small rise built in the center of Bexar, one of two in that location.

Around him other men ducked for cover behind the two-foot-thick west wall of the Alamo, spread out on the roofs of the officer's quarters. Holcomb held his position on the wall, his night glasses allowing him to see clearly the three Aztec warriors already starting to reload the cannon.

Behind them stood another Aztec warrior wearing a thin headdress and a wide robe.

From what Holcomb had learned over the last week of studying the Aztec society, the warrior looked to be a member of the Arrow clan. That meant he was in charge of the other warriors working the cannons.

The Aztec had less than a second to live. He just didn't know it. Holcomb already had the wind figured, had the distance figured to exactly 865 feet. He was ready, had his target in his sights.

As the shell exploded at the base of the wall of the Alamo mission twenty feet down to the left from his position, he fired under the covering sound, knocking the Aztec leader off the mound.

Holcomb then moved quickly, still covered by the echoing thunder of the cannon shot impact. He moved the gun sight to the second mound with another Aztec cannon twenty yards to the right of the first one. He picked the Arrow clan warrior clearly in charge standing behind the three working on the cannon, and shot, knocking him over backwards before his men even had a chance to fire that cannon.

No other person behind the Alamo wall heard his shots because of the explosion of the shell and the silence technology on the gun.

Beside him Berg DeWitt patted him lightly on the shoulder. "Nice shooting."

"Old skills come back quick," Holcomb said. "Two down, four or five thousand more Aztecs to go."

"Yeah, going to be nothing to it," DeWitt laughed, staring through night-scope binoculars at the cannons. "Just like Nam."

"We lost that war, remember?" Holcomb said, watching through the night scope on his glasses as the Aztec warriors scrambled around the cannons, pulling their dead leaders away from the mounds, leaving the cannons unattended.

"So we make up for that here," DeWitt said, focusing over the thick wall into the dark.

Holcomb glanced at the Vietnam vet beside him. DeWitt was a tall guy, maybe six-two, and he had arms on him that could bench press more than Holcomb wanted to think about. The guy had military short hair and intense green eyes. He was originally from Montana and had served in Nam for two terms leading right up to the end of the war.

He and DeWitt were both dressed as frontiersmen of the time, in soft deerskin jackets, cloth pants and heavy boots. They both had on a poncho-like gray cloth against the chill of the night.

Along the top of the Alamo wall, the Texans and other fighters got back into position as the dust from the explosion drifted on the cool evening breeze, rifles poised and aiming into the pitch darkness of the night. Halfway down the west wall, Davy Crockett stood, staring into the blackness.

Holcomb just shook his head and looked away. The real Davy Crockett looked nothing like Fess Parker, the actor who had played him on television when Holcomb was a kid.

The real Davy Crockett was short. That had been a real disappointment.

TWO

May 18, 1981
Portland, Oregon, USA

HOLCOMB SAT on the park bench staring out over the calm waters of the Willamette River, not really paying any attention to those walking the path behind him or the boats floating past on the river. The day had turned warm and brought hundreds out of their homes and offices to enjoy the afternoon sunshine and beautiful spring day along the waterfront.

Holcomb hadn't noticed any of it. He had just come from a doctor. All he could remember now from the conversation was the word "Cancer" and "two months to live."

It didn't seem real, but it had been the third opinion, the third doctor, actually. He hadn't trusted the first two, hadn't believed them. But now it seemed there was no doubt. He was dying and there wasn't a damn thing anyone could do about it.

A young woman laughed, the sound high and light, floating on the soft breeze. Before learning of the cancer, he would have sat here, watching her, enjoying the sun and the afternoon. He had spent many a warm afternoon on this bench, and even knew some of the nearby shop owners by name. This bench, beside this path in the narrow park along the river, had been his favorite place in the city. He called it his spot, and anyone he dated or his few friends at work knew where to find him on nice days. And Portland, in the spring and summer and fall, had a lot of nice days.

Now, the sound of someone laughing just annoyed him. How could anyone be enjoying a day like today? He had just been given a death sentence. There was nothing worth laughing about today. He stood and, without a look at the beautiful calm river or the park around him, turned and headed back into the center of the city.

His apartment was on the third floor of an old converted hotel six blocks from the river and he didn't notice the walk, other than the few times he bumped into someone. All he could think about was dying. He had faced enemy fire a lot of times in Nam, had killed more than his share of the enemy, but never in all that time had he worried much about dying. Now that death faced him, like a train coming head on, he didn't know how to deal with it.

It just made him mad, actually.

One thing for certain, he had no intention of going the way the first doctor at the VA had described, sitting in a hospice the last few weeks, medicated so that he wouldn't feel the pain. He had bought a pistol after that little talk just for the occasion and now, with a solid third opinion, there sure didn't seem to be any reason to put off the end. He would face it just as he had faced most things in his life.

Head-on.

He had no family since his parents had died in a car wreck the year after he got back from Nam, and even though he was liked for his dry sense of humor at work, he didn't have any real friends to speak of, just a few old buddies from Nam. He was just too much of a loner to let anyone close. At least that's what his last girlfriend, Sandra, had told him.

He hadn't argued with her. She had been right. No one would really miss him, and there certainly wasn't anyone to take care of him in the next two months. Only the VA and he doubted they really wanted to see him at this point either, after the fuss he had made about getting a second and then a third opinion.

He had no real money except the little bit his parents had left him and his job driving a city bus could be filled in ten minutes.

The pistol would do everyone a favor.

He opened the door to his single-bedroom apartment and tossed the key onto the small kitchen table after kicking the door closed behind him, leaving it unlocked.

The place still smelled of the eggs and bacon he had made for himself for breakfast. It had been a good last meal for a condemned man.

The apartment had been a pretty good place to live, so no point in staining it all up with his blood. He'd leave the world in the bathroom, in the tub, with the curtain shut. He just hoped someone found him quickly so that the smell wouldn't ruin everything.

"Not having a good day, huh?" a voice said from the big chair in his living room to the left of the main door.

Holcomb spun around to face a man sitting in Holcomb's favorite chair in front of the television. The guy had long gray hair combed back, dark eyes, and tan skin. He looked Native American or Mexican descent. He had on standard Oregon casual, jeans and a tan button-down dress shirt with his sleeves rolled up.

The guy was clearly not the standard robber that Holcomb would expect going through these apartments. He'd been robbed twice in his four years living here, both times by hippie-types looking for drug money.

Two steps and Holcomb had the pistol out of the kitchen drawer and pointed at the guy.

The guy didn't even flinch. "Thought you were going to use that on yourself?"

Now the guy was just pissing Holcomb off. No one knew his plans. And no one but his doctors and a couple people at the VA knew about the cancer. He hadn't told anyone, not even his friends at work. So how could this stranger know what he had been thinking?

"Nice of you to do it in the shower," the guy said, nodding. "Saved a lot of clean-up and they found your body in ten minutes because your neighbor heard the shot, so no real smell issues. A young married couple moves in here next month. Nice folks. You would have liked them, but of course, you'll never get the chance to meet them, will you?"

Holcomb couldn't let the guy confuse him. He focused, got his mind clear like he used to do in the service before a mission.

"Who the hell are you and what are you doing here?"

"Just call me Kontar. I know, strange name, but my father was Egyptian on his father's side." The guy shrugged as if any of that meant something.

Holcomb waved the gun in frustration. The guy was really starting to make him angry. And a soon-to-be-dead man wasn't a good person to piss off.

"What I am doing here?" Kontar asked, smiling. "Actually, I'm here to recruit you to help in a fight for your country."

"Yeah, right," Holcomb said, leveling the gun at the man. "Ten seconds to tell me the truth or they end up cleaning this place after all because of two bodies. As you seem to know, it will make no difference to me."

"You won't believe the truth, but I'll tell you anyway," Kontar said. "I know you are about to kill yourself because of terminal cancer because I am from the future. Actually, looking back from my time, you killed yourself in that bathroom back there, curtains drawn, that gun in your mouth. Because you have no family or real friends, we figured you to be a perfect candidate to help us out with a mission to save your country.

"And which government agency do you work for?" Holcomb asked, shaking his head. "The nut-ball service?"

Kontar shook his head. "I don't work for your government. I work for the Inca Nation. But the survival of your country is wrapped up in the survival of mine, which is why I need your help."

"In the future?" Holcomb said, still not believing a word this nut case was saying.

"Actually, no," Kontar said. "I need your help in the past. Since you're going to die anyway today, or in a few months from cancer, I have a mission for you first."

"A suicide mission," Holcomb said, disgusted and about ready to shoot the guy. "Right?"

"Of course," Kontar said, smiling, showing perfect, very white teeth. "But considering what you were about to do in your bathtub, I figured you wouldn't have a problem with that."

THREE

February 24, 1836
Alamo Mission, Bexar, Republic of Texas

WHEN THE SHOOTING from the other side of the long Alamo compound

started, it woke up Holcomb. He had dozed off against the west wall, his gun across his legs.

DeWitt snorted and came awake beside him. They watched as the Texans on the south wall laid down covering fire for someone coming to the gate. A few moments later the large wooden gate was opened in the wall built between the south buildings of the mission and the church itself. Five men came through leading twenty horses loaded down with supplies.

"Looks like we're eating tonight," DeWitt said.

"Yeah," Holcomb said, taking in the scene in front of him. They had come in just after dark last night and he hadn't gotten much of a chance to look around, since they went right to the wall and cut down the cannon fire from the Aztec cannons.

The Alamo grounds were a lot larger than he had ever imagined from the movies and stories he had been told. Between the buildings along the west wall and the barrack wall on the east, it was a good half a football field wide, and one and a half fields long.

A cannonade had been constructed right in the middle, large enough to let cannons turn in any direction and high enough to see over the walls in all four directions.

There were also four cannons along the west wall, two on the top of the building on the north wall, four along the south wall, and three in the back of the old church facing east. In the fort there were twenty-one artillery pieces of different caliber, an impressive fortification.

A guy by the name of Neill had managed to turn the old mission grounds into a pretty impressive fort in the months before they arrived.

From what Holcomb could tell, there had to be a good hundred and fifty men here already, mostly volunteers like he and DeWitt were posing as. Two names from the history books of Holcomb's time were in charge and he and DeWitt got to meet them both.

Travis led the Texas Regular troops while Bowie seemed to be in charge of all the volunteers. Both men seemed much smaller to Holcomb than their legends led him to believe.

And Travis was very, very young.

DeWitt and Holcomb were put under Bowie with the volunteers, but at the moment Bowie seemed to be sick and Travis was doing just about everything. Considering how young the kid was, Holcomb found him impressive. Even Congressmen Crockett nodded to Travis as the man in charge.

Supposedly, there were other teams from the future in the mix, but Holcomb hadn't really spotted any in the short time he and DeWitt had been inside, since everyone was dressed for the time period and didn't stand out.

Supposedly, the Incas were also supplying much needed ammunition and food to the fighters inside the Alamo without anyone knowing about it, but both Holcomb and DeWitt had their own supplies in the form of small pills as food. Interestingly enough, the pills were filling. Not much fun to eat, but enough to keep them going.

They both also had their medicine to keep them going long enough to die for the cause. DeWitt had less time left to live than Holcomb, and at times coughed so hard he spit up blood.

Holcomb watched, his back against the west wall of the Alamo, as four men shut the gate at the other end of the compound and Travis welcomed the new volunteers and the supplies they brought.

Holcomb had to admit that there were some brave men here, fighting for a cause they felt was right. Many of them had families and children at home they would never see again. Even if they lived and became a prisoner of the Aztec, they would be sacrificed and their hearts eaten, as was Aztec custom with war prisoners of this time period.

Death was the only way out of this battle.

Holcomb watched the small celebration around the new arrivals and wondered if he would have had the courage to fight this fight if he wasn't dying anyway. He hoped so. Sometimes, your country, and a way of life you believed in, was worth fighting and dying for. He had thought that at first, when he joined the Army and was sent over to Vietnam.

When he got home, he hadn't been so sure anymore.

He just hoped this time the fight was the lives and the blood and the pain. Davy Crockett and all the other men here sure seemed to think so.

FOUR

Unknown Date, 23rd Century
Cuzco, Inca Nation

HOLCOMB FELT like his brain was about to explode. Kontar had been trying to explain time travel and different universes to him and a guy by the name of DeWitt for the last half hour and none of it seemed to make sense.

They were in what looked like a standard conference room, inside a huge building with no real character, inside the vast city of Cuzco, the capital city of the Incas.

Flying in on some strange plane with porthole-like windows, Holcomb had been stunned by the beauty of the 23rd century city spread out below. But as Kontar said, there wouldn't be time to look around. Holcomb, with his cancer, just didn't have that much time left. But he had no doubt at all that he was in a future city from what little he did get to see. No city on his earth in his time looked like Cuzco.

He had been shown a room to sleep for the night, a change of clothes and shower. After what felt like a short eight hours, he was given a breakfast that tasted a lot like cold Cream of Wheat cereal. He was assured it was good for him and would give him extra strength. Bacon and eggs would have tasted a hell of a lot better.

After breakfast, there had been yet another physical that once again confirmed what the doctors in his time had told him.

He didn't have long to live.

Great, a fourth opinion confirmed yet again he was going to die, and not even the medicine in the 23rd century could save him.

After the physical, he had been introduced to another Vietnam vet from the east coast and put in a plain meeting room with tan walls to get their first briefing. If the first thirty minutes of this briefing were any indication, he and DeWitt might not live long enough to get through the lectures, let alone fight for their country.

"Okay, hold on a second," Holcomb said, holding up both his hands in a show of surrender. "Let me see if I got any of this right."

"Thank you," DeWitt whispered, shaking his head.

"DeWitt and I are from a timeline where the Spanish win over the Incas and the Aztecs and the Mayans. That forms what we know as Mexico and all the Central and South American countries. Right?"

"Correct," Kontar said, nodding.

"Good, got my own history correct then," Holcomb said.

DeWitt actually applauded him.

Holcomb went on. "You say we are sitting in a timeline where the Aztecs and the Incas both win against the Spanish and keep them out of Central America and South America. And you hate each other. Correct?"

"Yes," Kontar said.

"And in this world, the United States still exists in pretty much the same configuration as it does in our time line."

"It does," Kontar said, clicking something in his hand.

The wall behind him showed an image of North and South America. The Inca Nation was South America, the Aztecs held Central America and Mexico, and the United States looked normal, as did Canada.

"So why are we fighting at the Alamo again?"

"Because, if the Texans don't hold off the Aztecs at that time and win, this is what the world looks like by 1850, just a short time after the Alamo battle."

The map on the wall changed to one showing the United States cut off below Georgia with a line extending to the Mississippi and then up, with the rest showing the color of the Aztec nation.

"Without the Texans winning against the Aztecs, the Aztec/American war is never fought," Kontar said

"Like the Mexican/American war in our world," DeWitt said.

"Correct," Kontar said. "When the Aztecs discover gold in California, they wipe out all English and European settlers on the west coast and cut off all westward expansion with the help of the native tribes. They then buy the Louisiana Purchase from the United States and basically close off the area. In this timeline, the Aztec take over all of North America in the late 1920s while Europe was still fighting what you call World War One. With the vast resources of North America, the Aztec become very powerful and we fall to them in 2010."

Holcomb didn't much like the look of that map showing all of North and South America as bright red Aztec Nation. Not one bit.

"How many timelines does that happen in?" DeWitt asked.

"A great number," Kontar said. "See why the battle at the Alamo is so important?"

"Actually, no," Holcomb said. "In my timeline, the battle of the Alamo was lost, and it made no real difference at all, other than as a rallying cry. If I have my own history correct, that is."

"You do, but it does in these time-lines," Kontar said, pointing to the ugly map showing all red of the Aztec empire covering everything. "If the Aztec win the battle of the Alamo easily, they simply sweep across Texas and don't stop. They defeat the Texas army easily under Sam Houston and take Louisiana and Florida easily as well. Only a truce with the United States stops them at that point, but that's too late."

"Santa Anna, in our timeline, had thousands of troops," Holcomb asked.

"How many is the Aztec going to bring against the Alamo?"

"The War Chief will lead four to five thousand warriors," Kontar said with a straight face.

DeWitt just snorted.

Holcomb laughed. "You expect less than two hundred men to stop five thousand Aztec warriors?"

"No, I don't, actually. But with a few modern weapons to help out, you can slow them down and do some real damage, enough so that Houston and his men, with a little help as well, can stop them."

DeWitt shrugged and glanced at Holcomb. "We're both dead anyway in a few months, better to go out fighting for our country, even though this isn't really our country."

Holcomb nodded. DeWitt was right. It was much better than sitting in a hospice drooling on a bib waiting to die, or standing in a bathtub with a gun in his mouth.

Besides, he had always wanted to see the Alamo, ever since he was a kid. Looked like he was going to get a real close look at it.

FIVE

February 28, 1836
Alamo Compound, Bexar,
Republic of Texas

THE COLD NIGHT had broken into a warm day, letting the dust and the dry wind swirl through the large compound. In the distance, the sounds of thousands of Aztec warriors chanting and moving equipment echoed over the rolling hills. Travis reported to everyone that the Aztec numbers were still under two thousand, but growing by the day.

And the great Aztec War Chief was still a few days from the Rio Grande. He would have thousands of warriors with him.

Kontar had told him and DeWitt the Aztec War Chief's name, but Holcomb had forgotten it at once, since it was long and had more consonants in it than vowels by a margin of five to one. He'd never been that good in school with the English language, so learning Aztec names in a few days time just didn't seem to be worth the effort in his final weeks alive.

He was just glad that the Spanish had gone into Florida and across into Texas and Southern California when defeated by the Aztec and Inca nations. Otherwise, the Alamo would have had some other strange name as well.

Holcomb was now very sure, after five days in the Alamo, that there were numbers of other teams from the future inside the Alamo. He and DeWitt had been given permission by Travis to fire when a target was clear, since more than enough ammunition and food had somehow managed to be brought to the fort, both from outside supplies coming in from Sam Houston and the Texas government, and also from missions outside the walls searching surrounding buildings now abandoned by the settlers of the area.

So all night and all day, the sporadic sounds of gunfire cut through the air.

The number of men inside the walls still numbered less than one hundred and sixty, but with enough food and firepower, spirits were high at the moment.

Holcomb and DeWitt had both kept any Aztec warrior from poking his head up within hundreds of yards of the Alamo west wall. The two Aztec cannon placements on the mounds in the town were nothing more than a killing field for the two men. Aztec warriors would rush up onto the platforms to try to load the cannons, or even move the cannons off the platforms, and DeWitt or Holcomb or both of them would make the warriors pay with their lives.

Other teams down the wall and on both end walls had been doing the same to the other Aztec cannon emplacements, so unlike the history that Holcomb had studied of the Alamo in his timeline, this time around the constant cannon bombardment of the walls of the Alamo wasn't happening. That allowed the men inside to be more rested and since they had better food and lots of water, they were going to put up one very nasty fight when the time came.

Also, the fort walls were not beaten down by the week of bombardment, meaning that it would be a lot harder for the Aztec warriors to get inside.

One day, while walking the west wall, Travis had noticed their accuracy and asked them about it. Holcomb had simply said, "Kentucky practice. I can knock the left eye out of a squirrel at two hundred paces."

DeWitt laughed. "And I can knock the right one out at the same time from three hundred."

Travis had just laughed and moved on. The kid was smart enough to not question his luck. Holcomb wished a few lieutenants back in Nam had been that smart. They and a lot of their men would still be alive.

Well, actually, they hadn't been born yet, since this was 1836, and in a different world where Aztecs were a powerful nation. Holcomb just shook his head at the thought. All of this was just confusing.

Twenty paces to their right, three men laughed and Holcomb watched as they worked to raise a cannon a precise amount, using some sort of measuring device that didn't look like it belonged to this period of time.

After a moment, they looked pleased and called Travis to watch, having him focus on one of the cannon placements in Bexar that Holcomb and DeWitt had been guarding.

As one man signaled to fire, Holcomb covered his ears. The old cannons were amazingly loud. The explosion still rocked him and sent dust swirling in all directions.

DeWitt coughed a few times, hard, but then recovered. That cough wasn't sounding good.

Travis didn't seem to mind the sound of the explosion, and neither did Crockett on the other side of the cannon. Both just stood their ground and stared at the intended target.

Holcomb followed their gaze and a moment later one of the Aztec cannons just exploded, flipping over backwards and flying into a hundred pieces.

The three men manning the cannon cheered, as did all the men up and down the wall who had been watching.

"I didn't know those old things could be that accurate," DeWitt said, shaking his head in amazement.

"They can't," Holcomb said, laughing.

DeWitt stared at him for a moment, then laughed as well. "Nice to know old Kontar and his people are covering all the bases. Maybe we're going to have a fighting chance here."

"Well, we'll be fighting, that's for sure," Holcomb said. He had no illusion that they had any chance of surviving.

SIX

Unknown Date, 2300
Cuzco, Inca Nation

HOLCOMB STOOD at the table in an indoor firing range and studied the fake antique gun in his hands. It looked old, right out of the eighteen hundreds, modeled after the type of long rifle you saw Davy Crockett carrying.

It was a Kentucky rifle with brass inlays on the long butt and along the wood under the barrel. It even had marks and wear, making it seem like it had been used a great deal and carried in a saddle holster.

But this rifle, under the disguise was far, far more.

Even though it looked like it fired the old style ammunition, it didn't. Hidden in the long stock was a clip that held fifty high-powered rounds. The used shells were stored in the long wood area under the barrel until removed. The rounds looked no bigger than a 22 caliber, but Kontar assured him that the small shells and tips had more length and velocity than a sniper rifle of Holcomb's time.

And even more amazing, when fired, the gun spit out the same smoke and smell that a Kentucky rifle did when fired.

The only problem would be carrying the amount of ammunition they would need, reloading the clips into the butts of the rifle, and hiding the spent shells. That would be hard, at times, but workable, Holcomb was sure.

In the service, both Holcomb and DeWitt had been top marksmen, but Holcomb just couldn't believe he would be able to hit the side of a large building from a hundred yards with the fake old gun, even though it felt a lot lighter than it looked and balanced perfectly in his hands.

"Try it," was all Kontar said, smiling at both DeWitt and Holcomb.

"Too stupid for words," DeWitt said. "We're all going to die, why worry about pretending to be from the time period."

"Because the Aztecs of this world have time travel as well," Kontar said.

That fact stunned Holcomb right to his core and made his stomach twist. It hadn't occurred to him that the two sides would be evenly matched.

"So we're not so worried about hiding your presence from the locals inside the fort," Kontar said, "but from the Aztecs outside the fort who are from our time period. If they can't tell who our plants are, if any in the timeline you are going to, and who are just locals, you'll live longer."

"Super," DeWitt said, shaking his head. "We're not only fighting five thousand Aztec warriors in 1836, but Aztec agents from the future? What's the point? Just shoot us now."

"The point is," Kontar said, looking first at DeWitt, then focusing on Holcomb as if he was going to understand more than DeWitt, "that we don't know which way this timeline will fall. We do know that much of the outcome will come down to this one battle, and we're hoping the Aztec do not know that as firmly as we do, and once they discover that fact, we will already have won the day."

"So this is the first timeline your two people have fought over?"

"No," Kontar said, shaking his head. "We are fighting across many, many timelines at once, actually. We have turned the tide in other timelines by helping Sam Houston, by winning at the battle of New

Orleans against the Aztec, by driving them back with surprise attacks out of Georgia, but never once have we tried to stop them at the Alamo before."

"How do you keep all this straight?" DeWitt asked a moment before Holcomb could ask the same question.

"It isn't easy," Kontar said. "But this timeline is the one I focus on, that I am in charge of."

Holcomb was shocked. "You're telling me that the fate of millions of people and your very culture's existence rests on your shoulders alone?"

"No, my culture is right here," Kontar said, indicating the building and the firing range around them. "I'm just trying to help other timelines follow this culture, to get the chance to develop to this point."

Holcomb could feel his head wanting to explode again. "So tell me, how many timelines that you know about developed to this point without outside help?"

"None," Holcomb said. "We had help in our past as well in the form of a very special gift from someone far, far into our future. But we're not allowed to talk about that."

Holcomb just shook his head and tried to focus again on the fake antique rifle in his hands. He knew guns. Guns he understood. Time travel just gave him a headache.

"Ahh, well," DeWitt said, picking up the rifle and taking a stance aiming down the range at a human-shaped target one hundred yards away. "I'm going to die soon anyway. This way might just be fun."

He pulled the trigger and the loud sound filled the range at the same moment as a perfectly shaped hole appeared where the middle of the nose of the target figure would be.

DeWitt turned and smiled. "I'll be go to hell, this thing actually works."

Kontar nodded. "Wait until you see what the pistols and the grenades shaped as rifle rounds will do."

Holcomb held the perfectly balanced gun in his hands. At least in this war, he was going in well armed. Outmanned, but with real fire power.

SEVEN

March 1, 1836
Alamo Compound, Bexar,
Republic of Texas

HOLCOMB WATCHED from his normal spot on the west wall as over thirty troops arrived, riding through the covering fire and into the compound.

"Part of Gonzales' ranging company," DeWitt said. "If I remember my history correctly, those are the last reinforcements we're going to get."

"Unless Kontar changes the history," Holcomb said.

"Oh, yeah, forgot about that part. We can only hope."

At that moment the boom of an Aztec cannon filled the air.

Holcomb glanced up, waiting and watching for the flaming fireball coming at them. The Aztec had brought in more cannons and were now firing what Kontar, in a briefing, called "Flaming Arrows" from a greater distance and hidden from direct line of sight behind buildings.

It took exactly three shots for the cannon crew down the wall to narrow in on an exact location and destroy the cannon every time an Aztec cannon started firing, but in the meantime, when the Flaming Arrows landed, they

seemed to catch anything near them on fire. Holcomb figured they were more annoying then damaging, since there wasn't that much besides staircases and window frames made of wood inside the big compound. All the rest was thick rock and mud walls.

This shot landed short of the wall and caused no damage at all in the hard surface.

Very few Aztec cannon shots had hit the thick walls, so the fort didn't look much worse for wear than when Holcomb had arrived.

He and DeWitt had just kept knocking down any warrior out there that moved within range. And the accurate range of the fake rifles they had in their hands was almost frightening. They seldom missed, and it seemed neither did the other few sharp-shooting crews from the future placed along the walls. That kept the Aztec warriors a great distance away.

The great War Chief couldn't be very happy about his troops not getting close to the fort. He and the main band of warriors still hadn't arrived yet, even though they had crossed the Rio Grande three days before. Holcomb and DeWitt had talked a lot about what they thought the War Chief would do when he arrived. The only conclusion they had was that he would send his men in a full assault against the walls, just as Santa Anna had done.

It would cost him hundreds and hundreds of lives, but it would get the job done fairly quickly, even against weapons from the future.

DeWitt nudged Holcomb and got him to turn away from staring out over the empty and silent town of Bexar that would be San Antonio in his timeline. "We got company."

A man with a long moustache and carrying a rifle and a large knapsack was coming up the wooden stairs toward them. He looked to be tall, maybe six foot and then some, with large arms and a slight limp on his right side. He had a cowboy hat pulled down low over his eyes to shade from the bright sun.

Both Holcomb and DeWitt started to stand, but the man signaled they stay in position behind the wall and then knelt in front of them, pushing his hat back.

"Stacy," the guy said, sticking out his hand.

"Sergeant Ben Stacy, from California?" DeWitt asked, taking the guy's hand and pumping it like it was old home week. "I'll be go-to-hell. What are you doing here?"

"Same damn thing you are, it seems," Stacy said, smiling. "Committing suicide by Aztec. I was hoping you were still alive when I got here. Kontar said you most likely would be.

"Fit as a fiddle," DeWitt said, lying.

Stacy laughed. "Yeah, me too." He glanced around. "So this is what the Alamo looks like. Bigger than I expected."

"Me too," DeWitt said, then broke into a coughing fit before he could say another word.

"He gets all choked up seeing old friends," Holcomb said, sticking out his hand. "I'm Holcomb. Snatched right out of 1981. Lung cancer, about a month left if I survive this."

Stacy smiled and took his hand. "1986. Prostate cancer, don't want to think about spending that much time left. Riding a damn horse was painful enough."

"Yeah, understand that," Holcomb said, trying not to laugh. "Welcome to the fight."

Stacy dropped the leather satchel and waited until DeWitt's coughing fit passed with a little help from an inhaler he kept hidden in his shirt pocket.

"This is from Kontar," Stacy said, indicating the leather pouch. "I told Travis down there it was personal stuff from your family. It's actually more clips, hidden in the shirts, and about fifty small grenades with six-second delays once you twist the caps."

"How is our old friend Kontar?" Holcomb asked. "He have any idea how things are shifting in the fight?"

"Haven't seen him since you have," Stacy said. "I was put in with those men down there three weeks ago so I could get in here and deliver this and help you two in the fight.

"Before he recruited me?" DeWitt asked, looking puzzled.

Holcomb just patted DeWitt's arm. "Time travel, remember? Don't worry about it."

"Gives me a headache just thinking about it," Stacy said.

"Me too," both Holcomb and DeWitt said at the same time.

All three men laughed and then Stacy took up a position on the wall beside them.

It felt good to have another fighter with them, another Nam vet. Holcomb had no doubt he was going to die in the coming fight. But he didn't mind so much and wasn't afraid of it at all. There were a lot worse ways to go.

EIGHT

May 20, 1981
Portland, Oregon, USA

KONTAR HAD spent the afternoon trying to explain everything, then left, giving Holcomb two days to decide and get his affairs in order if he decided to go.

After the strange man with the white teeth left, Holcomb had gone back to the park, sitting and thinking about how crazy it all seemed, yet how right it was as well. He had watched kids playing in the grass, a couple kissing on another bench, a boat going past with a woman sunning herself in a bikini on the bow.

In other words, a normal spring day in the park.

He had figured, just as his father had said, that this world was worth fighting for. That's why he signed up for Vietnam. But coming back, it had gotten so confusing. Nothing was as black and white as his father had explained it to be.

But now Kontar had given him straight black and white talk. He needed Holcomb's help in a fight to help the United States to even exist in a different timeline. Aztecs were a warrior race that still believed in human sacrifice, even into the 23rd century when Kontar was from. The United States and the Inca Nation were the beacons of freedom of human rights and freedoms in Kontar's time. And the survival of one depended on the survival of the other, it seemed.

Holcomb didn't pretend to understand, and Kontar promised to explain even more before the mission started.

Kontar had also promised that if Holcomb came along, Kontar's people could help someone or some member of Holcomb's family if he wanted. But Holcomb had no real family, so he had told Kontar that he would think about that.

Sitting on that park bench, in that park, two hours after Kontar had left, Holcomb had decided to go. He might not have his name in any history books, but if he helped at the Alamo and it made a difference, at least he would be part

of a fight that an entire nation would remember.

He gave his notice at the bus garage, talked to a few friends there, and then went back to give notice on his apartment. What surprised him was how many people, both at work and in his building, seemed genuinely sad that he was leaving. He might not have that many good friends, but he clearly had people who liked him, and he liked them back, and some of them would even miss him.

One elderly woman down the hall even brought him a small plate of sugar cookies for a travel snack. He'd only seen her a few times in the hall, and couldn't remember her name, even though she knew his. She told him that he just made the place seem safer. She was going to miss that.

He had never noticed any of it. He just felt he had been walking through the world alone. It seemed he had been far from alone.

This time around, Kontar knocked on the apartment door and Holcomb answered, a small bag on his shoulder that included his pistol and bathroom supplies and a few changes of clothes. Everything else he was leaving with a note on the kitchen table.

"Seems you have decided," Kontar said, smiling as he backed up and let Holcomb step out and pull the door closed.

"Just one favor to ask," Holcomb said as they headed down the wide hallway toward the staircase.

"Ask and I will do what I can do," Kontar said.

"If you can, I would love to have you use what little money I have left in the bank and add some to it and set up a small college scholarship fund for kids of city bus drivers. Put it in my name if you would, even though no one will remember who I am."

Kontar glanced at Holcomb as they went down the stairs to the lobby, clearly puzzled. "We can do that, no problem at all. That's very nice of you."

Holcomb shrugged. "Always thought about going back to school. Just never got around to it."

"What would you have studied?" Kontar asked.

Holcomb laughed. "History. I always loved history."

Kontar laughed. "With luck, for an entire culture in a different timeline, you're going to help make some history."

As they went out the door and into the bright light of the warm spring day, Holcomb said, "That's why I'm doing this."

NINE

March 5, 1836
Alamo Compound, Bexar,
Republic of Texas

THE SUN WAS EASING BEHIND the low hills to the west. Holcomb, Stacy, and DeWitt had been firing consistently all day, picking off any warrior that moved in the direction of the Aztec camp, just as they had done for the past four days.

Travis had reported that the War Chief and the thousands of warriors with him had arrived earlier in the day. And as history in Holcomb's timeline had shown, no more men came to help those inside the Alamo. They were going into battle with thousands of Aztec warriors with around two hundred men.

But so far, the men inside the walls were in good spirits. No real damage had been done to the walls of the fort thanks to the sharpshooters keeping the cannons at a distance. The fort had stayed a safe little island in a sea of death. Holcomb had no doubt that was about to change. If the Aztec War Chief followed Santa Anna's plan, he would attack tomorrow, on March 6th.

But many historians and many of Santa Anna's own officers had thought it stupid to attack directly at the fort. But that had been in another timeline, with another commander and a much weaker Mexican army. The Aztec War Chief was known for just taking what he wanted. There didn't seem to be any doubt in anyone's mind he was coming hard and soon. The key would be how much damage the men inside the walls could do to the Aztec force before they were killed.

DeWitt used an inhaler to stop a coughing fit and Stacy used the time to refill the clip in his rifle, tossing the empty shells over the wall wrapped in a small cloth bag. The bag had a special acid inside it that ate the shells and turned them into dust in a matter of days. The shells themselves were designed to deteriorate quickly anyway. No one in ten years would dig up any shells or signs of anything from the future at this sight.

"Incoming," a voice shouted and all three men went back to staring out over the wall.

Holcomb was shocked at what he saw.

Coming at full run, directly from the center of the city, were about fifty warriors, their war cries filling the air.

"All four sides," Travis shouted from a perch atop the center cannonade. "They're coming at us from four directions."

Firing started up at once, the sounds covering the cries of the warriors. One right after another the cannons of the fort fired, filling the air with smoke, the booming sounds echoing over the countryside.

Holcomb, Stacy, and DeWitt fired as well, Holcomb taking a warrior on the right and killing him, Stacy aimed at the left, and DeWitt the middle.

The cannons sent more warrior bodies into the air, and each of them fired five more times before the firing eased to a stop with no more warriors to kill.

The wave of warriors hadn't even made it to within a hundred yards of the fort on any side.

"That was just a test," Holcomb said, staring at the bodies strung along the field between the fort wall and Bexar buildings. "The War Chief wanted to know how strong we are."

"He sacrificed two hundred men to test us?" Stacy said, shaking his head.

"Sure seems that way," DeWitt said.

Suddenly Holcomb realized what he had said. With any test, someone had to be looking at the results.

"Watch for movement in the distance," Holcomb said, flipping his glasses to binocular vision and studying the roofs and walls of the city buildings. "Lower War Chiefs had to have been watching so that they could report back."

Beside him, Stacy fired and a brightly adorned warrior spun and fell about two hundred yards out.

Holcomb caught sight of another warrior staring at the scene from the top of a building and put a shot between his eyes.

A few of the other sharpshooters on the other walls were also firing, taking out anyone who might show their face.

DeWitt laughed. "The great War Chief ain't going to like any of this."

"We just pissed him off is all," Holcomb said.

"So, when do you three think he will attack us?"

Holcomb spun around away from the wall at the same time as DeWitt and Stacy to see Travis kneeling behind them.

Holcomb couldn't think of a thing to say to the leader of the fort. And clearly DeWitt and Stacy were just as shocked.

"Look," Travis said, "I know you three have military experience from some place I am not familiar with, as do a number of others who are volunteers here. And you are the best shots I have ever had the pleasure of watching. I'm just glad you are all here helping Texas in this fight."

"It's our honor, sir," Holcomb managed to say. Stacy nodded and DeWitt coughed as he nodded his agreement.

In the last week he had only said a passing hello to Travis. He figured he and DeWitt and Stacy were staying under the young officer's notice. Clearly they hadn't.

History always said that Travis was both smart and very brave. He had just proven history to be correct.

"What just happened was clearly a test," Travis said, "and you sharpshooters cut down the number of reports the War Chief will get about the results. Any theories about what's next? Will it be a full attack tonight or any chance he might just leave us and go around?"

"He won't attack at night," Holcomb said and again both his friends nodded. "From everything I know about the War Chief of the Aztec, fighting at night has little honor. They will prepare at night, and they have no problem in small skirmishes at night, but if they come in full attack, it will be at first light."

He had learned all that from Kontar in the distant future, but he wasn't about to tell Travis that.

"And he won't go around us either," Stacy said. "He can't show any weakness to those under him or they will challenge and kill him."

"Agreed," Holcomb said. "They're coming in full force at first light tomorrow."

Travis seemed to think about that for a moment, then nodded. "I agree."

He stood and saluted Holcomb and Stacy and DeWitt. "Thank you, gentlemen, for the honor of fighting and dying beside you."

With that he turned and went down the stairs and back toward the sick room where Bowie was being cared for.

"This is a long damn ways from Vietnam," DeWitt said after a long moment of silence.

Down the wall, Holcomb noticed that Davy Crockett had been watching the exchange. He gave Holcomb a thumbs-up and went back to watching out over the wall.

For the first time, Holcomb knew completely that what he did in this fight really mattered. Dying for this cause was the right thing to do. He knew now what his father had described about fighting in World War II.

"This doesn't even feel like the same world," DeWitt said, shaking his head.

"Actually," Stacy said, "it's not, remember?"

Holcomb glanced once again at Davy Crockett, one of his childhood heroes. "Tough to forget."

TEN

March 6, 1836
Alamo Compound, Bexar,
Republic of Texas

THE MOMENT THE SUN tipped an edge over the hills in the east, the Aztec flaming arrow cannons filled the sky with streaks of fire, sending rolling thunder over the fort and the peaceful sunrise of a Texas morning.

The night had been long and quiet, with only an occasional shot cutting the

stillness from a sharpshooter who picked off a warrior stupid enough to show himself.

"Here we go," DeWitt said as the cannons went off, bracing himself against the wall.

"It's been my honor," Holcomb said, glancing at the two men on either side of him that he now called friends, "to fight with you."

"I will remember these days for as long as I live," Stacy said, smiling.

"That's going to be at least another thirty minutes," DeWitt said. "If we're lucky."

"I'm hoping for more like an hour," Holcomb said, laughing.

A moment later, thousands of Aztec warriors seemed to appear out of nowhere among the buildings of the town and the gullies of the hills around the fort.

Waves and waves and waves of warriors.

"Make that thirty minutes after all," Holcomb said, starting to fire.

The sounds of the exploding cannons, and thousands of rifles being fired at once smashed into Holcomb as he fired off one round after another into the ranks, trying to pick off any warrior who looked to be dressed better than any other.

He went through his first clip in a matter of twenty seconds, reloaded, and went back to firing, cutting down warriors in the front lines so that others behind them might trip over the bodies.

It was like facing a sea of ants. The Aztecs swarmed everywhere, screaming and firing as they ran.

One bullet nicked the top of the wall near Holcomb and sent sand into his face, but luckily nothing got into his eyes behind his protective glasses given to him by Kontar.

Beside him, DeWitt was grazed by a shot across one arm. He just swore, wrapped the surface wound in a piece of cloth, and went back to firing, his inhaler stuck in his mouth like a bad cigar.

Holcomb just kept firing, through another clip and then another, his shots always dropping a warrior. And every warrior he killed was one less to fight against Sam Houston and the others defending Texas and the rest of the United States.

The cannons of the Alamo kept up a constant bombardment of the rushing warriors, smashing five and ten at a time into the air.

Suddenly, DeWitt tapped his arm and pointed out at the town's buildings. The main wave of the warriors were now only a hundred yards from the bottom of the west wall and closing fast, and on the buildings of the town, well decorated and brightly colored Aztec warriors had climbed up to watch the fight.

And one in the center looked to be the top War Chief himself, not more than nine hundred feet away.

The idiot was too arrogant to know he couldn't be killed.

Holcomb tapped Stacy and pointed to what DeWitt had shown him. Stacy glanced up, then smiled and nodded.

Holcomb used the old hand signals from Nam to indicate in the intense sound of the battle the way the three of them should fire. Stacy would take the ones on the right side, Holcomb would take the top War Chief in the middle, and DeWitt the chiefs on the left side.

Then on the count of three, they all fired, ignoring the wave of warriors approaching the wall below them.

Holcomb knocked down the War Chief with a shot directly between his well-painted eyes.

Before the others could react around him, Holcomb killed two more of the War Chief's top lieutenants, while DeWitt and Stacy cut down the others on either side.

If nothing else, they had cut the head off of the snake. It would grow a new one quickly enough, but with luck that might give Houston and his Texan army some time and a real fighting chance.

All three of them went back to firing at the rushing warriors below as the remaining brightly dressed war chiefs scattered back into hiding.

When the leading wave of the warriors reached the base of the wall and started trying to toss ropes with hooks over the top, Holcomb grabbed a few of the pen-sized grenades, twisted the caps, and dropped them as beside him Stacy cut a rope and then did the same.

Other warriors were bringing ladders at the walls. Others behind the leading waves were moving cannons into position.

There were just too many. But the Aztecs were paying a very, very high price for this attack.

Along the wall, other defenders followed suit, firing over and over and tossing explosive charges into the mass of warriors coming up at them from the base of the twenty-foot wall.

But nothing seemed to slow the warriors down, they just kept pouring at the wall.

Holcomb went back to picking off the warriors trying to set up cannons to fire directly at the wall from close range. Beside him, Stacy leaned forward to drop a few grenades. Suddenly he spun backwards, a gaping hole in the back of his head from a shot that blew his skull apart.

He went over backwards and then tumbled down the stairs.

Holcomb gave his friend a quick salute of honor and went back to fighting.

Farther down the wall, Crockett was shoving a ladder away from the wall and butting two warriors with the hard end of his rifle, sending them back into the mass of death below.

Holcomb tossed half-a-dozen grenades along the base of the wall in front of him and DeWitt and Crockett.

The smoke from the explosions and the gunshots drifted so thickly it felt like trying to fight on a thick foggy night along the ocean. Only this fog smelled of gunpowder and sweat and blood.

Lots of blood.

DeWitt jumped up and moved to his right along the wall, firing at a warrior trying to breach over the top of the wall. Then he dropped a grenade at the bottom of the ladder and fired downward into the mass.

Suddenly, he dropped over backwards, a bullet hole directly between his eyes.

They had all been wrong. It didn't look like they all were going to last fifteen minutes.

At a half dozen places along the wall the warriors were coming over the top.

Holcomb took his last ten grenades and twisted the caps on all of them, tossing them at different places along the wall at the bases of ladders.

A shot ripped through his left arm, spinning him around and sending waves of bright red pain across his eyes.

His vision cleared quickly and he dropped his rifle and grabbed his pistol, firing as he went.

Crockett moved toward him, firing and butting at warriors reaching the top of the wall.

"Retreat to the church!" he shouted.

"I'll cover you," Holcomb shouted back and Crockett nodded and scrambled down the staircase to the middle of the compound where dozens of Texans were retreating toward their last stand in the church.

Holcomb kept firing, protecting his childhood hero as much as he could, until a shot ripped through his left shoulder and

he went over backwards, tumbling down the stairs to the hard dirt at the bottom.

Somehow, he managed to keep the gun in his hand.

A moment later, Crockett appeared in his vision and yanked him to his feet, pulling him toward the church.

Holcomb let the pain clear his mind and he focused one last time, firing at a warrior who was about to attack Crockett.

Then a shot cut through the Tennessee congressman, spinning him away from Holcomb. The shot had caught him in the chest, but he was still alive.

Now it was Holcomb's turn to pull his hero to his feet and stumble onward.

But it wasn't to be.

More fire from the right.

More pain cut through Holcomb's legs and back.

He and Crockett went down.

An Aztec warrior with a brightly painted face loomed over Holcomb.

Holcomb struggled to turn over, pushing himself in the dirt.

Crockett tried to get up to fight, but the warrior cut off his head with a quick swing of a sword.

All Holcomb could do was smile at the ugly painted face of the Aztec as the warrior raised his sword yet again.

Holcomb knew that they had accomplished what they needed to accomplish. He was sure of that. They had slowed the Aztec army and caused enough damage that Houston could defeat them.

This would be a good world he had helped create.

And maybe in Portland, Oregon, in this timeline, there would be a nice park on the river for people to enjoy. He hoped so. He loved that park, especially on warm spring days.

And as the warrior's sword came down to cut off his head, Holcomb just kept smiling.

It was going to be good to be remembered after all.

USA *Today* Bestselling Writer

DEAN WESLEY SMITH

Chapters 16-18

THE ADVENTURES OF

HAWK

What came before...

Nineteen-year-old Danny Hawk, his uncle, and his best friend Craig, were in Cairo to look for his missing father. Danny had witnessed the death of his only contact in Cairo, Professor Davis, because the professor had Danny's father's journals.

Danny knows that the men who had killed the professor were now after him and the journals. Danny finds the journals and gets his uncle and friend to safety in an airport hotel where he tells them what happened. They decide to keep searching for Danny's father and try to rescue him.

Along the way, Danny and Craig find some help from a street kid named Bud and twins from South Africa who had worked with Danny's father.

They managed to escape the men chasing them twice so far, Danny wasn't sure their luck would hold a third time.

THE ADVENTURES OF HAWK

CHAPTER SIXTEEN

August 20, 1970
Khan Al-Khalili bazaar, Cairo, Egypt.

DANNY HAWK felt like he might end up with a sore neck at any moment because he was twisting around so much, looking at the crowds around him, like every man or woman could be after him.

And they just might be.

He kept waiting for the knife to be thrust into his stomach from a man walking past, or a gunshot to rock him backwards into a booth. His imagination was making everyone look like a Hydra League member out to kill him.

He stared at everyone's hands, looking for the tattoo of the snake's head rising out of a pool of water that indicated Hydra League membership. Or at least Danny thought it did. The two men who had killed the professor both had the tattoo.

And in the crowds of this bazaar, there were thousands and thousands of people crammed into the streets.

Thousands of possible enemies.

There was an old man sitting on an ancient WWII motorcycle. Could he be the enemy?

Or what about the sinister-looking jewelry vendor with the thick brows and a gold tooth?

Anyone could be the one who kills him and takes his father's notebooks.

Anyone.

That had Danny scared to death, gripping his backpack with a death grip that made his hand ache.

The narrow streets of the bazaar felt like it must have felt a few thousand years ago. The smells of rich food, new carpets, and incense filled the air like a thick shield. Everyone was dressed in the traditional loose Arab robes, and all the women had their heads covered. The street was so jammed with booths, small tents, and people that it was almost impossible to move anywhere.

Since Danny and his best friend, Craig, were Americans, still dressed in their jeans and light shirts, everyone in the bazaar looked at them with suspicion, while at the same time seeming to want to sell them something.

Danny kept a firm hand on his backpack, which held his clothes and his father's original journals, and checked it every time it got bumped.

After twenty halting paces into the crowd, Danny felt the tug of Bud's hand on his shirt. He was yanked hard down and to the right, close to a stone wall.

"Get down!" Bud shouted to the other three.

A moment later, a shot rang out over the bazaar and a bullet smashed into the wall near Ed Black, one of the twins, not more than ten feet from Danny.

The echo of the first shot sent the thousands of people in the bazaar into a panic. Everyone tried to get out of the way at the same time, all moving in different directions.

The sounds of the screams and shouting was deafening.

Chaos.

A second shot rang out. It hit the wall close to Danny, between him and the twins, and just above their heads.

"Too close!" Craig shouted from behind Danny.

People screaming and running smashed into Danny as he tried to stay down and against the wall. He got kicked hard twice, and had yet another man trip over him a moment later.

From what Danny could see, his four friends were taking the same punishment. He had no idea where the shots had come from, but they were clearly aimed at the five of them. And where they were crouched, they had no real cover.

"The shooter's on the far roof!" Bud shouted, pointing up through the swirling crowds at the other side of the bazaar. At that moment, another shot cut through the screams and shouting and a man fell just a few feet from Danny.

"Follow me!" Bud shouted and headed along the right side of the bazaar, staying low.

Bud was short, and he looked more like a bum because of the tattered clothes. But Danny already knew the clothes were just a disguise to make Bud not be noticed in his many scams and tricks on tourists. Bud had lived on these streets for years. He could move through the bazaar crowds like a ghost, and Danny was noticing that Bud never seemed to miss a detail. It was a special talent he had, and Danny was happy to have him helping them stay alive right now.

Staying low, below the level of the frightened crowds, Danny ran along the wall, following Bud.

Craig was right behind him, and the twins brought up the rear. The twins were from South Africa. They were nineteen as well, Danny and Craig's age, but they clearly had had a much harder life, with their father being killed revolting against the South African white government.

Danny could only tell them apart by the fact that Ed wore a white earring in his right ear, and Ernie wore one in his left ear. They dressed the same in casual Egyptian clothes and sandals, and their dark eyes and black skin made them look distinguished.

Their passion was archeology and language, and they had actually worked on Danny's father's last dig. Last night, in a hotel room, they had translated all of Danny's father's notebooks into English. Languages were their special talent, and one that already came in very handy.

Another two shots sent stone chips flying from the wall near Danny.

Another man fell face first onto the street.

Danny had to get out of these crowds. Too many innocent people were getting hurt.

All this was because of the notebooks Danny carried on his back.

His father's notebooks.

His father had clearly found something big, so big that it had gotten him kidnapped. From what Danny had read in the notebooks, his father had found some of the Hydra Journals. Those were the ancient clues that led to whatever history had called The Fountain of Youth.

The Hydra League was an ancient group that for over six thousand years, since before the first pyramids, had protected the Hydra Journals. Two of the League's members had killed Professor Davis for the research notes, and now they were after Danny.

Danny had to stay alive and keep the notebooks safe. He and his friends were his father's only chance of rescue.

They ran past booth after booth, staying low and against the stone walls of the buildings. There were no more shots. They must have outdistanced the shooter for the moment, but Danny had no doubt the man, or men, would be right behind them.

Two-story buildings blocked some of the mid-morning sunlight from reaching the street, and Bud stayed in the shadows, leading them at full run through the venders.

Suddenly Bud turned into an alcove and went down a dark side alley. The intense sounds of panic in the bazaar was cut off by the narrow alley like someone had thrown a switch. It became only a background rumble, like waves on a distant beach.

At a fast run, they all went up a long, narrow staircase without handrails and turned left at the top toward the twins' apartment.

"Everyone all right?" Bud asked, stopping for a moment in the narrow hallway as Ernie Black pushed past and fumbled to open a door across from their apartment.

Danny nodded, trying to catch his breath as he glanced around at his friends. All of them looked like they had escaped the shooter, at least this time.

Next time, they might not all be so lucky.

"We also rent this apartment under another name," Ernie said, indicating a door he was fighting to open.

"I really don't think it's a good idea to stop here," Craig said, glancing back down at the staircase behind them.

"We're not," Bud said.

"I need to hide these," Danny said, patting his backpack and his father's original journals. The twins still carried the copies that they had translated last night in the hotel room. But the men chasing them were after the originals.

Ernie shoved the door open finally. Everyone crowded inside except Bud, who said, "I'm going to see how far behind that shooter is." He turned and headed back down the stairs toward the alley.

The room was tiny, the size of a small bedroom, and completely empty except for two chairs and a small wooden table with a scarred top. A window led out to a rooftop.

The twins' other apartment was across the hall.

"Why two apartments?" Danny asked, turning from the window. "One for each of you?"

Ernie shook his head. "Safety." He pointed to the window. "Another way of escape from this top floor. We're going out that way."

"Why?" Danny asked. "Something to do with what my father found?"

Ernie shook his head. "Our father."

"The South African government?" Craig asked before Danny could.

Ernie nodded. "They killed our mother trying to get to us. We were very vocal after they killed our father, and led demonstrations against them. We are criminals in our own country."

Danny was shocked. That was the exact reason he had sent his uncle home to protect his mother, in case the Hydra League would go after her to get to Danny and the notebooks.

"I'm afraid," Ed said, "that if we help you, we will all also be running from not only the ancient and powerful Hydra League, but the South African government."

Ernie nodded. "In fact, it may be

some of their operatives shooting at us, not the Hydra League."

Danny didn't much like the sounds of that, but at this point, he had no choice. He needed their help if he was to ever find his father. He smiled. "Well, at least that will make it interesting."

Danny just wished he felt as confident as he had tried to sound.

At that moment, Bud slammed into the apartment and quickly closed and locked the door.

"Three men in brown suits," he said breathlessly. "Headed up the stairs."

"Hydra?" Danny asked.

Bud shook his head. "I don't know. Couldn't see their hands. But I've never seen them before and they're all carrying big guns."

"Great," Craig said. "Now we have even more people out to kill us."

CHAPTER SEVENTEEN

August 20, 1970
Near the Khan Al-Khalili bazaar,
Cairo, Egypt.

BUD RAN TO THE WINDOW and pushed it up and open. "Let's go."

"We'll be right behind you," Ed said as he moved to one corner of the room and quickly pried up a loose floorboard. It didn't come easily, but it was clear Ed knew it would come.

"Put your father's journals in here," Ed said as Bud climbed out of the window and onto the roof. "We have paid for this apartment for a year. They will be safe."

Danny quickly took the notebooks out of the pack, knelt down, and shoved them between the floor joists, off to the right

under a board still in place. If anyone did pry the board off, they would never see the notebooks.

Outside the door, the sounds of heavy footprints filled the hallway. It sounded like a herd of elephants had filled the building. Danny wasn't sure if the sound of his pounding heart was louder, though.

Ed quickly and silently replaced the board. It looked like it had never been removed. Danny knew that if something happened to the five of them, no one would ever find his father's work. It didn't seem like the right thing to do, but at this point, anyone who Danny might send those journals to would more than likely be killed. And Danny just couldn't put someone else at risk, no matter how much work his father had put into the research.

Ernie was half out the window, and Bud and Craig were already running across the rooftop.

"Hurry," Ed whispered to Danny.

With one last look at where he had hidden his father's life work, he ducked out the window and onto the hard, white sand of the flat rooftop. From here, he could see mostly roofs and walls of buildings. Laundry was hung in different places, blowing in the hot wind, and on another roof, a couple of children played a game in the shade.

Ed came out behind him and carefully closed the window. Then the two of them ran to follow the others. From inside the building, the sounds of someone banging on an apartment door could be heard even outside. Those men weren't going to be far behind, that was for sure.

"Run fast," Ed said breathlessly from behind Danny. "You have to jump."

Danny didn't have time to ask how far or when. He could see when.

Right in front of him Ernie, at full run, leaped into the air and disappeared downward over the edge of the building.

Danny wanted to ease up to the edge and look at what faced him, but instead he just kept running. If a fall killed him, so be it. More than likely it would be a quicker death than having the men behind him catch him.

He hit the edge of the roof in mid-stride and full running speed and jumped.

"Oh, nooooooo!" he shouted as he flew over the hard stone of a dark alley two stories below.

The distance across the alley to the next building, which was lower than the one they were on, was a good eight or nine feet.

He focused on it, willing himself to make it.

Everything seemed to move in slow motion as he sailed through the air, finally landing solidly on the other roof, stumbling, but still running.

Ed cleared the alley right behind him.

Ahead of them, Ernie turned and quickly started down a metal ladder attached to the side of the building. It led into yet another alley.

Danny got to the ladder as below Ernie reached the ground and then ducked inside a building. There was no sign of Bud or Craig.

Danny half climbed, half-slid down the ladder, hitting the ground hard enough to jar his knees, but not hard enough to hurt himself.

The door led into a long, dark hallway that went through the middle of the entire building. On the other end, through a door, Bud was waiting like a doorman, holding open a cab door.

They had come out onto a main street of Cairo a few blocks to one side of the bazaar.

Danny piled into the back of the cab with Craig and Ernie.

A moment later, Ed jammed into the crowded back seat with them, then Bud slammed the door of the building closed and climbed into the front seat beside the driver.

Bud said something to the driver in Arabic that was clearly instructions. A moment later, the cab sped off, moving at full speed down the narrow side street and finally onto a wide boulevard.

All of them fought to catch their breath as the cab swerved through traffic, putting distance between them and the men with the guns.

Danny was sweating like he had never sweated before, and the hot wind coming through the open window didn't seem to help much.

They had escaped again.

For the moment.

Finally, Danny breathlessly asked Ernie, "Where are we going?"

"Your father's last dig," Ernie said. "You said you wanted to see it, remember?"

"Yeah," Danny said, sitting back in the seat and wishing his heart would stop racing. "But that was before people started shooting at us."

CHAPTER EIGHTEEN

August 20, 1970
Cairo, Egypt.

"STOP HERE," Bud shouted, pointing to a place beside a food cart on the sidewalk near the four lane highway. The cab crossed two lanes and almost slid to a stop, half up on the sidewalk.

"What's wrong?" Craig asked, looking around, his blue eyes wide with worry. Craig and Danny were both from the Pacific Northwest, and before this trip to Egypt, their biggest fear was making it to work and their college classes on time.

They were both in far, far over the heads.

Bud didn't say anything and motioned for them to stay in the cab.

Danny had no idea what the short Egyptian kid was up to.

Bud jumped out, talking quickly to the man in the food cart. A moment later, Bud started handing into the back seat what looked like wrapped meat sandwiches and warm bottles of Coca-Cola.

Food. Bud was getting them food.

It looked and smelled like heaven to Danny. He had forgotten they had skipped breakfast that morning and had had no time to eat in the bazaar. They needed food and drink, and Bud had been the only one to think of it.

It was like a fast pit-stop in a sports car race. Less than thirty seconds later, Bud was back in the cab and the cab was again speeding toward the western edge of town.

Bud said something to the cab driver in Arabic, then handed him a bottle of Coca-Cola.

The man seemed very happy to have it.

The wrapped meat tasted like a mild Sloppy Joe. And Danny had never thought a warm Coke could taste so good.

Danny ate, watched the neighborhoods of Cairo flash past, and thought about what he had read in his father's notebooks last night. Those notebooks were the key to all of them staying alive.

While reading them, it had become clear that over a decade ago, his father had decided to try to track down the historical background for the myth of the Fountain of Youth. From the dates in his journals, it had taken a few years for his father to get any traction at all on the goal.

Then the famous engineer Taccola came into the research about the time Danny would have been in his early teens. Taccola lived in 15th Century Siena and was known for being ahead of his time in inventions concerning the movement of water. During the last of his life, Taccola had become focused on Egypt and had actually disappeared there in 1458.

In hieroglyphs, Danny's father had written a simple phrase that Taccola had found.

"Belief. The Water flows uphill."

His father had then later labeled that phrase "Hydra Journal Entry One."

Danny had no idea what that meant, and it seemed from what he read, neither did his father.

Napoleon was next in his father's research. It seemed that the French leader had been focused on discovering in Egypt a way to give his troops fantastic strength and long life. It seemed Napoleon didn't find what Taccola had found, but something different, which Danny's father had labeled "Hydra Journal Entry Two: The birth of a snake, the path of elephants."

His father had found reference to the Hydra League in some ancient texts and on stone hieroglyphs. As Danny read, it became clear that his father became more and more worried that the ancient organization still existed. And that he believed that some of the members might have been alive for far longer than humans normally lived.

By the end of his notes, it had become clear Danny's father believed the Hydra

League did still exist, and its purpose was to only allow those worthy to find the Fountain of Youth.

He knew there were ten parts to the Hydra Journals, that they must be followed to find eternal youth, and he again underlined the word "Map."

His father had then underlined another key phrase. "Fountain of Youth. Not Water. Something else."

His final entry in his notebooks was "Hydra Journal #3: Under the teaming masses, the river becomes clear, the path muddy."

Danny looked out at the buildings of Cairo flashing past. He had no idea what to do next. And he didn't even want to admit to himself how scared he was. He just kept those thoughts pushed back, out of the way, covered with the idea that he had no choice.

To find his father, he had to find the Fountain of Youth, and he had to find that Fountain by following a trail of ancient riddles.

He had never been much good at solving riddles. They just made him angry, and now his father was somewhere at the end of an ancient riddle, protected by men who thought nothing of killing innocent people to protect their secret.

Impossible.

Finally, with one last drink from his bottle of pop, Danny looked around at his friends crowded into the cab. "Do any of you have any idea what to do next, when we get to the dig?"

"We follow the clues," Ed said.

"That's our only logical path to the next clue," Ernie said, "and then the next."

Craig laughed. "Yeah, that's going to work."

"Belief: The water flows uphill," Bud said from the front seat, shaking his head. "What in the world does that mean?"

"You must put yourself in the shoes of ancients who lived six thousand years ago," Ernie said.

"The water flows uphill was a belief about the Nile in ancient times," Ed said. "And on a map with North up, the water of the Nile flows uphill as well."

"Wish I'd paid more attention in history class now," Craig said, shaking his head.

"But the Nile is a very long river," Danny said, at least glad that he now understood the first Hydra Journal Entry. The easy one. "How does that help us?"

"It doesn't," Ed said.

"Unless you have the second clue," Ernie said.

Bud shook his head. "The birth of a snake?"

"The headwaters of the Nile," Danny said, suddenly realizing what that phrase meant. "The Nile is a long snake on a map."

"Exactly," Ed said.

"And the path of elephants?" Craig asked.

Both twins just shrugged.

"So, we go to the headwaters of the Nile, find an elephant, and follow it," Bud said, shaking his head. "Where will that get us? And that third journal entry seems really crazy."

"That it does," Ernie said. "But if we go to the head of the snake, we may find something that will help us understand it."

"And maybe find the next riddle?" Bud asked.

Danny turned to the twins. "What are we going to see at my father's last dig?"

"Not much, to be honest," Ernie said. "More than likely, by this time, since it hasn't been protected, blowing sand has filled back in much of it."

Danny nodded. He had thought as much. "Then I don't need to see it. It might put us at risk again. They might be watching the site, assuming I would go there. We need to get out of this city. Let's find a way to get started up the Nile."

"Anything is better than hanging around here waiting to get shot," Craig said.

The twins nodded, so Bud turned to the driver and gave him new instructions in Arabic. A moment later, the cab was headed south, toward the edge of Cairo.

They rode in silence for a few minutes, then Craig laughed. "This had got to be the biggest wild-goose chase ever imagined. Actually, an ancient, deadly wild-riddle chase."

"True," Bud said, "but with a fantastic treasure at the end."

For Danny, the treasure at the end would be finding his father alive.

Continued in the next issue...

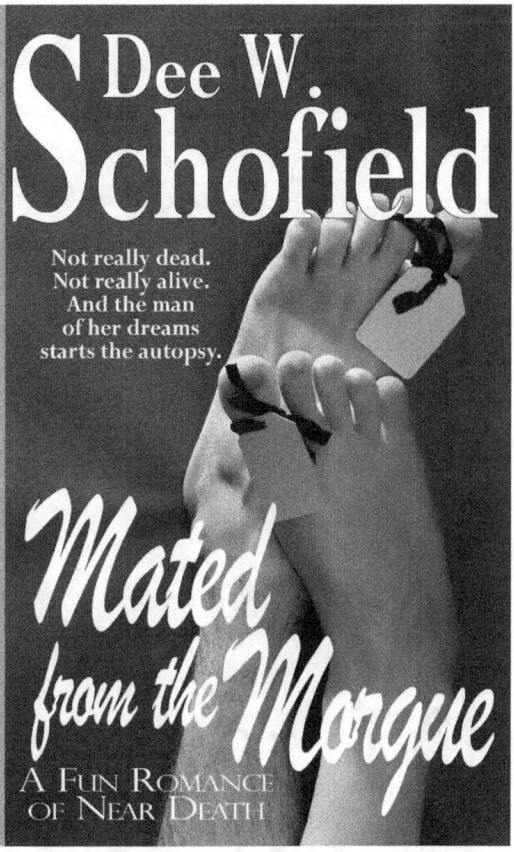

USA *Today* Bestselling Writer
DEAN WESLEY SMITH

He Saved the Kids by
Making the Neighborhoods
Bulletproof...

NEIGHBORHOODS

Continuing the Fiction River *series of showcased stories, 'Neighborhoods' got started one night when I was watching the Mayor of Chicago talk about how they were going to stop the violence. Then, in the same newscast, the Congress of this country couldn't even pass a simple gun registration bill. So, I had the thought that the only way to save the kids was to either get them out of the neighborhood or make their neighborhood bulletproof.*

I have a five-year degree in architecture, so I used that background to design a building that would work for security, schools, power, green living, and support the people living there without creating even more Projects that had failed in the past.

Then, to give the people a decent chance to make it, they had to have their homes paid for completely, so their money went to education and food, and so much more. So I used the idea of crowdsourcing both the initial investors behind the scenes and out front for the actual purchase of the apartments built like modular homes.

Scary fact is that this would work, even though it seems like science fiction at the moment. Especially with a couple of floors as wind tunnels and solar on the sides. This would be a money-generating building without any rents, or just low tenant fees.

NEIGHBORHOODS

May 2016

THE NEWS COMING over the big screen television made Big Ed's Bordeaux turn almost bitter to his taste. He set the glass aside in disgust and kept watching.

Heat shimmered outside the cool, air-conditioned comfort of his recreation room in his penthouse apartment. Around the apartment the city of Chicago spread out, stretching along the lake in both directions as far as anyone could see.

Big Ed sat in his big leather chair, especially designed for his six-four height, his feet up, his slippers kicked off, as he watched the Chicago evening news, watched the carnage of innocent children being killed.

Nothing seemed right. Everything in the world felt off, out of kilter for him and this city he loved. Outside, all over the city, all over the world, everything seemed to be coming apart.

Guns couldn't be controlled, kids died in the streets every night, and the summer was predicted to only get hotter. And heat meant more innocent people dead.

It made him angry, sad, and disgusted.

Something had to be done, but not a soul could figure out what that should be.

All anyone could do was watch.

He tried another sip of his wine. The bottle had cost him almost seven hundred dollars, yet the flavor he had savored a few minutes before now twisted his stomach as story after story flowed across the screen in front of him.

Like most nights, the mayor came on, vowing to stop the violence, but he had been saying that now for years and he hadn't managed to do a thing about it. It just got worse.

Not one person knew what could be done. No one had any ideas at all. And Big Ed had no doubt that if this continued here and in the other cities around the country, the world would soon follow.

Something had to be done, but here he sat, comfortable in his large apartment above Lakeshore Drive, watching just like a regular person watched a baseball game from the stands as others struggled with the problem and failed over and over.

Big Ed considered himself anything but regular. Just the idea of "being regular" made him angry. So far in his life, he had proven he was far, far from regular. A self-made millionaire, he prided himself in being unique in everything he did.

Even in casual evening clothing, he looked elegant. No one ever caught him messed up or even underdressed in the slightest. He took pride in that, and the art collection that covered his walls, and the collections of books and magazines stored in special rooms throughout the penthouse.

He took pride in being able to help artists establish themselves, help start-up companies get going, support the right charities and projects to make the world better.

A perfect dresser, a collector of fine art and books, wealthy beyond his dreams, his life should have been full. He should have felt satisfied.

Yet now, sitting here in the luxury of his apartment, he felt empty and helpless. On this hot evening, he could do nothing but sit and watch the news once again report the latest sad death of some child with real promise, gunned down without a reason.

Behind him, the door to the media room banged open. He didn't bother to turn around. It could only be one person, his good friend and attorney, Carl.

Carl dropped into the overstuffed leather chair beside him. Carl was just about as opposite to Big Ed as any person could get. He normally never got out of jeans and a dress shirt with rolled-up sleeves. His dark hair seemed to never be combed and was always too long. Always.

Big Ed always looked dapper and perfectly dressed compared to Carl. Yet Big Ed admired Carl for his intense brain and drive and ambition. The two had been friends for decades, and their tastes in women and art were the same.

Carl was the only one allowed to come into Big Ed's private media area without even knocking. They were that close.

"Someone's got to do something about this," Carl said, pointing to the news.

"I've been sitting here thinking the same thing," Big Ed said. "But what?"

Carl only shrugged as Big Ed once again tried his wine, then pushed it away in disgust. Nothing was going to seem right, taste right, feel right from this moment forward. Not until he tried to solve the violence problem this city (and every city in the country) faced every single day.

He was tired of being just a normal person who sat and watched.

Disgusted, he clicked off the news and stood, heading toward his office that occupied one corner of the entire floor of the building.

Over his shoulder, he said to his best friend. "Come on, we've got a city to save."

"Oh, oh," Carl said. "Here we go."

Big Ed just smiled as he kept striding toward his office. Every time Carl said that about one of his hare-brained ideas in the past, they had worked just fine. But right now Big Ed just wished he had an idea.

Any idea.

No matter how crazy it might seem, any idea was better than sitting there, watching children die, and doing nothing.

June 2016

ONE MONTH LATER, Carl finally uttered the words Big Ed had been expecting. "You can't do that."

"Sure I can," Big Ed said, smiling at his friend who had already downed two bottles of water since coming into Big Ed's climate-controlled office twenty minutes before. Outside it was another one of those days, with temperatures coming close to a hundred and the humidity at the same level. The city was bracing for yet another night of violence, while at the same time trying to get people to cooling shelters where possible.

Sweat dripped off Carl's face, and his t-shirt was stained.

"A brutal Chicago summer day," was what one newscaster called it.

"No, this time you really can't," Carl said. "I know how much money you have, and it's not enough to even build one of those complexes. In fact, just starting it would break you, and you'd be out on the streets. Then I'd have to house and feed you, and your tastes are a tad bit beyond my budget."

Carl pointed at the very rough building model taking up the middle of the room. Actually, it was four buildings reaching forty stories into the air. Each one covered four city blocks, and was connected every ten levels over the streets by corridors.

When it was done, it would be completely self-contained and would furnish its own power, heat, water, everything. Nothing would be on the two lower floors, but restaurants and shops would be included on third and fourth floors.

Big Ed had worked with an entire firm of architects over the last two weeks, ever since he'd woken up with this idea in the middle of the night. The model of the prototype alone, in rough form, had already cost him just under twenty thousand to be rushed to this point. But seeing even the rough model, he now knew it would work.

He stared at the model for a moment, then turned to Carl. "You got the investors lined up for the engineering companies?"

"Four brand new engineering companies are incorporated and off the ground," Carl said. "Investors are coming a little slower. You're going to need to talk with some of them, give them the old presentation of whatever this is going to be."

"Oh, I will," Big Ed said, smiling. "They hear the possibility of exclusive patents and long-term sales income, and they'll be on board and pouring in money, no problem at all."

Carl snorted and said nothing.

Big Ed knew that reaction from his friend. A "I'll believe it when I see it" reaction. It was typical from Carl— but Big Ed had always delivered in the past."How about the land companies?" he asked.

"All set up," Carl said. "Investors are coming a little easier into those because there's land under their investments. Not good land, but land."

"It will be great land in time," Big Ed said, pointing at the model of the large four-building complex. "How soon can we have the first four-block site under wraps?"

Carl shrugged. "We got top realtors on it as I speak. Maybe a month for the first full four-block site."

Big Ed nodded. "Hold off on any of the old factory grounds that will take major EPA cleanup, since they'll take some time. But try to have a few new corporations ready to buy those up when you can. We want every possible block of land we can get on the South Side."

Carl again only nodded and took another long drink of his water. Then he said, "Getting you in as an investor on these companies is not cheap. I'm buying in as well, and we're both in a few million at this point as minor investors. But that's going to go up as I set up more and more companies."

"By the time it's all said and done, I don't plan on us spending much of our own money on each complex," Big Ed said. "And that money should be returned in time if we do this right. Who knows, we might even make a profit."

"What else?" Carl said, laughing.

"And after we get the first couple complexes up and people see how this will work, others will want to buy in. I promise you that."

Carl snorted again, shook his head, and dropped down into an office chair. He put his tennis shoes on the coffee table and took another long drink of water from the bottle.

"So, explain it to me," he said. "Because I sure can't see how you'll build a complex of forty-story buildings without more millions than you and I could scrape together on a good day."

"We get investors to only build the frame and utility cores," Bid Ed said, smiling. "Like a big shell of a building with the public and business areas in place."

"That alone is going to take some major investors," Carl said, shaking his head, "to even get that far."

"Not the way this will be designed," Big Ed said, smiling. "Investors in green energy, green living, are going to be jumping at the chance to toss money at the building when they see the plans."

"So why only build the core structure?" Carl said. "Why not build the entire thing, walls, apartments, and all?"

"Because," Big Ed said, smiling and staring at the model, "we want the people on the streets to have their own place to live, a place that is safe. And it needs to be paid for as well, otherwise this won't work."

He walked over and took out a square from one side around the thirtieth floor and held it up for Carl to see. "Modular construction."

And then Big Ed showed Carl everything he was planning. Slowly and carefully, as much for Carl as for himself, working to see if in his explanation he could find even one thing that might stop this idea.

And after an hour of talking and Carl asking questions, Big Ed couldn't think of one major problem that would stop his idea.

Neither could Carl.

September 2016

BIG ED was feeling the excitement. Things were getting closer and closer.

They'd had their share of problems in the last two months, all the while keeping the idea tightly under wraps.

Zoning had been a huge issue, and if this had been any other city and any other area of the city, the politics might have gotten in the way. But Big Ed knew who to get on the side of the building to move things along, who to get to approve permits, who to get to just look the other way. He bribed no one, but he made sure that the violence in the streets and the deaths that still happened every day would be blamed on anyone who didn't support this project.

And when that hadn't worked, Carl and his massive firm of lawyers had swooped in and just plain overwhelmed anyone who wanted to stop the plan with more paperwork and filings and suits than anyone could possibly handle.

Just over two months after explaining it all to Carl, the architects had delivered their full model to Big Ed's office in his penthouse.

On any new idea that came out of the design and engineering sections of the buildings, Carl had filed patents for Big Ed and all the investors of the varied companies.

There were now more than sixty patents pending for various ideas developed in the buildings, the electrical

systems, the wind tunnels, the solar arrays, the water systems, and the rest. These would be buildings like no other buildings in existence, and that took new inventions along the way to accomplish.

Big Ed had no doubt that if this worked, he and Carl and the investors would be very rich just from a few of those inventions.

Outside, the early fall weather was giving the city a break from the hot nights of violence, with a touch of chill in the night wind off the lake. But it was only early September, and there were still many hot nights remaining before they were through this summer of death.

And the newscasts made it clear that the violence still continued.

Through more than fifty holding companies and more investors than Big Ed wanted to ever think about, Carl had bought enough square blocks of the city to hold twenty-five of the four-block square complexes. All but two had the zoning worked out. Six were on the sites of old steel mills and factories, so they had cleanup issues that would take a year or more, but those would be ready in time if this first complex worked as planned.

And Carl had the multiple corporate structures together for the next steps in the process. The important step, as far as Big Ed was concerned.

During the last two months, another of their companies, again with the help of start-up capital and investors, had bought and refurbished an entire manufacturing plant on the lower South Side. It was being retooled right now, with production starting within another month.

It was so exciting to be so close to getting started, Big Ed almost couldn't sleep. And that was very rare for him.

Normally, things didn't bother him much. But this project was different, very different. He was risking everything on this, and he knew it.

He and Carl stood staring at the model delivered by the architects.

"It sure doesn't look like much," Carl said, shaking his head.

Big Ed had to agree. It didn't look like much at all. Just skeletons of four buildings. The third and fourth floors of all four buildings were connected over the streets, then again on the tenth and eleventh floors, then again on the twenty and twenty-first floors, and then on the top five floors.

Those connected floors were solid and had walls on the outside so he and Carl couldn't look inside the model. But the rest of the building looked unfinished. Plus with no structure but pillars and a central utility core, all four buildings looked like they were sitting on two-story-high stilts. The entire thing was just massive framework and utility areas and elevators and staircases. You could see completely through any open floor.

"You have the contracts for the tenants done?" Big Ed asked, staring at the model.

"They'll be on your desk by the end of the week," Carl said, "and we can go over them. My office is double-checking them now, assuming the funding works."

"Will the contracts stand up to challenge?" Big Ed asked, never taking his eyes from the model.

"They will," Carl said. "And all the security regulations have been researched and opinions given. We're clear under the Jobs Act. And all zoning restrictions have long since been cleared as well on all the sites." Big Ed didn't hear a moment of hesitation in that answer, so he nodded

and turned to his friend. "Construction on Complex A starts in four weeks. Still think we can keep a lid on this once we start building? A lot of people now know what we're doing."

"All we can do is try," Carl said, shrugging. "But not that many have the full picture yet. We have all the land purchases well hidden under layers of companies, and the production plant ownership is so deep, no one is going to trace it to you or me or anyone connected to any of these sites. Besides, this idea's so crazy, who's going to believe it, anyway?"

Big Ed laughed and went back to staring at the ugly frame of the model. Carl did have a point.

Crowdsourcing a building to save the world was just flat crazy.

April 2017

IN THE END, it cost Big Ed just under sixteen million of his own money to design and build Complex A and invest in all the various companies involved. A minor amount compared to the total cost of the four-building structure. Yet it had strained him financially and if this didn't work, he was going to be back looking for a job.

No one really had paid much attention to a massive construction project going on in a burnt-out neighborhood on the South Side of Chicago until all four buildings started to climb above ten stories in their framework. And the third and fourth floors of all four buildings were connected over the streets below forming two-block-long tunnels. That was hard to ignore by even a press used to ignoring events on the South Side.

And when people noticed, reporters starting digging into the construction and the project.

But they learned little. Carl and his team had everything covered and blocked. And none of the investors were talking, which surprised both Carl and Big Ed. It seems the people who had tossed money at one stage or another of this project believed in it as much as they did.

The four buildings reached their full height of forty floors with the news doing weekly reports on them and adding nothing new. The plans were on file with the city, but all the plans showed could be seen from the street, for the most part.

They were called the "Buildings of Mystery" by the press. Big Ed and Carl and the hundreds of investors in the various projects just called it all Complex A.

Now, Big Ed stood with his friend Carl in his media room in his penthouse apartment, again staring at the television that had forced him into action the year before. Carl stood beside him. Both of them just stared at the screen, hardly moving.

The press conference was about to start about Complex A. It would be now or never. Were they both going to be broke and laughed at for building a massive eyesore, or maybe, just maybe, had they done something that actually might help save the city—and the world?

This was the turning point.

The smiling man who walked onto the stage and faced the cameras was Devon Conrad, the president of the board of directors for the Complex A corporation, named simply Complex A Incorporated. Big Ed and Carl had helped put him in place not only for his passion for the project, but his ability to speak to the media.

They had booked the big and plush Hilton Chicago Grand Ballroom for the press conference, and set the stage perfectly to showcase something of this size.

Devon turned to face the cameras with a smile that seemed to be reassuring instead of condescending. He stood six feet tall and had the square jaw of a superhero. His dark silk suit shouted that he was a man with more money to spend than he knew what to do with.

In reality, Devon was personally rich, and he'd been an investor in a number of the companies before Carl and Big Ed offered him the front position on Complex A. Now, like Big Ed and Carl, he had money in all the companies.

Devon and Carl and Big Ed had gone over every word of Devon's speech and planned out where they thought there would be troubles. Devon was as prepared for this as he could be.

Devon started the conference with all the basic thank-yous that the press had come to expect, then made a motion and a drape moved back beside him to expose the model of Complex A.

Big Ed's stomach twisted.

Carl said, "That thing is truly ugly, you know."

Big Ed said nothing. To him it was a thing of beauty, a thing of his dreams.

The model looked exactly as the four buildings did from the street. Four building frames connected on varied floors over the streets. Big Ed had to admit, it did look half-finished to the normal eye. But he hoped the world would love the look as much as he did when this press conference was finished.

Then Devon started to talk about the violence on the streets, the children dying for no reasons, and behind him on a huge screen images from newscasts flashed past, detailing out quickly what everyone already knew: The streets were not safe for a normal family to live and raise children. Period.

"So how does a building complex like this help the crime issue in this and other cities?" Devon asked as the news feed stopped.

He paused for perfect effect. "In Complex A, we give families a completely safe place to live, to raise their children, to shop, to work, and have their children go to school. All without fear."

There was a murmuring among the reporters, looking first at Devon and then at the framework of the four buildings.

Devon smiled and moved a step over to the model. "Notice how the building is up on its frame with nothing on the two ground floors but the central core?"

He tapped the empty space on the lower two floors and a knocking sound echoed over the quiet. "There will be bulletproof glass all the way around the base of each building. The only way into each building complex will be through a series of doors leading to a security station in the center of one building. No guns or drugs will be allowed in any building. Everyone entering the buildings will be scanned and searched. No exceptions."

Again the crowd of reporters started to erupt, but he held his hands up for silence and surprisingly to Big Ed, they honored him. Devon was good, of that there was no doubt.

Devon pointed to the two floors that spread through all four buildings and were closed in except for windows. "On the third floor will be grocery stores, clothing stores, and a few restaurants. The fourth floor will contain schools for all levels, from preschool through high school. The residents of the four buildings will be offered jobs in all aspects of the businesses and schools on the two floors and they will be paid fair wages."

Devon pushed on before anyone could interrupt. Big Ed and Carl and Devon knew this was a critical point. Devon had to keep going now, or all was lost.

Devon pointed to the next two series of closed-in floors going upward. "These will contain community areas, indoor parks, playgrounds, and so on."

"Then he pointed at the top five closed-in floors. "Of course the roof will be open park area and gardens, but the five floors below will be hydroponic gardens watered by cured wastewater in each building. Each building will grow more than enough fresh food for all residents year-round and be able to sell the extra to local markets for a profit."

"Don't stop now," Big Ed whispered to the big screen and Carl only nodded.

Before the reporters could break in, Devon pushed forward. "The third floor from the top will be laced with wind turbines and electrical storage areas. Since the wind in Chicago seems to always blow one way or another, there are over three hundred various sized electrical turbines that will generate electricity around the clock."

Big Ed could tell that Devon now had the full attention of the reporters trying to grasp an entire floor of electrical-generating wind turbines.

"On all areas of all four buildings," Devon said, gesturing to the outside areas, "that get sunshine at any time of the year, the sidings are designed to be solar panels gathering electrical energy. Between wind and solar, each building will generate so much power, it will not only supply all the energy needs of the residents, but each complex will sell power back to the main grid. Each building will sustain itself from the power sold and make a profit after city and land taxes—"

The room exploded in a thousand questions being shouted all at once.

Big Ed glanced at Carl.

Carl smiled. "Here we go. The key to all this is now. We're either going to save this city or go broke very quickly."

Big Ed just nodded, almost afraid to speak. He wanted to sit down, to make himself relax, but he just couldn't do it. Everything turned on what Devon was going to say next.

So he just stood and stared at the screen, his hands at his sides.

The reporters were shouting, but Devon just stood and smiled, holding up his hands for silence. When he could finally be heard he said, "I'll answer all your questions shortly, and we have packets with all the details to hand out to everyone to make sure all facts are correct. But…you haven't heard the best part yet."

The reporters all fell silent.

Devon smiled and pointed at the model. "Aren't you wondering why the building is nothing but a frame?"

His question sort of just hung there.

Big Ed had hoped for that exact reaction.

Devon took a square block from under the podium and held it up for everyone to see.

"This is a modular, three-thousand-square-foot apartment," he said. "It can be designed to contain two, three, four, or five bedrooms. It will have two and a half baths and a large kitchen and dining area. There are many designs to choose from for each one."

On the screen behind him, suddenly different apartments floated in and over each other showing living rooms, modern

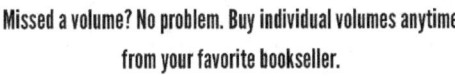
75

kitchens, bedrooms, family rooms, and so on in many varied colors.

Devon smiled. "These apartments are the size of apartments many of the rich people of our fair city live in."

He walked over to the model and slid the apartment block into one side of the building. It clicked into place.

Then Devon turned to the camera, looking suddenly very serious.

"Each apartment will be completely owned by a family. They will pay no electricity, no house payment, and if they choose to work so many hours in the shops or restaurants or schools or security or gardens or utility areas of the building, they will not even pay tenant's fees."

Before anyone could shout a question, Devon went on. "Their families will be completely safe inside their homes. All windows are bulletproof, as are all exterior walls. Each apartment will have a view. There are no halls in this complex. Each apartment opens onto a large open public area in the center of each floor. The apartments are only positioned around the outside of each floor."

The room started to erupt one more time, but Devon used the command in his voice to silence it. "Please hold on for one more important fact."

Right there, Big Ed knew he and Carl had picked the right man for the job.

"Each apartment unit for all of Complex A is in the first stages of production, built by a plant right here in Chicago. Each apartment will be modular construction, built in the factory to save costs, and then raised into place by cranes. But before we can get a family moved in, the family must first buy the apartment. Of course, we know the families that need protection from the violence of the streets are the families that can least

afford to move. And our desire is that every apartment be paid off completely on the day that every family moves in."

Devon stared at the reporters. Then smiled again.

"We have over two hundred families signed up to move in now, with hundreds and hundreds more in the process. Complex A can hold around six hundred families. But each of those families need help, help from everyone out there who wants to see kids grow up without being shot, to live free of violence, to get top educations, and live to be productive citizens of this wonderful city."

Devon smiled. "The apartments are going to be sold at cost to each family with no profit at any step. Let me repeat that. No profit at any step will come from the sale of the apartments to the families."

He paused again for a moment, then went on. "And with the modular construction, the costs are very low. Some families have agreed to sell their homes for payment on an apartment, others who are only renting have no way to pay for an apartment. And that's where we all can help."

Again Devon got serious.

Big Ed waited for it, wondering if this was going to work or not, his stomach so cramped up he felt like he was going to be sick.

Devon looked into the camera. "Each family approved for an apartment in Complex A has been set up on Crowdsourcing Help to help fund the apartment."

On the screen behind him, a URL address appeared in large letters for the site they had created just for this project.

"There are videos and background information on each family on each project. All the details are there. Also each family has a donation fund set up at all local banks to help as well. Any extra money raised will be moved to another family. No one will make a profit from the funds donated."

Again, Devon paused and the reporters, shocked to their cores, all stood there silently, letting him finish. "For years we've all wondered how to save the children and innocents of this city. Now we have a way to not just sit in front of the televisions and wish we could do something. Now we can actually do something."

He stared directly into the camera as if talking to everyone watching. "You can help a family get into a self-sustaining apartment and into a new and safe life, with great schools and great jobs. But many need your support."

Devon looked around the shocked room. Then he really hit them with the final punch. "Over the next two years we will build at least two dozen more exactly like Complex A on the South Side of Chicago. All will be four-building-construction, all holding around six hundred families per complex."

On the screen behind him was an artist's rendering of the South Side of Chicago with towering complexes going off into the distance surrounded by green parks and wide roads. It looked almost like a scene from a science fiction novel instead of something that could happen in just a few years.

"The land has been purchased and the plans are under way for all of the new complexes. The buildings alone will supply over one third of all the power needs for the entire city."

Devon let that sink in, then hit them with his final punch. "In the very near future, families in this city who used to be afraid to walk outside their own home will live in safety, their children will go to great schools, and well-paying jobs will be available to anyone in the building in all areas of life."

Devon smiled. "Before I take any questions, I want to make one thing very, very clear. The residents of each building can come and go as they see fit, go to school where they want, move if they want. But no drugs or guns will ever be allowed in any of these buildings. At least

the children in each building can play in safety, go to school in safety, and the entire family can live and work in safety if they so choose."

Devon took a deep breath and looked sad and intense at the same time. "Maybe the day will come when the citizens of this fine city can turn on the news and not have to watch a story of an innocent child being killed. So please, support a family or two or a dozen, depending on what you can afford. The families of this city want to move to safety into buildings being built right in their own neighborhoods. They just need your help. Every dollar helps."

Then he nodded and smiled at the camera. "Now I will be happy to take any questions."

The conference room exploded.

Big Ed muted the television and dropped into his chair, trying to catch his breath. There were going to be a lot of people who hated this idea. But in time, he could imagine many neighborhoods between the tall buildings being parks and open lands instead of war zones. The families who wanted to sell their homes were selling homes to corporations who would hold the homes and in time clear the land for parks.

It was going to take time, but this was a new century. No one said that they couldn't invent a new meaning for the word neighborhood.

Carl started pacing, the phone to his ear. Then suddenly he laughed sort of high and insane-like and hung up.

He sat down in the chair beside Big Ed, stretched out and stared at the ceiling, smiling.

"What was that all about?" Big Ed asked, staring at his friend. He had never, in all the years of their friendship, heard Carl make that noise.

"Break out a bottle of the best and most expensive wine you got," Carl said, his eyes closed as he shook his head slowly from side-to-side.

"Why?" Big Ed asked.

"Because in the first two minutes after we announced, forty of the family Crowdsource accounts got completely funded. At this rate, the first building will be funded completely by tomorrow. And by the end of the week, we might have Complex B. funded as well."

All Big Ed could do was smile. He sat back and stared at the screen where a year before he had watched children dying, and wondered what he could do to stop it.

Now six hundred families would be moving to safety very, very soon. And after that another six hundred.

They hadn't saved the entire world, but it was a start.

A damn good start.

 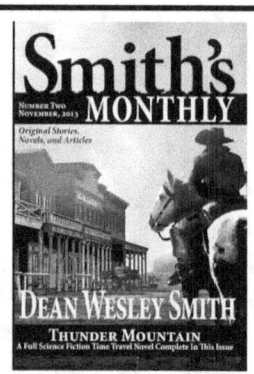

Coming Next Issue in Smith's Monthly
Poker Boy's first novel!
The origin story of his team.

USA TODAY BESTSELLING AUTHOR

DEAN WESLEY SMITH

KILL GAME

A COLD POKER GANG NOVEL

USA Today *bestselling writer Dean Wesley Smith takes you into the world of his acclaimed novel* Dead Money *with a brand new series focused around a group of retired Las Vegas Police detectives playing poker and solving cold cases.*

They call themselves the Cold Poker Gang. And they have been very, very successful in closing old cases.

Retired Detective Bayard Lott hosts the weekly games at his home. As a brand new detective, his very first homicide case had gone cold over twenty years earlier. But retired Reno detective Julia Rogers, new to the Cold Poker Gang, suggests they look at that case again for personal reasons.

From that simple suggestion spins one of the strangest and most complicated murder mystery puzzles seen in a long, long time.

KILL GAME
A Cold Poker Gang Novel

PART ONE

CHAPTER ONE

May, 1992
Downtown Las Vegas, Nevada

THE IDEA JIM HAD on a warm early-summer evening was to find the rumored place for afterhours dancing called "The Path." Jim had just graduated high school, the proud class of 1992. He was headed next year to Stanford, full academic ride, and he was really looking forward to getting out of the desert in a couple months. He had been born and raised here and was excited about living somewhere else. Anywhere, actually.

Jim stood barely five-nine, had long brown hair, and a moustache he was doing his best to grow and mostly failing.

Sharon, his girlfriend over the last six months, also now graduated, wasn't happy he was going so far away. She had been offered a scholarship at UNLV and had taken it. So between them there was a tension of the coming split.

Sharon was actually taller than Jim, with long blonde hair and skinny legs that seemed to always be stuffed into jeans a size too small. She had also done some light modeling and as she aged, she just got better looking.

Jim had no idea what she saw in him, but they always had such a good time together. They had two hobbies: Dancing and having sex in every place they could imagine or risk.

Tonight they were thinking of doing both at the same time. They had heard how really crowded the dance floor at "The Path" could be. Sharon had suggested, with a smile, that it might be fun to try a little "fooling around" on the floor while dancing.

Jim was game if she was. With Sharon, he would try just about anything. Logic often never played a part.

So they parked down on Paradise Road, about two blocks from the club, and headed down the sidewalk along the row of low warehouses, holding hands and laughing, the coming separation only a distant thing to ignore on such a wonderful spring night.

The club had an entrance off an alley into a large warehouse, but until two days ago, on Sharon's birthday, both of them hadn't been eighteen and old enough to get in, so they hadn't tried to find it.

Paradise had street lights and even though the area felt rough, both of them were native to the city and knew this really wasn't a bad area. They were as safe as they could be at midnight in Las Vegas.

Cars lined the street on both sides, so they knew they were in the right area even though they didn't know exactly where the club was. And between traffic on the street, if they listened hard, they could hear the pounding beat of the music echoing through the one-story buildings of the area.

"Maybe it's down here?" Sharon asked, pulling Jim into the first alley they came to.

Jim could tell at once they were in the wrong place.

And then the smell hit them.

The putrid smell of something rotting in the heat. It was a cloying smell that seemed to make the air thicker than it actually was, and fill every sense. It turned his stomach instantly. He knew it was a dead person instantly. He had smelled that before. He had no idea how police who worked around dead bodies ever got used to the smell.

"What is that?" Sharon asked, stopping and covering her mouth and nose. After a moment she started to back toward the street, her eyes round and her skin pale.

Jim stood his ground. He had been with two friends last year up on Lake Mead when they found a floater near the shore. He knew that smell. Someone had died.

But there was no body in the alley. Just walls of warehouses. Not even garbage cans.

He stepped toward one wall and the smell decreased.

"Jim, get out of there," Sharon said from the sidewalk behind him.

He motioned to her that he would be right there, then stepped toward the other wall. Originally a white stucco wall, it was now stained with years of grime and lack of paint that he could see even in the dark shadows.

And the smell got much worse.

There was no door in the wall, just a nearby high window that was cracked slightly.

Someone was dead in that room beyond that window.

He turned and went back to Sharon, taking her hand. They went around to the front of the building, took down the address, then said, "We have a phone call to make."

He could see a pay phone a block away on the outside wall of a closed grocery store, so he started off in that direction.

"I thought we were going dancing?" Sharon asked, scrambling along in her high heels, working to keep up with his fast strides.

"We are," he said. "But we have to call the police first."

"Why?" she asked.

"That smell," he said.

"You are going to report a smell to the police?" she asked. "It was bad, but not a criminal offense I'm sure."

"I wouldn't be so sure of that," Jim said, letting go of her hand as they reached the phone and he started digging into his pocket for change.

"What do you mean?" Sharon asked, looking worried. There was one thing he really liked about Sharon. She was smart and knew he was smart, so they trusted each other on a lot of things.

"I've smelled that smell before," he said, as he dropped the coin into the phone and pushed zero for operator."

He glanced back at her puzzled expression.

"Near the body I found up at Lake Mead."

She put her hand over her mouth and even in the strange lights of the street, he could see she had lost most of her tan very suddenly.

The operator answered and he was connected to the police. He gave them his name, his location, and the address of the building.

Then he said clearly, "I want to report a dead body."

CHAPTER TWO

September 2014.
Pleasant Hills.
Las Vegas, Nevada

RETIRED DETECTIVE Bayard Lott had just arrived home from the grocery store when the doorbell rang. It actually startled him, the high, ding-dong sound. It had to be someone trying to sell something, since no one he knew ever rang that doorbell. He didn't even know the stupid thing still worked.

He had his arms full of paper sacks of snacks and soft drinks for the evening's poker game. Plus a tub of Kentucky Fried Chicken he planned on having for dinner and to snack on the next few days as well. It smelled wonderful and made his mouth water as it filled the kitchen with promise.

He loved KFC. Never seemed to grow tired of it. A couple of his friends had said he was going to turn into a giant chicken leg if he wasn't careful and didn't balance the KFC with something green.

He only ever shrugged at that. As a detective, he'd seen worse.

It felt good to be inside in the cool air out of the heat of the early evening. It had to still be over a hundred degrees outside, far too warm for the middle of September. The fall cooling hadn't really started yet. Even being in an air-conditioned store and car, just getting between places was hot.

He dropped the supplies for the game and the chicken on the counter near the sink. The Cold Poker Gang met every

Tuesday night downstairs in his basement poker room. He lived for Tuesday nights, he had to admit.

Usually there were four or five playing, all retired Las Vegas detectives. They got together, played cards, told stories about whatever, and worked on cold cases for the city.

At sixty-three, he felt he still had a lot to give to police work and solving cold cases made him feel useful again. He liked that.

All the members of the Cold Poker Gang did. And he enjoyed the poker games as well.

And KFC.

Didn't get any better than a poker game with friends and KFC. His version of heaven.

The doorbell rang again.

"Yeah, coming," he muttered to himself. "Not buying anything anyhow."

He made sure none of the sacks would tip off the counter and glanced at the clock on the stove. It was still a good hour before the game started. His best friend and former partner, Andor Williams was the only one who ever came early. He knew it wasn't Andor because his old partner never rang a doorbell. It seemed to be against his religion, if he had one. He liked pounding his fist on doors for some reason.

Lott headed out of his kitchen and across the formal dining area and then the front room. His wife, Connie, had died three years before, and the living room looked like she was still here, sitting in her big recliner, watching the nightly news.

He hadn't really touched a thing in that room. It had been her favorite room in the house and now he hired someone to keep it clean, but mostly stayed in the kitchen and the basement and watched

television downstairs in his remodeled gaming room.

Trying to watch television in the living room just got him thinking of Connie too much and he did enough of that as it was.

Damn he missed her.

As he headed for the front door, he ran a hand through his still-thick gray hair and made sure his badge and gun were close by on the end table near the door.

He opened the door and was surprised to see retired detective Julia Rogers standing there, a Yankee's baseball cap pulled down over her light brown hair to shade her face. She wore her standard tan slacks and white blouse under a light dress jacket. At first glance she looked like a middle-management worker on her way home from work. But the baseball cap didn't fit that image at all.

Rogers had joined the game two months before on the recommendation of his daughter, Annie. He liked Rogers a lot. More than he wanted to admit to himself at times. He found himself thinking of her out of the blue.

But Connie had only been gone for three years and he just didn't feel ready to have another relationship, even though Annie was at him all the time to get out more and relax.

Annie had been the one to suggest he remodel the basement game room a year ago to make it all his. She was worried about him banging around in the house all alone with only the memories of her mother.

He understood that worry, but he still missed Connie every minute of every day. Nothing he could do about that. Connie was gone, he knew that. He was doing his best to move on with life. That was one reason he liked the Cold Poker Gang games so much.

Rogers actually had been a detective in Reno and had retired after having a bone in her leg shattered by a gunshot in a firefight with some drug dealers. She now walked with a slight limp that was hardly noticeable. She was only in her mid-fifties and had moved to Las Vegas to get to warmer weather and to play poker. From what Annie had told him, she was a good tournament player and had won her share of tournaments around town.

Rogers had bright green eyes that didn't seem to miss much and her sense of humor often kept all of them laughing. She seemed to have no trouble at all being the only woman in the Cold Poker Gang.

She seemed to have no trouble at all being the only woman in the Cold Poker Gang.

"Sorry to come early, Lott," she said, smiling as he opened the door to let her into the coolness.

He could tell her smile really didn't reach her eyes. Something was really bothering her.

"No problem. You can help me with the snacks and drinks."

"Love to," she said.

She followed him back into the kitchen where he grabbed a cold bottle of water from the fridge and handed it to her as she pulled off her baseball cap and shook out her long hair. Usually she kept it tied back, but for some reason today she hadn't done that.

Compared to his six-foot frame, she was almost tiny at five-two. But he had no doubt she was the toughest five-two you would ever want to meet in a fight. And he and Andor had taken her to the gun range off Las Vegas Boulevard and she was a better shot than both of them.

"Wow, that smells good," she said, indicating the chicken as he worked at the sacks, suddenly feeling very odd. Besides Annie, Rogers was the first woman who had been in the kitchen since Connie died. He glanced around, actually looking at the room.

He or Annie or the housekeeper had put away most of Connie's things from the kitchen, leaving it just kind of bare. Standard white appliances, gray stone counters, and a big stone-topped dining table with six chairs around it.

His cleaning service kept the kitchen cleaned and sparkling. But he seldom cooked much of a meal in it. And the fridge was full of take-out leftovers, usually boxes of KFC.

"The chicken does smell good, doesn't it?" he said. "You hungry?"

"I could use a piece. What can I do to help?" she asked as he unloaded sacks of chips onto the counter near the stove, plus a large bag of Peanut M&Ms for Ben "The Sarge" Carson. Sarge loved the things, but he often left most of a bowl full behind. Lott couldn't keep away from them no matter how hard he tried. So every week Lott had to buy another large bag.

"How about just sitting there at the table, work on a piece of chicken, and tell me what's bothering you?"

He slid the bucket of chicken over onto the table, then dug out some napkins and plates.

She laughed. "That obvious, huh?"

"I think the hour early sort of gave you away," he said, smiling at her.

"What?" she asked, smiling back at him with a grin he could really come to enjoy. "Can't a friend just come to talk with another friend without there being something wrong?"

"Of course," he said, shaking his head and going back to unloading the sacks of chips and pretzels. "But that's not the case this time."

"Got me on that one, detective," she said as she dug into the bucket and put a chicken breast on her plate, licking her fingers off after touching it.

Then she sat there in silence until he joined her at the table and took a leg and thigh for his plate. The smell was heavenly and he had half the leg gone before he glanced up at her.

"Not sure how to say this," she said.

"Quickly usually works for me," he said, "Like pulling a bad tooth."

She shook her head and laughed. "That's one way of thinking about all this." Then she looked him right in the eyes.

He sort of jerked. She really was better looking than he had thought and those intense green eyes seemed to just look through him. He had noticed her a lot over the last two months and had even admitted to his daughter that he enjoyed the games even more since Rogers had joined them. But until now he had never been alone with her and really looked at her.

Clearly there was a connection between them.

"I'm wondering," she said. Then stopped again and looked down at the bottle of water in her hands and the chicken on her plate.

"Wondering what?" he asked, not really pushing. Just trying to help her get it out. He kept working on his chicken, giving her time.

She again looked him directly in the eye. "I'm wondering if the gang might take on my husband's case."

"Your husband?" He finished off the leg and then wiped his hands. He had no idea about her past, but he had a hunch he was going to find out a lot more fairly quickly. And that idea actually excited him. He suddenly wanted to know a lot more about the beautiful woman sitting across his kitchen table from him.

"He was killed here in Las Vegas in May of 1992," she said. "Never solved."

That surprised him more than he wanted to admit. "What was his name? I don't remember a Rogers in the cold case files and I had just gotten my shield in 1992."

"Rogers is my maiden name. His name was Stan Rocha."

It was as if she had punched him in the gut. He pushed back slightly from the table. The chicken he had eaten suddenly seemed like a lump in his throat.

The Rocha case had been his first case as a homicide detective. He remembered clearly there had been no leads, nothing. Not solving that case had really set him back mentally early in his career.

She leaned forward, staring at him with a puzzled look. "You know the case?"

She must have been able to read his reaction as easily as he read her discomfort with coming here early for something.

"I do," he said. "Let's call Andor and get him over here early and see what he says. He's the one that gets the files from the Chief of Detectives each week."

She nodded and sat back.

"Are you sure you want this opened again?" he asked, looking at the worry on her beautiful face. "You know how cold cases can sometimes dig up things often far better left buried."

She nodded. "He and I were basically separated when he was killed. No real marriage left, not that there ever was one. But not knowing who killed him has eaten at me for twenty-two years now."

"I know that feeling," he said.

She frowned.

"Your husband's case was my first case as a homicide detective."

"Oh," was all she said.

CHAPTER THREE

September 2014.
Pleasant Hills.
Las Vegas, Nevada

JULIA WAS STUNNED at how attracted she was to Lott. Over the years, since her husband's death, she had dated a few times, and even had one relationship that lasted for a few years. But mostly the relationship part of her life had been shut off for a long time. She had just assumed it would always remain that way. There just weren't a lot of men looking for fifty-some-year-old retired police detectives with a limp.

And until she had been shot and then retired and moved to Las Vegas to be near her daughter, she hadn't noticed that she missed having a man in her life. But now, for some reason, since joining the Cold Poker Gang, she had been attracted to retired detective Lott.

More than she wanted to admit.

He had a calm way about him, and seemed frighteningly smart. She had

even caught herself a few times looking at his wonderful head of thick, gray hair.

His daughter, Annie Lott, was one of the best poker players in the world and her boyfriend, Doc Hill, was pretty much acclaimed to be the best. Julia had met and liked them at a few tournaments, and sat next to Annie at one tournament for a few hours.

When Annie, who also used to be a Las Vegas detective, learned that Julia was a retired detective, she told her about her father and the Cold Poker Gang. It had sounded wonderful and it had turned out to be to be even better than Julia had imagined it might.

Julia looked forward to Tuesday night now. Fun poker, fantastic company, and so far she had been involved in solving two cold cases, which had given her intense satisfaction, something she hadn't felt as an active detective in Reno for years.

And she loved the banter between the detectives, just like she had never left her department. She hadn't realized how much she missed talking with people who were blunt, funny, and trying to solve bad things that had happened to people. The gunshot wound had given her an out, but many times she wondered if she should have taken it.

Now she needed to have some answers as to what happened to Stan. And if the gang would take on the case, she might actually get the answers, good or bad, and feel like finally she could move on with her life.

They sat in Lott's kitchen, eating the wonderful-smelling KFC chicken and talking while waiting for Andor. They went from talking about the late-season heat wave to what Annie and Doc had done this summer up in the Idaho Wilderness.

"They keep wanting me to go with them once," Lott said, shaking his head.

"Sounds like fun to me," she said. And it did. Four days rafting in wilderness area down the River of No Return seemed so distant from poker tables and murders, she loved the idea and had promised Annie she would try it next summer.

"Oh, no, you too?" Lott asked, shaking his head.

"The forces are pushing you toward the river," Julia said, laughing.

"The force is that daughter of mine."

"She is a force," Julia said, laughing and wiping off her hands after a second piece of chicken. She didn't realize just how hungry she had been.

"How come no more kids?" she asked, "If that's not being too personal."

"Not at all," Lott said, laughing. "Connie often joked I was more married to the job than her."

"I know that feeling." She loved his laugh and his grin. He was a very handsome man who clearly had loved his late wife.

She had loved Stan as well, but they just weren't making it when he was killed. In fact, their entire marriage had seemed just off somehow. He had seldom been around and when he was he seemed always too willing to please her.

She really hadn't wanted a passive, dull man for a husband. She had always imagined herself with someone strong, able to stand up for himself, and someone who could make her laugh.

A loud banging echoed through the house, making her jump.

"What the hell is that?" she asked, glancing around.

"It's either an earthquake or Andor," Lott said, shaking his head and standing,

indicating she should just stay put. "I'm betting on Andor. He's allergic to doorbells."

She laughed as Lott went to the door of the kitchen and shouted, "It's open."

A moment later she heard the front door open and then slam close.

"I smell chicken," Andor said as he came toward the kitchen.

"We left you some," Lott said, sitting back down and smiling at her.

He came in and nodded to her. "Rogers."

"Andor," she said, nodding back.

That tended to be most of their conversations except over a poker table. She liked Andor a lot. She had known other detectives like him. Outwardly like a bull in a china shop, but inside very kind and generous and smart.

He headed over to the fridge, took out a bottle of water, grabbed a plate and napkin and joined them at the big table. Clearly he was used to being in this house and making himself at home. She had never gotten that close to any of her partners in Reno.

She envied that.

Andor's wife had also died a number of years before and from what she had discovered, his entire focus was now solving cold cases. He seemed to have no other life at all that she knew of. She at least played poker and had lunch with her busy daughter Jane once every week or so. When Jane had time to squeeze her in, that was.

He grabbed a couple of pieces of chicken on his plate and started into it, pulling the skin off with his fingers and eating it with two hands, one sliver at a time like a giant vulture picking apart a carcass. He never picked up the piece from his plate.

She and Lott both watched him for a moment before Lott smiled at her and she laughed.

"He eats like that with everything," Lott said, shaking his head. "I've watched it now for a couple decades."

"Yeah, yeah," Andor said, still working at the chicken piece, his hands covered in grease. "Why the rush-over-early call?"

Julia was glad that Lott took the lead when he asked his former partner. "Remember the Stan Rocha case?"

Andor snorted. "That thing we could never solve? Drove us both nuts. Why?"

"Meet the widow," Lott said, pointing toward her.

That froze Andor with a sliver of chicken halfway to his mouth. He looked at her intensely.

Finally he asked, "Joke?"

"No joke," she said, staring into his dark, intense eyes. "Rogers is my maiden name. I never took his. We were separated and not getting along much when he was killed."

Andor dropped the sliver of chicken and wiped off his hands, then his mouth, shaking his head the entire time.

"Let me guess," he said. "You think the gang should open the case?"

"I do," she said.

Andor again just shook his head, then looked over at Lott. "And what do you think?"

"I think it's about damn time we clear that case. It drove us both crazy for a year."

"And you think now is going to be any different?" Andor asked.

"No," Lott said, smiling. "But now we have the time and we have family help." He indicated her and she smiled at Andor.

"You two are nuts," Andor said, shaking his head as he dug back into the

second piece of chicken on his plate. "But I'll ask the Captain next week."

"Thanks," Julia said, suddenly both excited and scared to death.

She needed to know what had happened to her husband. But at the same time she wasn't sure she really wanted to know. She wasn't sure Jane wanted to know either what had happened to her father.

But Julia had a hunch that, as good as the Cold Poker Gang was at digging into cold cases, she was going to find out no matter what, now that she had started this ball rolling.

CHAPTER FOUR

September 2014.
Pleasant Hills.
Las Vegas, Nevada

ANDOR SHOWED UP EARLY the following week before the gang was set to arrive. Lott had been in the kitchen getting a glass of iced tea. The summer heat still hadn't broken and even though it was only a week from the end of September, the temperature had gone past one hundred yet again. He normally didn't mind the heat, but this summer it had started early and was lasting longer and he would be glad when the cool nights were back.

Andor banged on the door and Lott shouted for him to come in.

By the time Lott had the pitcher of iced tea back in the fridge, Andor tossed a brown file folder on the kitchen table and went for a bottle of water.

"The Rocha case?" Lott asked, taking his tea and moving over to the table. The folder looked really thin, far thinner than he remembered it. And had a coffee-cup stain on one side. Somehow his memory had built this case into a huge investigation. It hadn't been.

The folder had the standard "Copy" stamped on the outside.

"That's it," Andor said, taking his bottle of water and joining him at the table. "I left out the murder scene pictures of the body. No point. Let's hope Rogers can add some details because that case is as cold as they come."

Lott sat across from Andor and opened the folder, letting the memories of the early case in his career flood back over him. Over twenty-some years as a detective, he had had a couple-dozen murder cases go cold on him. But this had been his first case as a detective. Period

And Andor's first case to go cold.

So they both remembered it clearly.

Male vic by the name of Stan Rocha, three shots, killed execution style, two in the chest, one in the head, at close range with a twenty-two. Body left in an empty warehouse off of Paradise Boulevard to rot. No way to trace the bullets, no shells left behind.

A couple kids smelled the body and called the police. The guy had been dead for a week.

Some mining company owned the warehouse, but were not using it for anything. The doors were all unlocked. No prints worth dealing with.

The case was cold almost from moment one. And that fact had driven them both nuts.

There was a notation in the file that his wife was a cop. They were separated, no issues, and that she was a cop in Reno and had been on duty all week. Andor had called and her chief vouched for that and they had ruled out Rogers as a suspect

almost instantly and hadn't even bothered to interview her, since she sent them a report on what she knew of her husband's travels, which wasn't much.

And Rocha had no other family that they could find, or that his widow knew about. And she had no idea what he was doing in Vegas. She had thought he was in San Francisco looking for work.

Lott looked at the last page of the file. Neither one of them had even put a hunch of who they thought might be a suspect.

There were no suspects.

Lott closed the file and sighed. He felt as hopeless now on this thing as he had back twenty-two years ago. He hated that feeling, almost more than anything else.

Andor just shook his head. "This one is going nowhere quick."

"We'll see what Rogers has to add," Lott said, sliding the file back to his partner. "She might have picked up some details after twenty years."

"I wouldn't count on it," Andor said. "From what she wrote in that report she sent. Looks to me this Rocha pissed off the wrong people and paid the price."

"Doing what?" Lott asked. He pulled the file back to him and opened it again to make sure his memory was right. "Says here he had no drugs on him or in his bloodstream. And only twenty-two bucks in his wallet."

Again Lott closed the file. The Cold Poker Gang had tried a number of cases like this one over the last year. No leads, nothing. And those cases, for the most part, were still sitting on his bar downstairs next to the poker table. Why did he have a hunch this one was going to join that pile quickly, even with Rogers' help.

They didn't come any colder than this case.

"So what do we do first?" Andor asked.

"Interview the widow after the game tonight," Lott said. "Show her the file, see if something clicks."

Andor shook his head. "I'll leave that one up to you, partner. I got a date with eight hours sleep after we're done tonight. Last damn thing I want to do is dream about the Rocha case."

Lott nodded and just stared at the thin folder.

There just wasn't much there. And twenty-two years in the past was a long time.

CHAPTER FIVE

September 2014.
Bellagio Hotel and Casino
Las Vegas, Nevada

AFTER THE GAME ENDED in Lott's basement at about ten, Lott had told her that he had wanted to interview her and brainstorm about the case. But he said he didn't feel right doing that in his own kitchen. Something about the fact that he had never done anything like that in the past kept him from wanting to do that now.

He had told her that he and Andor and other detectives over the years had sat at that kitchen table and talked about cases a great deal. But actually doing a sort-of interview in the kitchen didn't seem right.

So he had suggested to her that they go down to the Cafe Bellagio to get something to eat.

She had agreed at once. She told him she liked the place, since it had nice booths and comfortable tables and chairs, mostly surrounded by plants. It was

always open. She had eaten many a meal there while playing in poker tournaments.

They took separate cars to the casino and when she arrived, he was already being seated in a booth that looked out at the entrance and had more than enough privacy.

"You know all the cop short cuts?" she asked, laughing as she slid in across from him.

"That and I use valet parking," he said, giving her that grin she was starting to really like, more than she really wanted to admit. He had a strong chiseled chin, intense dark eyes, and a sense of humor she was just starting to see. He was fantastically handsome for a man of any age.

"That's cheating," she said.

"More money than the desire to walk in this heat very far."

"Yeah, there is that," she said. "This is my first fall down here. Does it ever cool down?"

"Eventually," he said. "At least I remember it does, but you know how old cop memories can be?"

"No, how?"

"Shot to shit," he said.

She groaned as the waiter handed them both menus and took their drink orders. Even though it was after ten in the evening, they both ordered iced tea. Clearly he was a late night person as she was. She liked that.

After they both had ordered — him a BLT and her a chicken salad — he turned to her.

"Are you sure about opening this? Got to ask."

She had asked herself that same question a dozen times over the last month and that many at least since last week. She needed to know what had happened, if that was even possible. And from the look of the thin file they had on the murder, they were all starting from scratch decades late.

And she really, really appreciated that he was worried about her feelings on this. Made her like him even more.

"I am," she said, nodding like she really was sure. "Let's do this. Fire away, detective."

Lott reached down and picked a lined yellow legal pad off the seat beside him and slid it to her. Then he put another in front of himself. "We don't trust only one of us to write everything down. We're going to find the answer in the details and we both need to figure out those details."

"Worried about our old memories, huh?" she said.

"That, and just making sure we miss nothing."

She nodded and pulled the legal pad in front of her. He slid her a pen so she wouldn't have to dig one out of her small purse.

She was relieved beyond words that he was organized on this, at least this much. The murder of her husband had been so much of a part of her life that she had put away, she had no idea how to organize any of this.

"Let me start," he said.

"Please," she said. "Thanks."

"Do you have any idea as to his family background?"

"Nothing," she said. "He didn't much like to talk about anything in his past and in the four years we were together and married, it never once came up. We eloped, so no one but us was even at the wedding."

"So you don't know anything about his mother or father or family?" Lott asked.

"Nothing," she said, feeling amazed that was still her answer after all these years. When he died, she half expected someone to contact her from his family, but no one ever did.

"That's where we start," Lott said.

"I agree," she said. "That's bothered me right from his death."

She wrote "Family???" at the top of her blank page and felt a lot better.

Then she had a thought while staring at that word. She looked up at Lott. "Maybe someone missed him at one point or another?"

"You mean if he disappeared, someone might have filed a missing person's report?" Lott asked, frowning at her.

"Exactly," she said. "He was in Reno on business when we met in May of 1988. We were married three months later. I sort of bullied him into it, I think. He traveled a lot during those marriage years, always on business of some sort or another. I think it had something to do with construction because he often came in dirty, like he had been on a construction site."

"So you thinking we look at missing person's reports from 1988?" Lott asked. "I like that." He went to writing.

She did the same thing.

"And not only 1988," she said, wondering why she hadn't thought to check earlier, "maybe he never told his family about me and when he was killed in 1992, they filed a report then."

"Well," Lott said, writing as she went to write her thoughts down as well. "That's going to keep us busy."

"Easier now than in 1992," she said. "But chances are it will be a dead end."

"At least it's a path," he said. "We don't have many good ones at the moment with this case."

"Boy, don't I know that," she said.

They were served their late-night dinners and after the waiter left, she decided to confess something to Lott.

"Promise you won't laugh?" she asked as she picked at her salad.

"None of this seems to be funny to me," he said, then took a bite of a fry that came with his sandwich.

"I never even knew exactly what his job was," she said softly. "Married for just short of four years and I didn't know what he did to make money. And after he was killed, no employer contacted me."

"Did he have money?" Lott asked.

She shook her head slowly. "This is the embarrassing part. I found out after he died he was taking my money. A little bit here, a little there. Even though he said he was supposedly making a living and putting money into our account, it seemed I was supporting us both."

"You have money besides your police salary?" Lott asked, his food forgotten.

"Not a dime," she said, just about as embarrassed as she had ever felt in her adult life. "He moved into my small apartment with me and he had his own car. I just never noticed because he seemed to be employed. But after he died I discovered all our money came from me."

"Con artist," Lott said. He grabbed his pen and marked it down on his paper.

"But there was nothing he could con me out of except living expenses," she said. "I wasn't even a detective yet and never talked about my job at home. I never brought files home, and he never asked."

"You got all his belongings still?" Lott asked.

"Tossed his clothes, but everything else I have still. Two file boxes is all."

"We need to go through that," Lott said. "You, me, and Andor."

She nodded and went to work on her salad.

"You were young and you had no way of knowing," Lott said.

She looked up into his smile. It made her feel a lot better that someone like him actually understood. She had never told anyone that information until now. Not even her daughter. She had tried to protect her daughter as much as possible from information about her father, what little information there was.

"Thanks," she said.

"So how long was he normally gone?" Lott asked.

"Sometimes up to two weeks or more at a time," she said. "Then he'd be back for three or four days, working at something around Reno, and then gone again. I was so busy being a cop, I hardly noticed, sadly."

"And you didn't pay for his travel?"

She had to laugh. "On my cop's salary?"

"So what was he doing?" Lott asked, writing on his pad as she wrote the same question on her pad.

"And where did he get the money for the travel?" she asked, adding the question to her pad as well.

Lott smiled and put his pad beside him, off the table. "Seems to me we have a lot of places to start."

"It does, doesn't it?"

She also put her pad beside her and for the next hour enjoyed a good meal and the great company.

If somehow she could put the death of Stan behind her, she might actually be able to really get on with her life. And having help doing that from someone as

handsome as Lott was making her feel better by the moment.

CHAPTER SIX

September 2014.
Pleasant Hills.
Las Vegas, Nevada

THE HEAT seemed to be breaking a little the next day when Rogers showed up at Lott's place about two minutes before Andor. Lott had really, really enjoyed their late dinner last night and had promised her a chicken lunch the next day, straight from the nearest KFC.

He had gone out about noon and gotten that, since she and Andor were both due at one. The chicken now smelled wonderful sitting on his kitchen table. He already had the paper plates out and a bunch of napkins.

Somehow, he had refrained from taking a piece early, but his rumbling stomach had told him a few times that he should do just that. There was just something about KFC that could do that to him.

This time Rogers knocked loudly instead of ringing the doorbell. When he opened the front door, she was standing there with two old brown file boxes stacked in her arms, smiling over the top one at him like a kid over a wall. The boxes were the reason for their lunch. They were going to look through Stan Rocha's last possessions.

She looked like she was dressed to go to work as a detective again. Her long brown hair was pulled back and she had on a white blouse under a light brown dress jacket and brown slacks.

He could feel a slight jolt as he saw her again. He was going to have to watch himself. He really was falling for her. He wasn't sure, honestly, what he thought about that.

He had no doubt his daughter Annie would be overjoyed.

And he had a hunch that Connie would be saying "It's about time." Right before she the cancer had finally taken her, she had made him promise he would move on with his life. He had promised, but not believed the promise. Without Connie, there honestly had seemed like no life to move on with.

But now, after three years, he realized just how smart his wife had been.

He held the door for Rogers and then took one box off the top as she passed him.

"Thanks," she said as she headed for the kitchen and he followed.

"Wow, that smells fantastic," she said. "Amazing how KFC uses that smell to sell chicken. I'm hungry."

"Me too," he said. "Haven't had much since the Bellagio."

She smiled at him as she set the box on the counter. "That was fun."

"It was," he said. "And productive. This morning, on the way to KFC, I came up with one more thing to add to the list. What had happened to Rocha's car?"

She jerked and then shook her head. "Never once thought of that either. I sure didn't get it. Damn, I really needed to pay more attention back when this happened."

"You were stunned he was dead," Lott said.

"Yeah, I had a lot of things going on. But I sure wasn't much of a detective on my own husband's murder."

"Were you a detective yet?"

She laughed. "Not for another three years."

"Well, I was," Lott said, "And it never occurred to me to wonder about a car. We just assumed he was killed somewhere we couldn't find and taken there."

"He might have been," she said.

"You remember the make and model number?"

"I do," she said.

He slid the second box next to hers on the counter. "You have the registration in these boxes by any chance?"

"Nope," she said, shaking her head, clearly stunned that she had never once thought of her husband's car. "I would have noticed it and that would have reminded me."

At that moment, Andor banged on the door.

"Grab yourself a bottle of water. Or there's iced tea in the fridge," Lott said, turning for the living room again.

"You want some tea?" she asked.

"Love some," he said over his shoulder.

He reached the small dining area and shouted across the living room, "It's open."

Andor came in, banging the front door closed behind him just as he always did. Lott loved Andor, but at times he moved through life like a bull in a china shop, not really caring what got in his way or what he broke.

"I'm starving," he said as he headed across the living room.

"I got the big bucket," Lott said, shaking his head and turning back into the kitchen.

"Perfect," Andor said.

When Lott got back into the kitchen, Rogers was pouring them both glasses of iced tea from the glass pitcher he had filled earlier.

As they sat down and dug into the chicken and corn-on-the-cob side that

Lott had added, he filled Andor in on what he and Rogers had come up with last night.

"So let me get this straight," Andor said after licking off his fingers from finishing his first piece. "We search for his family. We search missing persons from around the time of his death, give or take. We look through this stuff here, which is his personal information he left with you, and try to figure out what he was doing for money. And we search for what happened to his car. Right?"

"Got it," Lott said, nodding.

"Well," Andor said, shaking his head and smiling. "That's about a thousand more leads than I thought we would come up with in this case."

Then he turned and looked directly at Rogers. "What kind of car was he driving and you remember where it was registered?"

"1989 dark-green Grand Caravan van. He seemed to carry stuff in the back of his van that he kept covered, but I wasn't sure for what. Always assumed it was for his job. Nevada plates on the van. No clue from what part of the state. I never once rode in it."

"Did you two have a joint checking account?" Lott asked as he wrote down all that information on his note pad.

"No," she said, shaking her head and looking at the half-eaten chicken leg on her plate. "But I know he had a checking account because he carried a checkbook. But he left no records at my place."

Then she stopped and realized what she had just said. "Damn it all to hell! I never thought to check for that either."

Lott watched her as she shook her head in disgust at herself and marked down that note on the note pad as well. He did the same on his note pad. Sometimes there were records of abandoned money and accounts, but he wasn't sure if they could find any accounts or if they did if the accounts would show anything of value. But it was worth looking into. Maybe he could get his daughter Annie to help on that. She and Doc, her boyfriend, had resources to do that sort of thing.

"And you have no idea what your husband did for a living?" Andor asked.

"Besides something in construction because he often came home dirty, basically he lived off of me," she said. "I discovered that after his death. He stayed in my apartment after we were married and I sometimes cooked. But I have no idea how he paid for all his traveling, or where he went all those weeks he was gone."

As Lott ate another piece of the luscious chicken, she went on to explain to Andor the same details about the marriage and what she had discovered after her husband had died. And the realization that she knew little or nothing about the man she married.

"He was a very passive guy," she said. "Now that I think about it, it's hard to imagine he made anyone angry enough to kill him."

"Doesn't take anger sometimes," Andor said.

"Yeah," Rogers said. "Then what?"

No answer to that one.

Lott knew that nothing about any of this was adding up anymore than it did in 1992. But at least now they had something they could do, some things to trace down.

That was a start.

And a starting point was a lot better than they had had twenty-two years ago.

CHAPTER SEVEN

September 2014.
Pleasant Hills.
Las Vegas, Nevada

AFTER THEY FINISHED the chicken and corn lunch, Lott cleared off the big kitchen table and moved the first box over. The light from the afternoon sun streaming through the kitchen windows was filling the room with clear light, and the overhead light filled in even more. It was a bright and comfortable place to sort things. Over the years, he and Andor had done just that at this table numbers of times, usually making Connie disgusted at some of the things they had to sort.

But she had been amazingly supportive. He had asked her why she didn't mind them doing things like that at her kitchen table and she had said simply, "At least you're home."

As a detective, he understood that. She had mostly raised Annie with him just being in and out. Amazing Annie had followed him into police work after that sort of upbringing.

As Lott dropped the first box on the table, Andor looked inside and then dumped it out on the table, spreading out the folders and a couple pens and a few small notebooks.

Lott took out his yellow legal notepad and across the table Rogers did the same, frowning at the stuff on the table as if she hadn't seen it before. More than likely it had been decades since she had looked at it.

Lott picked up one of the spiral notebooks and opened it. Nothing. Totally empty from front to back.

"Where was all this stuff?" he asked Rogers.

"Stan kept a small desk in the apartment, plus some of this stuff was in his part of the closet and in his chest of drawers. I put receipts and stuff in the folders as I found them in his clothes pockets and such."

Andor nodded and picked up one folder.

Lott waved the notebook. "Empty." He dropped it back into the box.

Rogers slid him another notebook and it was empty as well. In the meantime, Andor was sorting receipts looking for anything that might give them a lead.

"How are you sorting?" Lott asked as Andor started two piles.

"One for Reno, one for out of the Reno area."

"Good idea," Rogers said, taking another folder full of receipts and starting into them.

Lott did the same with yet another folder, sometimes finding it hard to figure out even a name on some of the faded bits of paper. As detectives, they were used to this kind of work and used to doing it carefully. It always felt to him like a combination of doing a puzzle and a treasure hunt. Sometimes pieces fit, sometimes they found the one treasure that would lead them to solving the case.

For an hour they worked mostly in silence, getting through both boxes, sorting out pens and a couple of empty keychains with names outside of Reno on them, plus all receipts.

Then when they had all the Reno paperwork pulled and all items that were Reno-based back in one of the boxes sitting beside the table, they looked at the remaining piles in front of all of them.

"I got Boise receipts," Andor said, "Salt Lake receipts, Winnemucca receipts, and Las Vegas receipts."

"The same in this pile," Rogers said, indicating the one in front of her.

"Exactly the same with mine," Lott said, getting a little excited at the prospect of actually seeing Rocha's life have a pattern. "So we sort by city."

They went back to work and after another half hour had four piles of receipts from out of Reno filling the middle of the table.

"I had no idea he traveled this much and this far afield from Reno," Rogers said, shaking her head. "I sure wasn't much of a wife not knowing what her own husband was doing."

Andor laughed. "I doubt this had anything to do with you. My gut sense is telling me your husband had a con going of some sort and that's what got him killed."

Lott nodded. He agreed with his partner, even though the idea of that clearly hadn't made Rogers happy. He couldn't imagine how she was feeling discovering this, even after all these years.

They spent the next hour sorting through and getting a general timeline on the receipts for each town. It seems that over the years he went from one town to the other like he had a route.

Lott made out a timeline on his notepad of the general times Rocha had been in each city. It seemed, in general, his stays never seemed to last for more than three or four days at a time, usually once every three weeks. Just as Rogers had said was his pattern in Reno.

Then they focused on the Vegas papers since they knew the most about Vegas. Food receipts, gas, and so on.

"What's missing here?" Andor said after all three of them looked through the hundred pieces of paper from Vegas.

Roger shook her head, but Lott saw it almost at once when Andor asked the question.

"No hotel," Lott said. "Where was he staying during all this time here in Vegas over all these years?"

"Oh," Rogers said. "I'll be go to hell. Where was he staying?"

"These cover summers, winters, year-round for a number of years," Andor said. "He couldn't live in his car during the summers."

"And there were no other hotels that I saw in any of the other places either," Lott said.

"So who was he staying with?" Rogers asked. "In all of these places. No hotel receipts at all. None."

"We figure that out," Andor said, "and we might have our first lead."

"What the hell were you doing, Stan?" Rogers asked, staring at the piles of paper on the tabletop, as if they would give her an answer.

And Lott knew that eventually they might.

CHAPTER EIGHT

September 2014.
Boulder Highway
Las Vegas, Nevada

AFTER THEY GOT DONE sorting receipts on Lott's kitchen table, they planned their attack on the case.

Julia was stunned at how much she had already learned about her ex-husband. It had never occurred to her to sort those receipts like that. Or even look through them. After she got the news of his murder, she had just boxed up everything and tossed the two boxes in the top of a closet.

A couple of weeks after that she had sold his desk and given his clothes to The Salvation Army. She had just cleaned him from her life and gone back to work and having his baby. She still wasn't sure why she needed this solved now. Part of it was because she was attracted to Lott. She knew that.

And part of her knew she could never really be in another good relationship until this was cleaned up. Or at least until she made an attempt to clean it up.

But it was amazing how much more she now knew about her former husband than she knew when married to him. That just made her sad that her one and only marriage had been such a sham. What did that say about her?

After sorting the receipts, their plan was pretty simple. Andor was going to head downtown to the police station and see if he could get some searches running for missing persons in the Boise and Salt Lake areas, using Stan's picture and the make of his car. And see if the car was impounded back in 1992 somewhere here in Vegas.

The impound information would be quick, but the missing person searches would take time in two other states.

Lott was headed to the DMV before they closed to try to get a trace on the registration of the car.

And she was going to take the receipt addresses and names and see if she could make a pattern of the area where most of the Las Vegas receipts were grouped. Almost all of them were along the Boulder Highway, they knew that much from just

looking at them. They had figured that giving them a closer look might give them at least a center to work from.

It was almost six in the evening and the sun was low in the sky by the time she finished out along the highway. Most of the gas stations and grocery stores on the receipts were gone or replaced by newer stations. But the addresses kept everything in a pattern about a mile long.

Clearly he had mostly stayed in this area while here in Las Vegas, but there was little near the area except older subdivisions and a few small casinos and old highway motels that she doubted looked much better in 1992.

And since there were no receipts for a hotel, she didn't bother with them.

But she did cruise a few of the streets of the subdivisions in her Jeep SUV, just looking for anything that might strike her. All the homes were clearly already old in 1992. And there were also a number of older apartment buildings. Most of the neighborhood just looked tired and rundown.

Maybe Stan had family here?

Or a girlfriend?

At the time, Julia had no idea her husband had even came to Las Vegas. And he claimed he hated gambling. But right now she didn't trust anything he had told her.

Or her memory for that matter.

At six, she headed for the Bellagio and the café there to meet Lott for dinner. She really liked talking with him and he seemed to enjoy her company as well.

There was clearly a connection between them and she had no plans on trying to stop that connection. In fact, she wanted to spend even more time with him as this went along.

It took her almost a half hour to get from the Boulder Highway to The Strip and parked and into the Café Bellagio. She was stunned as she walked in that Lott was already there sitting with his daughter, Annie, and Doc Hill, Annie's boyfriend.

Doc and Annie had clearly already eaten, but Lott was just sipping on an iced tea.

As she approached, Annie looked up and smiled. "Detective Rogers," she said.

Doc stood up and shook her hand, smiling. Julia wasn't sure exactly what to say other than "Just Julia."

These two were two of the best poker players in the world and she had watched them on television and studied their games before even deciding to move to Las Vegas.

They both were tanned from all the time on the river in central Idaho this summer, and Doc was about as handsome as they came. Together, Doc and Annie made a striking couple. Both tall, young, and in great physical shape. They both seemed to just radiate youth and attractiveness, even though neither of them tried for that effect at all.

Julia suddenly felt like a little girl in front of two major movie stars, even though she had talked to them before and Annie had told her about the Cold Poker Gang and introduced Julia to Lott. It was one thing to talk with a person while sitting next to them in a poker game, another to talk with them away from the game.

Annie gave her a quick hug and then she took Doc's hand and said, "Time to go."

"Don't rush off on my account," Julia said.

"Dinner break on the tournament is almost over," Annie said. "I'm short-stacked so I might be back sooner than not."

Now Julia realized what they were doing. It was the regular weekly thousand-dollar buy-in hold'em tournament. She hadn't yet played in it because the entrance fee was still a little high for her budget. And with the focus on the case, she hadn't played any poker besides with the Cold Poker Gang for almost a week.

"We'll be here for a while," Lott said, smiling at his daughter. "Have fun."

"Will do," Annie said.

"Detectives," Doc said, nodding to both of them as he turned and went with his girlfriend back toward the casino and the poker room beyond.

"Those two are really something," Julia said as she settled into a chair facing across the table from Lott.

"And rich," Lott said, laughing. "They fly all over the world in a private jet and you ought to see the home they are building to the north of town. Plus they have a home up in Boise and Doc's father's home here in town."

"Yeah, I heard Doc's father was killed a year or so ago," Julia said.

Lott nodded. "Annie hadn't gone full-time poker yet and was still working part-time as a detective. That case is the reason they met. It was her last official case. Although, the two of them do some freelance work for the police at times."

"We'll, I'm glad she introduced me to you," Julia said, smiling at Lott.

He smiled back. "I'm glad she did as well."

They might have sat there just smiling at each other like a couple of kids for the next half hour, but the waiter broke the moment by starting to clean up Doc and Annie's dishes and asked Julia if she wanted something to drink.

She hoped to have more of those moments with Lott in the near future. She was really, really attracted to him.

And for the first time in a very long time, that felt wonderful.

CHAPTER NINE

September 2014.
Bellagio Hotel and Casino.
Las Vegas, Nevada

"SO, ANY LUCK?" Rogers asked him after the waiter had taken her drink order and left with Annie and Doc's dishes. She seemed to be in complete detective mode, leaving the personal out of this case for the moment.

"There were a lot of dark-green 1989 Dodge Caravans in Nevada in 1992," he said, shaking his head. "And none registered to a Rocha."

"So who owned the car?" she asked.

He sighed. "Damn good question. They are sending me a list tomorrow of names of people who owned that kind of van in 1992. I limited the results to the Las Vegas area, which will cut it down a lot to start, but it might not help."

"I have a hunch we can limit it even more," she said, smiling at him.

He loved her smile, but this time it seemed she had some real information she very much wanted to tell him.

"Those receipts were all around a few subdivision and apartment complexes out on the Boulder Highway. Unless Andor comes up with a van that was impounded, my gut sense is the van never moved from that neighborhood after Stan's death."

Lott felt a slight jolt of excitement that he always felt when there was movement on a case. There was a real chance that car might lead them right to some great leads as to what happened to Stan Rocha.

"Let's find out," Lott said, grabbing his cell phone and calling Andor while smiling at Rogers.

"Yeah," Andor said as he picked up his phone. He never answered a phone in any other way.

"Anything on the impound?"

"Nada," Andor said. "You?"

"Nothing registered to Rocha," Lott said, "but tomorrow I got a list of that type of van registered to others in this area coming. And the receipts led Rogers to a clear neighborhood area out on the highway."

"Perfect," Andor said. "Call me in the morning if anything comes together and we'll do a house call."

"Got it," Lott said, hanging up and smiling at Rogers.

"I assume he found nothing on the impound," Rogers said.

"He didn't," Lott said. "But he thinks we might be doing a house call tomorrow."

"Wouldn't that be nice," Rogers said, smiling a smile that Lott knew he would never tire of.

The next two hours were wonderful, with easy talk about both of their careers, her now-deceased parents, and even how she met Rocha.

And she got Lott talking about Connie through desserts of apple pie for him and a small bowl of vanilla ice cream with chocolate for her. It felt odd to talk about Connie to a woman he was interested in, but at the same time it felt natural. Connie had been his life for a very long time. If he and Julia had any chance of any kind of relationship, he had to be comfortable talking about Connie, and Julia had to be comfortable with that as well.

And she seemed to be completely comfortable.

They were still talking about Connie when Annie joined them, clearly surprised they were talking about her mother.

"You get into the money?" Rogers asked as Annie sat down and indicated to the nearby waiter to bring her a cup of hot black tea.

"Got my entry fee back at tenth is all," Annie said, shaking her head. "Doc is chewing up the tournament as he often does, huge stacks of chips. He took me out like I was so much trash."

"Wow," Lott said, "that sounds harsh."

His daughter laughed in a way that reminded him a lot of her mother. "At a poker table, there is no such thing as being nice to another player."

"I'm learning that on the Tuesday night games," Rogers said, also laughing.

"And taking all of our money at the same time," Lott said.

Annie patted his hand. "Ahh, too bad, dad. She's going to make you guys raise your game."

"She already has," he said, smiling at Rogers, who smiled back.

"So what case are you two working on that's keeping you out so late?"

"We're trying to figure out who killed my ex-husband here in Vegas back in 1992," Rogers said.

Annie just looked at her, blinking.

Lott laughed. It wasn't often Annie could be surprised, but that statement had done it, especially Rogers' matter-of-fact manner. Annie had lost her well-known poker face, not something she often let slip for any reason.

"It was my first case as a detective," Lott said. "You were about ten."

"The Rocha case?" Annie asked, glancing at Lott first, then back at Rogers.

Annie was showing her few years as a detective and knowledge of her father's cases. But Lott was surprised she remembered the name of the case. Granted, he had talked about it at times. But he hadn't realized Annie knew about it as well.

Rogers nodded. "I kept my maiden name and we were separated when he was killed. Never was much of a marriage."

Annie shook her head. "Didn't realize you were that cop from Reno. I made a slight run at that case in a slow week about a year after I got my shield," she said. "Got almost nowhere. You two having any luck?"

"Almost nowhere?" Lott asked, glancing at Rogers who looked as puzzled as he felt.

Annie nodded. "I went back into the evidence and pulled samples off the stuff they got from under his fingernails. It was mostly rock and dirt particles found to the north and west of the city. It was as if he had been digging out in the desert for some reason. He had the same material on his pants and shirt. All that led nowhere."

Lott nodded and smiled at his daughter. "Good thinking."

"Reports are under a separate file name, I think the file is titled Rocha two. Dated my second year."

"We'll get it," Lott said.

"Frustrating case," Annie said. "You guys make any headway?"

"Looking for his van," Rogers said.

Annie frowned. "I checked the DMV for Nevada and California to see if he had a car. Nothing popped."

"Under another name, clearly," Lott said. "We know the make of the van and we have an area off the Boulder Highway he stayed when in town. And we know he traveled from Reno to Winnemucca to Boise and then to Salt Lake and then here."

"But we have no idea why," Rogers said.

"You guys are making some progress," Annie said, nodding. "A lot more than I managed, that's for sure. Let me know if there's anything Doc and I can do to help."

"Oh, trust me, we will," Lott said, smiling at his daughter.

From there Rogers asked Annie a question about her mother and Lott sat back and listened to his daughter tell a woman he was interested in about his wonderful departed wife.

It didn't get any weirder or more uncomfortable than that.

CHAPTER TEN

September 2014.
Boulder Highway.
Las Vegas, Nevada

AT TEN IN THE MORNING, Julia had just finished her morning workout routine, a shower and breakfast, when Lott called.

"Andor and I will meet you in the parking lot of the grocery store on the northeast corner of Tropicana and the Boulder Highway."

"How long?" she asked.

"I'm leaving now," Lott said. "Twenty minutes."

"Got it," she said, and hung up.

She had an apartment down near the university off The Strip, so she was the closest to the corner than any of the three of them.

She strapped on her old badge and put her gun holster on and under her arm. The Cold Poker Gang had permission from the Las Vegas Police Chief, even though retired, to flash badges and carry their guns, since they were investigating murder cases for the department. That privilege came, Lott had told her, from them closing more cold cases than anyone in the history of the department. Which in turn gave the chief a good name and record.

She reached the parking lot first and parked her Jeep SUV off to one side so she could see the others when they came in. This was the neighborhood she had investigated yesterday, so clearly they had a hit on an address for the van.

She could feel the excitement building a little and scolded herself to remain professional. She doubted the van would be around still, but maybe they could get lucky and find someone who remembered who owned it.

She got out into the early morning heat when she saw Lott's Cadillac SUV pull in. It was only eighty degrees, but still felt warm to her for this early in the morning. It was going to be past ninety again today.

She had put on her standard work clothes; dark slacks, white blouse, and business jacket. The jacket hid her gun nicely. She had her hair pulled back and tied out of the way.

Lott pulled up beside her and motioned she should get into the back.

Andor was already in the front seat. Lott must have picked him up on the way.

"This the area you explored last night?" Andor asked as she closed the door.

"Square in the center of all the receipt addresses," she said, settling with relief into the air conditioning coolness.

"Great," Lott said, turning and smiling at her with that smile she was starting to like so much. "The van is registered to a Denise Miller about four blocks from here."

"Is registered?" Julia asked, her stomach twisting.

"Right from 1989 onward," Andor said as Lott took them out of the parking lot and away from the highway 'into the very old and rough subdivision to the east.

She forced herself to sit back and not jump to any conclusions. She focused on studying the houses. They almost all needed paint, none had any more than rocks and weeds for yards, and many of them had cars up on blocks in the driveways. A few of the homes were boarded up with sad-looking For Sale signs hanging in the front yards.

Lott pulled up in front of one house on the left. In the driveway she could see a van identical to her husband's. Only it needed paint badly since the dark green had turned a faded ugly and pitted olive color. It had a badly dented rear panel. And on the driver door there was a horseshoe-shaped dent that she remembered was on Stan's van.

Holy hell, it was his van, and even more amazingly, it looked like it was still being used. How was that even possible?

"I'll be go to hell," Andor said, staring at the van.

"That the van?" Lott asked, turning to look at Julia.

"Looks exactly like it," she said. "Right down to the horseshoe dent on the driver's door."

"How do you want to handle this?" Andor looked at Lott.

"We knock, flash badges, and talk," Lott said.

Andor nodded.

Julia nodded.

"No mention that you're his wife, got it?" Lott said, looking at her with a dark seriousness to his eyes.

"Copy that," she said, nodding.

She was feeling slightly in shock and was glad Lott was leading this. She couldn't believe they had found Stan's van. It hadn't even occurred to her to look for it after he died, and now because of a few receipts and some legwork with the DMV, they had found it twenty-two years later.

It didn't get any more amazing than that.

They climbed out and made it up the gravel sidewalk to the front door through the warming morning air without saying a word between then.

She forced herself to take slow, deep breaths of the warm air and stay in detective mode.

Andor banged on the screen door that hadn't seen a screen in a decade, let alone paint. The rest of the house looked just as bad, and the windows hadn't been cleaned in a decade. Moisture-stained drapes hid any look at the inside the house.

Julia stayed behind Lott, since there wasn't room for all three of them on the small concrete slab that served for a step up into the house.

She and Lott both scanned the front of the house in both directions. Old training kicking in, clearly.

After a moment a young man answered, maybe college age at most, swinging the door wide open.

"Yes?" he asked, his voice deep and exactly like Stan's voice.

Julia gasped and stepped back. The kid in front of them could have been Stan when she met him. Same dark hair, same dark eyes, same voice. This kid had on a UNLV tee shirt and jeans.

He was going to the same school as Jane, his half-sister.

Lott glanced back at her, clearly worried at the sound and more than likely the shocked look on her face.

"Your mother or father home?" Andor asked, flashing his badge.

Julia noticed that as Andor introduced all three of them as detectives, he made sure that he flashed his gun under his jacket in the process.

The kid stammered for a moment, then turned and shouted, "Mom?"

A woman about Julia's age appeared. She had bleached-blonde hair pulled back and was wearing a MGM Grand Hotel room service uniform. She was very thin and clearly smoked, since through the open door and hole where the screen used to be, a smoke-smell wafted over them.

Andor again introduced all three of them as she stood there, nodding.

"Are you Denise Miller?" Lott asked.

"I am," she said, nodding.

"You own that van?" Lott asked, pointing at the van.

"I do," she said. "But it mostly goes only between here and MGM. It's seen its day. Why?"

"We're actually looking for information about a man who used to drive it by the name of Stan Rocha."

At that, Denise Miller did something Julia would have never thought would be a response.

Denise laughed. A smoker's laugh, rough and ending in a cough.

Then Denise Miller said something that sent Julia back one more step.

"Someone finally dig up the body of that worthless husband of mine? After twenty-two years, it's about damn time."

Then the kid beside Denise asked Lott, "You found my father? Really?"

All Julia could do was gasp for the thin hot air and try to focus, as she had learned how to do over decades as a detective.

In fact, without that training, more than likely she'd just be sitting on the sidewalk right now.

She felt like doing that anyhow, but managed to remain standing and staring at a woman that had been married to her husband at the same time she was.

And had a son with him as well.

Luckily, that son-of-a-bitch husband of theirs was dead. He wasn't the type to face this kind of thing easily, even though this was all his mess.

And mess didn't begin to describe this.

CHAPTER ELEVEN

September 2014.
Just off the Boulder Highway
Las Vegas, Nevada

ANDOR, putting on his charm offensive as Lott had seen him do many times over the years, asked Denise Miller if they could talk with her.

She said sure. She said she had an hour before she had to be to work. She indicated they come in and took her son's arm and pushed him back inside away from the front door.

Lott stepped back and took Rogers' elbow. Then he whispered to her. "You okay? You want to wait in the car?"

She shook her head and took a deep breath, clearly finding a way to center and ground herself as all good detectives could do. "I'll be fine," she whispered back.

Lott wasn't so sure how fine she would be. She had just learned that her former husband had been a bigamist and had a son. That kind of news would send anyone spinning. And from what he could tell from Rogers' eyes, she was clearly in slight shock.

"You sure?" he asked.

"Fine," she said, her voice firm. With that she came back into her eyes and looked into his.

He nodded. With that she squared her shoulders, took a deep breath, and stepped up and followed Andor into the smoke-smelling small living room.

She stood to one side, leaning against the wall near the door as Lott followed Andor around and sat on the cloth couch that had seen far more wear than Lott wanted to think about as he sank down into the soft brown cushions.

Denise sat in a big, worn recliner facing a large-screen television and the kid went over and stood behind her and to one side. She didn't pop up the footrest, but instead sat almost sideways in the big chair, facing the couch.

The room was cluttered with old music albums and a few other chairs covered in papers and a couple of shirts.

The place was clearly lived in and seldom cleaned. The drapes over the two windows kept out any hint of sunshine and the smell of bacon mixed with the smoke smell.

"We need some basics, first, if you don't mind," Andor said, putting his nicest smile that had a way of making people relax a little, especially women about his age. He took out a notebook and opened it to a blank page.

Lott didn't move and neither did Rogers. It was normal for only one detective to take notes in situations like this. This time it would be Andor. Lott was glad he was, since Lott was worried about Rogers.

Denise smiled at Andor and said, "Sure, fire away."

Lott managed to not laugh. Andor could charm a woman without hardly trying, so when he turned it on, the women he interviewed seemed to just melt for him. And it certainly wasn't because of his looks.

"You were married to Stan Rocha from when to when?" Andor asked.

"From the spring of 1988 to the day he disappeared in 1992," she said. "I guess technically I'm still married to the jerk unless you find his body or something."

"I'm sorry to have to tell you, but Stan Rocha was killed in May of 1992," Andor said fairly bluntly. "He was shot and left in a warehouse downtown."

"Shit," the kid said, his voice rough.

Denise just shook her head. "I always sort of knew he was dead, but didn't hear about that. I don't read the papers much. I figured one of his lost mines had killed him with a cave-in or something."

"Lost mines?" Andor asked.

Lott was very glad Andor asked that question or he would have. Out of the corner of his eye he saw Rogers stand up away from the wall.

"Sure, that's all he did. He searched for lost treasure and lost mines. He called it his job and figured that any day he would strike it rich. He was sometimes gone for a month out there in those deserts. So he was shot, huh? And I assume, since you are here now, you never found out who did it."

Lott started to open his mouth, then closed it. He glanced over at Rogers who looked just as shocked as he felt. Why would an old buried treasure or lost gold mine get Rocha executed?

"Anyone who would want him dead back then?" Andor asked.

Denise shook her head. "He was a freeloader, of that there was no doubt. He hated anything that looked or smelled like real work. But he was a general nice guy, docile as a lamb, too much at times."

Lott again noticed that Rogers was nodding slightly. That was similar to some things Rogers had said about Stan as well.

"Unless he ran across something in the desert that he shouldn't have," Denise said, "I can't imagine why anyone would kill him. He didn't gamble and had no money except what little I gave him to keep him going searching for mines."

"You have any of his research material," Andor asked. "That might help us a lot discover what got him killed."

"Oh, sure," Denise said. "Boxes of the stuff that was in his closet, his desk, and mostly the van. We sold all his picks and shovels and stuff, but kept all the paperwork."

"So you ever try to figure out where he vanished?" Andor asked.

Denise laughed. "He'd been gone almost two months when I really started to think something was wrong. When I looked at his paperwork, he was digging into lost treasures all over Nevada and into Idaho and Utah. No clue where he was. And he never told me much of anything, to be honest. Tight-lipped guy. When he didn't come back, I just figured he either had bailed on me and his new baby, or a cave-in got him."

"Sorry to bring you the bad news," Andor said, keeping his charm on full

burn. Lott figured it was going to be lucky they got out of there without this woman offering to take Andor into the back room by the time he was finished. Over the years, Andor had had a lot of those offers, but never once took a woman up on it. He had been devoted to Helen, his now-dead wife, and never once gave any of the offers even a second thought.

Denise just shrugged. "As far as we were concerned, he's been dead a long time."

The kid nodded, but Lott could tell he was shocked. Before this visit he had a father lost in a mine cave-in, not shot in a murder.

"If you wouldn't mind getting all of Rocha's stuff for us," Andor said, smiling and standing. "We'll let you get on to work."

She smiled and stood, giving the look to Andor that Lott knew was a "I'm single, call me" look.

"Do you know where my dad is buried?" the kid asked.

Lott nodded. "I'll have the directions brought over."

Denise patted her son's arm, clearly understanding that he was having some trouble with all this.

"Come on, Roger," she said to her son. "Let's get your father's stuff for these detectives."

Lott started to open her mouth, then said nothing. He turned to Rogers, who was staring at the kid.

Then she said softly to Lott, "I'll wait in the car."

After she was out the door, Lott turned to Denise. "I don't mean to pry, but why did you name your son Roger?"

"Stan said it was on old family name and I liked it," she said. "Roger wasn't even a year old when his father disappeared."

"Sorry, for the bad news, kid," Andor said.

"Just find who killed him," Roger said.

"That's what we hope to do," Lott said. "And we'll keep you informed when we do."

"Thanks," Denise said, leading them to a closet at the end of a narrow hallway where she had stored the six boxes of Stan Rocha's work.

Boxes that might just get them closer to who killed him. If they were lucky.

And Lott knew at this point they were going to have to be very lucky.

CHAPTER TWELVE

September 2014.
Off the Boulder Highway
Las Vegas, Nevada

AS THEY CARRIED out the boxes from Denise Miller's house to his car through the warming morning air, Lott decided he had a couple more quick questions to ask Denise.

"Did Rocha have another car besides using your van?"

"Sure," she said, nodding as they reached the back of the Cadillac and he got the back gate open. "It was a 1985 Chevy Impala. Nasty green color. But he liked taking the van when heading out in to the desert for any kind of long trip. He said it allowed him to sleep in the van if he needed to."

Andor nodded to Lott at the answer to that question as he put a box in the back of the Cadillac and turned to Denise. "So he took the Impala the day he left here and never came back?"

"He did," she said, nodding as she took a box from her son and handed it to Andor to put in the back of the Cadillac.

Rogers was turned around slightly in the back seat listening. Lott hoped she was doing all right. He would know soon enough, but he couldn't imagine how she could be. Her dead husband had another family and had named his son after her. Didn't get much weirder than that.

"So do you know if he had any family other than the Rogers?" Lott asked.

"Oh, sure," Denise said, smiling at Andor. "His parents and brother live in Boise. I called them a few years ago to see if they had heard from Stan and they hadn't. They were both still alive, as well as Stan's brother, still in Boise. Now I know why they hadn't heard from him. But honestly, he and his parents were never close, at least that's what he told me."

"You got their number and names?" Andor asked, giving Denise his biggest smile.

"Sure, come on back into the house and I'll get it for you with the last couple of boxes."

Andor nodded and followed Denise and her son back into the house.

Lott watched him go and hoped that Denise would let Andor out of there with his pants on.

Rogers was shaking her head. She got out and moved around behind the Cadillac with Lott. He wanted to touch her elbow, but it was clear she had her footing again and was doing all right.

Or at least as well as possible considering all the weird things she had just learned.

"This is making no sense at all," she said, glancing back to make sure Denise and Andor had not yet come back out

of the house. "How come on the police report I was listed as his wife? And she was never notified?"

"I honestly don't remember," Lott said. "But I agree, we need to find that out. It doesn't make sense. Not a lick of sense, actually, since she was here in town."

At that moment, Andor and Denise came back out, both carrying another old brown file box.

Lott took the one from Denise and put it in the back of the Cadillac while Andor did the same with the other box. They all just about filled the back area of the SUV.

"One more question if you don't mind," Lott said, remembering one more detail they needed to know. "Did Rocha have any family in Salt Lake or Winnemucca?"

Denise looked puzzled, then shook her head. "None that I knew of. He said his best friend, a woman by the name of Julia, lived in Reno. But he didn't say much else beyond that about any other family or friends outside of Boise."

"Thanks," Andor said, reaching out and shaking her hand and smiling, holding onto her hand just a little longer than he needed to, another of his many tricks. "I hope you don't mind if I call you if we need more questions answered."

"Any time, detective," she said, smiling back at Andor as Lott took Julia's elbow and got her around to the back seat and then closed the door. She looked to be in complete shock, and Lott didn't blame her at all.

Andor waved at Denise from the passenger seat as Lott got them headed down the road.

Then Andor turned back to stare at Rogers. "You all right?"

"I've been better," she said, her voice firm and clearly angry. "But I'll be fine.

The bastard's been dead for over twenty years after all. Lucky for him."

"Yeah," Andor said, turning around and giving Lott a high-eyebrow look. "Doesn't' make it sting any less."

"Got that right," Rogers said.

CHAPTER THIRTEEN

September 2014.
Off of the Boulder Highway.
Las Vegas, Nevada

JULIA FELT like she was in shock as Lott took them back through the subdivision toward her car. She wasn't completely sure she could drive at the moment, and she needed to get her feet under her from all this new information about her former husband.

She always knew she had never really known him, but now she was questioning everything about her own judgment.

How could she have missed so much?

What in the world had been wrong with her?

She needed answers now a lot more than she had when she suggested they start down this road.

Lott glanced back at her, then said, "Anyone up for some lunch?"

"Wendy's," Andor said. "One about a half mile in toward town."

Rogers smiled. He was taking care of her. And right now she really appreciated that.

Lott laughed and then looked back at her. "You like Wendy's hamburgers, Rogers?"

"Not so much," she said, "but I love their chicken sandwich and their baked potatoes. So it sounds perfect. Thanks."

"Wendy's it is," Lott said, nodding. He went past the parking lot with her car and turned onto the Boulder Highway.

In ten minutes they were ordering and were shortly tucked off at a table to one side. The lunch rush was still a good forty-five minutes away, so no one was sitting close to them at all.

She was very glad for this idea of lunch. She was already feeling better. Lott really seemed to already know her. And part of her really liked that, and that he cared enough to figure out something to help like this.

They all made small talk for a few minutes while they dug into their sandwiches and hamburgers and fries. Cops were notorious for not eating well and clearly the three of them weren't that concerned even after decades of being in the field. But she had to admit, Wendy's food was one of the best in the fast food world. But it was still fast food.

Finally Lott reached down and pulled up the yellow legal pad he had brought in with him. "We need to get a plan going on this."

"We're making a ton more progress than I thought we would," Andor said, also getting out his notebook. Then he looked at her. "Sorry, Rogers, for the hit this is causing you."

"Lott asked me if I wanted to open up this part of my past," she said. "I know digging into cold cases is often like turning over a pile of rotted and molding boards and seeing what bugs scatter. So I can handle it. Just ignore me if I stagger for a moment."

Andor laughed.

"Deal," Lott said.

"So what's next?" she said before taking another bite of her chicken sandwich. She was surprised that it actually had some chicken flavor to it and a nice light pepper kick. She remembered it being good, just not this good. Not something you normally get in fast food.

"I still have missing persons searching old files in Winnemucca, Boise, and Salt Lake," Andor said. "Those might be in sometime this afternoon."

"I think we should run a pretty good check on that Denise Miller," Lott said. "She might know a lot more than she's letting on. I wouldn't put it past her to have put three shots in Rocha when she discovered he was married to Julia."

"I agree," Andor said.

Julia was glad that neither one of them had asked her opinion on that. She thought they needed to do the same thing, but coming from her it might have sounded off. And she wasn't sure if it was her gut instinct or old feelings that had her thinking that something about Denise Miller felt off.

"What about the building he was found in?" she asked. "Now that we know Rocha was into mining and old treasures, would the owners of that building back in 1992 have a connection anywhere else in the state? It was a mining company that owned it, right?"

Lott nodded and looked at Andor, who was also nodding. Then they both added that to their notes.

"We always wondered why he ended up there," Lott said, "and how anyone knew it was empty and unlocked. I know exactly who to help us with that search."

"Who?" she asked.

"Annie and Doc," Lott said.

Andor nodded.

"Why them?" she asked.

"They have some amazing ways of getting information and links buried in old files," Lott said. "Far more than we

have. Not sure if it's completely legal and I honestly don't want to know."

Julia was surprised. She knew that Annie and Doc sometimes helped on cases, but she didn't know that. "How did they get that ability?"

"Money," Andor said, shaking his head. "More money than anyone else in this city, actually. More money than two good-looking people of that age should ever have."

"I wouldn't know about that," Lott said, laughing. "But they made some contacts when they were working on his father's death."

"Same one where the President's friend and Chief of Staff were killed?" Julia asked.

"Same one," Lott said.

She dropped the subject at that. If Lott trusted his daughter and Doc to get the information, then they were good as far as she was concerned.

"So we also need to put traces and impound searches on that Impala," Andor said.

"Back to the DMV for me," Lott said. "They love me there."

"I'll check the missing persons," Andor said, "and get someone going on the impound of the Impala, see if that happened."

"What do you need me to do?" Julia asked.

Lott glanced at Andor. "Head home, take a nap for about two hours, change into your sorting clothes, and meet me and Andor back at my place in three hours. We have a lot of boxes to sort."

She appreciated the thought. And she planned on doing part of it. "Tell you what. I'll only take an hour-long nap to get my feet under me, then get on the internet and see what I can find for books on lost mines and treasures around this part of Nevada."

"Perfect," Andor said. "And check the old bookstore down on the corner of Sahara and Industrial. Who knows what they might have as well. Those folks in there seem to know more about Nevada history than anyone in the state."

"That I can do," she said. "Someone is going to have to contact his parents and let them know their son is dead."

Lott glanced at Andor.

"Let's wait until we have a few more answers first," Andor said.

She agreed and nodded her thanks to Lott, then quickly finished off her chicken sandwich in two bites as the other two stood.

Typical. She was always the last one still eating. Especially with other detectives.

Over the years, she had left many a meal half-eaten. At least these two were kind enough to let her get close to the end before heading to the door.

CHAPTER FOURTEEN

September 2014.
Pleasant Hills.
Las Vegas, Nevada

JULIA ARRIVED at Lott's home and parked out front of the well-kept two-story home. It was clearly a loved place with a green lawn and desert plants arranged with care in great patterns in rock gardens. Lott hadn't gotten there yet, since his car wasn't in the carport attached to the house where he normally parked it.

More than likely he had gotten hung up at the DMV. She didn't envy him that

task. She had spent her time in the DMV up in Reno over the years. They had been friendly people, at least in Reno, and she always bought them small Christmas presents every year.

But even with nice people, the task of searching old databases was never easy or fun.

Before she came over, she had managed to find a good dozen books on lost treasures and mines in Nevada online, and a few more that covered the entire Southwest, from California over through Utah and Arizona. Stan had no receipts from Arizona, so she had ignored books on that state. She had managed to get three of the main ones she had found online from the bookstore that Lott had suggested. One, a book titled Nevada: Lost Mines and Buried Treasures by McDonald had been published in 1981 before she had met Stan, so it might have been one of the books he used. Or at least knew about.

It would give them a start if they found an area he might be working.

Earlier, after getting back to her apartment, she had actually made herself lie down for a short time. That, and the lunch, had helped her get her mind back and she now felt fine again.

She supposed it shouldn't have surprised her that Stan had another wife. As Denise had said, he was a freeloader.

For all she knew, Stan also had wives in Winnemucca and Salt Lake. Now if she and Lott found them, those extra wives wouldn't surprise her. If he had to marry while freeloading, that would only make sense. He clearly had had the ability to remember who he was with at any time and keep his stories and different lives straight.

But what bothered her a lot was why

they had called her as his wife and not Denise, right here in town. That made no sense at all.

And why he had named his son after her? He hadn't lived long enough to have anything to do with naming Jane. He was dead before she had been born, so Julia had named her new baby daughter after her own mother.

Now she was going to have to tell her daughter that her father had been a bigamist and that she had a half-brother about her age.

That wasn't a conversation she was looking forward to.

Over twenty years after his death, Stan was still driving her crazy.

At that moment, Lott pulled into his driveway, waving at her and smiling through the tinted windows as he went past.

Just seeing him made her smile. She couldn't believe that at her age she was falling again for someone. She couldn't even remember how this had felt all those years ago, before meeting Stan.

She hadn't even felt this way with Stan. He had just been someone easy to hang around with, who didn't mind her being a cop, and who was pretty decent in bed. She had a hunch that if she really looked at it, she used him as much as he used her.

It would have been nice, though, if he could have helped raise Jane some. But he clearly hadn't lived long enough to even know that Jane was coming along. Julia had planned on telling him the next time he was in town. But instead got a phone call about his murder.

She climbed out into the late afternoon heat. It was just around 3:30 and the temperature in late September still had to be over ninety, easily. She had no doubt this heat and weather were going to take

her a few years to get used to.

She moved up behind Lott's white Cadillac as he climbed out and opened the back hatch. Then he went to open the backdoor as she reached for the first brown box.

It was light, so she grabbed another and took two into the back door and the coolness of the kitchen.

"Where shall I stack them?" she asked.

"Against the wall in the kitchen dining area," he said, going past her for a load.

Clearly this wasn't anywhere near the first time he had done something like this.

Working quickly, they had the nine brown file boxes out of the car and into the coolness of the dining area. The boxes were clearly dirty and smelled of smoke after all the years in Denise's home.

"You have some fresh boxes?" she asked. She had spent her years in and out of smoke in bars and restaurants and people's homes, but there was still nothing worse than the smell of smoke built up on paper and cardboard over decades of time. It had a rich, thick, rank smell like something long spoiled.

He wrinkled his nose and nodded, turning toward an area off the kitchen that looked like a storage room.

He came back a moment later with a stack of ten fresh file boxes from Staples, not yet put together.

They quickly put the boxes together, dumping the contents of each of Stan's boxes into a fresh one without looking at any of it and then tossing the old box outside into the carport.

It only took a few minutes and when they were done and had lids on the boxes, the smoke smell was mostly gone.

"Much better," he said, nodding, clearly relieved. "Good idea."

Then he stopped, faced her, and looked her squarely in the eyes.

She was again startled at how intense his gaze was and how handsome he was when he looked at her like that.

"Are you all right?"

"Honestly," she said, "that was a shock, especially the part where he named his kid after me. But I'm fine now. Got past it."

"You sure?" he asked, clearly worried, as she would have been in his spot.

"Completely sure," she said. "It's been over two decades after all that he's been dead. I didn't like him much anymore when he was killed."

"Fair enough," he said, still looking into her eyes with that fantastic gaze of his.

"But there is one thing I need," she said, looking at him with her most intent stare, as if she was going to ask him for the secrets of the world.

"Anything," he said, being very serious right back.

"A glass of that wonderful iced tea of yours."

Then she smiled.

It took him an instant, but then he laughed, shaking his head as he turned toward the fridge. "Yup, you're fine."

With that she laughed, and honestly, that felt great after how the day had already gone.

CHAPTER FIFTEEN

September 2014.
Pleasant Hills.
Las Vegas, Nevada

LOTT ENJOYED THE FEELING as he and Rogers settled in with their iced teas and starting looking through the boxes from Denise Miller's home. He was very glad Rogers was going to be all right. He had worried about her all afternoon since leaving her at her car.

And when he realized he was worrying about her, he felt startled and surprised. It was the same kind of worry he used to feel about Connie. A kind of worry that was anchored in actually caring for a person.

They started off by sorting receipts again, making sure that all the receipts were in the four major areas that they knew about, plus another pile for the ones they couldn't read or that were not in Winnemucca, Boise, or Salt Lake.

They tossed the Reno and Las Vegas receipts back into a fresh box unless it was something unusual or that they couldn't figure out.

They put all the maps and books and notebooks into another box. They were through the second box and had the third one dumped out on the table when Andor banged on the front door.

"Open!" Lott shouted and Andor came in, stomping through the living room like he always did.

Lott glanced at Rogers who was smiling much like Connie used to smile every time Andor did that. Andor sounded more like a monster approaching than a retired detective.

"Any luck at the DMV?" Andor asked as he came in and went to the fridge to get a bottle of water.

"Nothing," Lott said. "But they are running the same searches they did on the van on the Impala for me. They'll have it tomorrow.

"So he didn't own that car either," Andor said, shaking his head and sitting down at the end of the kitchen table.

"How about you?" Rogers asked.

"No Impala impounded anywhere around the city from 1992 to 1995. Nothing. So I have running searches for the car in other areas outside of the metro limits."

"Good," Lott said. "And I called Annie and asked her to search the records of the building and compare it to outside interests of any type. She said that she and Doc and their friend Fleet would get right on it."

"So we have a ton of irons in this fire," Andor said.

Lott couldn't agree more. A lot more than he had expected them to have at this point. He half expected them to be playing cards every week with no leads at all.

Now, as Andor sat down and took a long drink from the bottle of water, Lott could tell his partner wasn't giving all the information. After working together for almost twenty years, he knew that look on Andor's face.

"So spit out the rest," Lott said, pretending to sort receipts and not look at Andor.

"Sometimes you are a damn kill-joy," Andor said.

Lott glanced up at Rogers' smiling face and winked.

"We got two hits on the missing persons search," Andor said, smiling. "One four months after Rocha's death in Winnemucca and another the same month in Salt Lake."

Then he frowned and looked at Rogers.

"Let me guess, both were from his wives," she said, shaking her head in clear disgust.

"Got that in one," Andor said. "Sorry."

Lott stared at Rogers, who clearly didn't seem to be bothered by it. And from what he had seen of her over the last four months, she didn't have that good of an emotional poker face.

"It's starting to figure," Rogers said. "And after this morning I expected it."

"How's that?" Lott asked, clearly puzzled as to why Rogers was now taking this news so well.

"He was a freeloader, plain and simple," Rogers said. "And he was in search of some lost treasure. No sane woman was going to let him do that and help support him unless he married her. And more than likely if he had even told me what he was doing, I'd have booted his ass down the road sooner than I was doing."

Lott had to admit that she was right on that.

Andor looked at her, frowning. "Are you saying it's one thing for a husband to be a freeloader, another for a boyfriend to be one?"

"You got it," she said. "Women won't stay with freeloaders very long as boyfriends. Husbands who don't work are as common as sand on the beach."

Lott had to agree with her on that as well. He'd seen that more times then he wanted to think about.

"Got any idea how long he was doing this sort of thing?" Andor asked.

"I got a hunch these boxes are going to help answer some of that question," Rogers said, pointing to the stack of banker boxes. "But I don't think he was any older than me when we met, so it had to only have been a little over four years at most. Maybe a few more, but it would take a few years to come up with this kind of plan I would think."

"Denise said she met and married him in 1988," Andor said.

"Same year for me."

"So what do we do about these other wives?" Andor asked.

"Same thing we do with his parents in Boise," Lott said. "We wait and see what else we can come up with first."

Suddenly Lott noticed that Rogers frowned and sat back.

"Something wrong?"

She laughed. "With this case, just damn near everything. You have the official police file on this?"

"On the counter over there," Lott said, pointing toward the stove. "And I got the second one that Annie started as well with it."

Andor and Lott went back to sorting the paper on the table as Rogers moved over to the file. After a moment she said, "I thought I remembered that."

"What?" Lott asked.

"Small caliber killed him."

"Twenty-two," Andor said, nodding. "More than likely from a rifle at fairly close range."

"Twenty-two rifles are often used as saddle rifles," she said.

"You thinking he might have been on horseback when he was shot?"

She shook her head. "No idea. But just thinking that a twenty-two is an odd weapon choice to kill someone in an execution-style murder in a city like Las Vegas."

Lott nodded. She was right about that. It was very odd for downtown Las Vegas. But now that they knew Rocha spent time out in the desert, it was less and less odd.

Rogers sat at the table and looked at both of them. "So, tell me, gentlemen, why did you call me as his wife and none of the rest of the other women he was mooching off?"

"I thought about that and looked it up," Andor said, scooting back his chair and going for the official file by the stove.

He flipped it open, went in a couple of pages and then pulled out a sheet.

He handed it to Rogers who stared at it for a moment.

"Rocha's driver's license on him when he was killed was issued in Reno," Andor said. "He had you down as wife and next of kin."

"I'll be," she said, shaking her head and handing Andor back the paper.

Then she turned to Lott. "Did the DMV have a statewide database on driver's licenses in 1992?"

"Sure," Lott said. "But I'm betting that Rocha had no issue at that point getting fake driver's licenses for each family. My gut sense is that the license for Reno was the only real one. Or the one he had on him because his next stop was Reno."

"So where did those extra licenses end up?" Andor asked.

That question stunned Lott and he grabbed his notebook and quickly wrote it down.

"He must have had a place all his own somewhere," Rogers said, shaking her head. "But I have no idea how he could have afforded that."

"Nope," Lott said, suddenly having a flash of insight. He smiled at his two friends. "I know exactly where all his secret stuff is stashed."

"Where?" Andor asked.

Rogers looked at him just as puzzled.

"Tell me if I'm wrong," Lott said. "We're dealing with a guy here who liked to be taken care of, right?"

Rogers nodded. "He liked it when I made the decisions for him like what to eat or what to wear somewhere."

"And from what I saw of Denise this morning," Lott said, "she would have treated him the same way."

"Mother," Rogers said, nodding.

Lott smiled. "We'll find all his secret stuff stashed safely at his home where his mother could take care of it all."

"Looks like someone's going to Boise sooner rather than later," Andor said.

"As soon as we get this all done and find out some results of some ongoing searches," Lott said.

He had a hunch they were just starting to scratch the surface of this case. And going to Boise would only be part of the key to who killed this freeloading bigamist.

And with four known wives, there was now some pretty clear motive. Men over the centuries had been killed for a lot less.

PART TWO

CHAPTER SIXTEEN

October 2014.
Foothills.
Boise, Idaho

DOC HILL'S big Cadilac SUV rode in silent comfort as Lott drove it slowly up the winding road into the foothills above Boise. Doc had let them use it because, as he said, it was just sitting in his garage doing nothing.

Lott couldn't believe how beautiful this town was, and how rich. The higher they went up the hill, the bigger the homes seemed to get. The home they were looking for was a mansion, plain and simple. He had been to Boise once before and liked it, but clearly he hadn't seen much of it.

Beside him, Rogers rode silently, staring at the homes and huge lawns and carefully trimmed shrubs and shaking her head. She was clearly as surprised as he was about how much money they were driving past.

"You know your in-laws were this rich?" Lott asked as they finally stopped in front of one of the highest and largest homes on the entire street. It had a tall black iron fence around it and monitored gate across the driveway. From what Lott could tell, the driveway wound through some trees farther up the ridgeline to a circular driveway in front of a three-story mansion that could hold a dozen of his homes and not even break a seam.

"Not a clue," Rogers said. "I didn't know I had in-laws, actually. Stan seemed poor and acted poor right down to every detail. For heaven's sake, he drove a three-year-old van with a dent in the door."

Lott just shook his head as they sat there in the comfort of the big car, letting the air-conditioning keep them cool in the afternoon heat of early October. None of this made any sense.

From the moment they started finding out about Stan's many wives, nothing seemed to add up. And they weren't one inch closer to who might have killed him. And they had a lot more questions than answers, now. And a lot of suspects, none of whom felt right to Lott.

They never did find the Impala. It wasn't impounded and there were a lot of them registered in those years after his death, but not to anyone that seemed connected to the case in any way.

And the boxes had been full of receipts and maps and charts and old books. Until they got an exact lead, the maps and such would make no sense. As Andor had said, the boxes were more of a lost treasure than anything Rocha had been looking for.

And then, when Annie and Doc came back with the results of their search on the building, it turned out they had discovered that Stan had actually owned the warehouse where his body had been found.

That had shocked Rogers almost as much as finding out Stan had other wives. Maybe even a bit more.

Stan's company had specialized in mineral rights, which explained a lot of the old maps and documents they found at Denise's home. The company owned upwards of fifty parcels of land around Nevada and had bought mineral rights on a hundred more.

And almost all the holdings were of land where a supposed lost mine or treasure might be located. Stan really had been searching for lost treasure, but doing it with a big corporation.

There didn't seem to be any other shareholders in the company, at least that Annie and Doc could find. All records were privately held in the Nevada corporation. And Nevada, being a state that prided itself on being business friendly and nonintrusive into corporate affairs, didn't have any records other than that Stan was the majority shareholder and ran the company and was the only name on all the documents.

After Stan's death, the company went on for another dozen years and then was finally bought by a mining consortium for an undisclosed amount of money in 2005. They could find no idea as to who got the money or Stan's shares.

Annie and Doc and their crew of researchers had no idea what the company did except buy land, mineral rights, a few water rights, and a dozen different warehouses. But Annie had promised him that they would keep digging.

Annie had gotten interested in the case, since she also had made a run at it when she was a detective. So when Lott told her that they needed to get up to Boise to visit Stan's parents and brother, she and Doc offered to fly them up on their private jet. The two of them had a tournament they had planned to play in at the Bellagio, so they couldn't go along. Which left the private jet with its huge brown leather seats, soft carpet, and wonderful food served by a woman named April to just Lott and Rogers.

Lott had to admit, that was the type of flying he could get used to. Annie and Doc had offered a few times over the last year to take Lott on a flight, but until this case, he had had no real need to leave Las Vegas.

Now he might find more reasons.

Rogers flat loved the plane, at one point over a glass of wine saying she needed to play more poker.

Lott knew that this jet had been earned by Doc being such a good poker player, but more of it was because his best friend, Fleet, knew how to invest and make money grow. Lott knew the two had been a team since they were in college together, Doc making the cash from poker, and Fleet investing it.

Then when Doc's father had been killed, Doc had inherited another not-so-small fortune.

Lott had asked Annie once how much money Doc had. She had laughed and said, "Trust me, Dad. You don't want to even know."

And now, with the help of Fleet as well, Annie's winnings at poker were making her wealthy as well. Connie would be proud of her daughter, Lott was sure. He sure was.

He glanced over at Rogers who was just staring at the gate of the big mansion. "You ready, Detective?"

She took a deep breath and nodded. "Take the lead," she said.

"Glad to," he said, climbing out into the dry, warm air. It wasn't as warm as Vegas, but still plenty warm enough.

They moved up to the big gate. There was no sign, only an address.

Lott pointed at the bell beside the gate with a speaker above it. "Andor would hate this."

Rogers laughed. "No place to knock."

Lott smiled at her. She would be fine. The two of them had really come to like spending time together over the last week, mostly eating dinners together. And the flight up here this morning, besides being in luxury, was comfortable between them as well.

He just hoped that once this case was over, they could continue spending time together. He was starting to enjoy not eating alone every evening while getting to know her.

"Yes," a voice came back through the speaker.

"Detectives Lott and Rogers," Lott said into the speaker.

"I'll be right down," the man's voice said.

Lott glanced at Rogers. That was not at all what he had expected. They had called ahead and made an appointment to talk with Carl Rocha, Stan's brother.

And they had both hoped to have a word with Stan's parents as well.

A man looking to be in his late fifties came striding down the driveway. He was dressed in tan golf slacks, a tan short-sleeved golf shirt, and brown loafers.

"Stan's brother," Rogers whispered. "The likeness is scary."

Lott nodded as the gate opened.

Carl Rocha introduced himself with a firm handshake, then asked, "Would you mind if we talk in your car?"

Lott shrugged and turned and led the way. He had Carl climb into the front seat and Rogers climbed into the back behind Lott. She moved to the middle so she could see Carl as well between the big front bucket seats.

Lott turned in his seat so he could see both Carl and Rogers.

"Sorry," Carl said after Lott got the car started and air-conditioning going. "Mom's having a rough day and I didn't want to upset her anymore."

"We understand," Lott said. "Thanks for seeing us."

Carl then did something that Lott was not expecting. He looked back at Rogers. "I assume you are one of Stan's wives? The Detective from Reno?"

All Rogers could do was nod.

How the hell had he known that?

CHAPTER SEVENTEEN

October 2014.
Foothills.
Boise, Idaho

JULIA SAT THERE STUNNED for a moment at Carl's question.

"You are correct," she said. "I was Stan's wife in Reno. I was the one informed about his death. I didn't know he had family, let alone other wives. He never mentioned a thing about his life, otherwise I would have contacted you at once."

Carl nodded. "I know you would have, Detective." He then asked the next logical question that Julia would expect a rich person with a mess on his hands to ask.

"Why investigate my brother's death now?"

Lott explained about the group of mostly retired detectives who worked on cold cases for the Las Vegas Police. "Your brother's case was my first case to go cold as a detective. So I have a personal interest in getting it solved."

"And I joined into the group when I retired and moved to Las Vegas," Julia said. "So how did you know about your brother having a number of wives?"

Carl shrugged. "He told me."

"You're kidding?" Julia asked, again shocked. "That's not like people who do that sort of thing. They are usually very secretive about it. Did he tell you why?"

Carl nodded. "Sure. He said he loved you all and just couldn't help it. Honestly, I tried to get him to get professional help, but he didn't want it. I just kept hoping that the house of cards he was building with all four of you wouldn't come crashing down."

Julia laughed slightly and Lott glanced at her with his worried look she was starting to really like.

"That makes sense for the Stan I knew," she said. "He hated hurting anyone's feelings. He would rather just go along with something instead of complain at all."

Carl nodded. "That was my brother. From a distance I sort of kept track of all four of you for a time after he disappeared. Stopped about ten years ago after it was clear Stan wasn't coming back either here or to any of you."

"And I assume you have kept this all from your parents?" Lott asked.

"I kept everything about his four wives from them except this news about his death," Carl said. "I didn't know he had been murdered until I got a call from Denise Miller after you spoke to her. I told my parents then that Stan was dead. I think they knew, but having it confirmed really set them back. Especially mom. She somehow, after twenty years, kept thinking he would walk in the door at any moment."

Julia couldn't think of anything to say to that.

"We met Denise," Lott said after a moment of silence.

Carl nodded. "She's a real piece of work, that one. Never met her, but the phone calls are always interesting. She's the only wife Stan told about his parents."

"Do your parents know they have grandkids?" Julia asked.

"I have three kids," Carl said. "At the moment that's enough for them. Detective, realize my father has Alzheimer's and doesn't remember anyone anymore and my mother has congestive heart failure. Both of them have very little time to live. I see no point at this time in their lives to change anything."

Julia nodded. "That honestly makes sense. I'm sorry to hear that."

"Don't worry, Detective," Carl said. "On my parent's death, all three of Stan's children will be cared for with trust funds and college paid."

"Three?" Lott asked.

"His wife in Winnemucca had a young girl right before he vanished, or as it turned out, was killed."

"And the other child?" Lott asked.

"My daughter," Julia said, looking at Lott with a puzzled look. "She was born three months after Stan was killed."

Lott looked at her, his mouth open.

"You're kidding?" Julia asked, now starting to suddenly get worried. "I didn't tell you I was pregnant with my daughter Jane when Stan was killed?"

Lott shook his head.

"I'm very sorry," Julia said to Lott, suddenly worried about how he would feel. "She's majoring in biochemistry at UNLV. It's why I moved to Las Vegas in the first place, to be close to her. She's so busy, we seldom talk. Not sure why I never mentioned her."

Then Julia turned back to look at Carl. "I am sure she will appreciate anything coming from her father's family, since she never knew him. But there is no need. She's doing fine with scholarships in the meantime. That's not why we are here. We want to find out who killed Stan."

Lott said nothing.

"I understand," Carl said, nodding.

Julia really hoped her surprise hadn't hurt what she was starting to enjoy with Lott. The subject of her daughter had just never come up. She hadn't been hiding it. Or at least she didn't think she had.

Dammit all to hell. What a stupid oversight on her part. She was proud of her daughter, just as he was proud of Annie.

She and Lott would have to talk when this was over. She really wanted what they were building to continue. She enjoyed his company far, far more than she wanted to admit at times.

Also, she wasn't looking forward to letting her daughter know she had a half-brother and a half-sister. That was a task she had been avoiding since they had talked to Denise.

When they got back, it was time to have that conversation as well.

CHAPTER EIGHTEEN

October 2014.
Foothills.
Boise, Idaho

LOTT HAD BEEN SHOCKED at learning about Julia's daughter. He had to admit that. She clearly was proud of her daughter, and clearly hadn't been hiding her from him in any fashion. It had just never come up.

And that worried him because he was really starting to fall for this woman and he realized he knew almost nothing about her. After all the years with Connie, knowing everything there was to know about Connie, he guessed he just sort of figured he would automatically know a person he was attracted to.

But that was clearly not the case. A very dumb assumption on his part.

She looked worried about him not knowing about her daughter. Clearly she also was concerned about something getting in the way of what was growing between them.

Well, as far as he was concerned, it wouldn't. He just needed to adjust his thinking some and enjoy getting to really know another person. Something he hadn't done since he and Connie had met back when he was still a traffic cop.

"So," Lott said, deciding to focus back on Carl while they had him trapped in the car. "What happened to your brother's corporation?"

Now it was Carl's turn to act surprised. "What corporation? Except for the money my parents sent him to live and an old Impala, he had nothing more than the clothes on his back."

Rogers looked at Lott and he nodded. She reached into a folder beside her on the back seat and pulled out all the information they knew about Stan's business. And with luck, Annie and Doc and Fleet would be digging up even more in the next day or so.

She handed the paper to Carl who studied it, clearly shocked. Lott had watched a lot of people pretend to be shocked. This was real.

Carl really, really hadn't known his brother ran such a large business. Rocha really had a way with secrets, that's for sure.

After a moment, Carl looked up. "Breyfogle Incorporated?"

Lott nodded. "Named after a famous lost mine to the west of Las Vegas. Your brother's company bought up land, mineral rights, and water rights all over Nevada, almost always where there was a rumored hidden treasure."

"Plus they owned three warehouses in Reno and a dozen in Las Vegas," Rogers said. "His body was found in one of the warehouses his company owned."

"We didn't know he owned the building at the time," Lott said. "We only discovered all this just lately in this new investigation."

"So what happened to all this after his death?" Carl asked, frowning as he continued to study the paper with all the assets of the corporation listed that had been found so far. "There was a lot of money here."

"That's what we just asked you," Lott said. "We have people tracing this, but so far we have run into a dead end. Whatever happened to this corporation was very, very carefully covered up. And, of course, Nevada corporation laws make that fairly easy to do."

"This isn't possible," Carl said. "My brother was a free spirit. Smart as they came, yes, but not the corporation type. And I have no idea where he would have gotten the money for all this."

"Parents didn't fund him in any way?" Rogers asked.

"No," Carl said, shaking his head. "I've five years older than Stan and was already doing the family books and accounting when he left college. I did the books both for our family corporations and my parent's personal money. I know of every dollar they sent him. And it wasn't much. Not enough to start this."

Carl waved around the paper and then handed it back to Rogers who put it back in the file folder.

"Did Stan have any friends in college that could have helped him with his treasure hunting?" Rogers asked.

That was a good question that Lott hadn't thought of.

Carl shook his head. "He was a loner. He had a girlfriend for the last couple years of college, but he told me she wanted to get married and he wanted to go search for lost treasure."

"A woman he didn't marry," Rogers said, laughing.

"Yeah, wondered about that after he started into marrying all of you," Carl said, shaking his head. "He did all that marrying in one year. 1988."

"When did he leave college?" Lott asked.

"1986 was when he graduated," Carl said.

"The corporation was incorporated in late 1989," Rogers said. "And started buying land shortly after."

Suddenly Lott had a thought, one that Stan's brother and Rogers wasn't going to like much if he was right.

"So I assume," Lott said, "that when Stan came home, he stayed here with your parents."

Carl looked puzzled. "Stan never came home. Not once from the time he left to go treasure hunting."

Rogers jerked and looked at Lott.

"Tell me," Rogers said, "was his college girlfriend rich?"

Carl nodded, looking puzzled because he seemed to know he had missed something. "Very. Why?"

"And she had access to money, even being young?"

"I think so, why?" Carl asked. "She had a huge trust fund that she came into when she graduated. You think she funded up Stan?"

Rogers nodded. "I can't imagine the man I married saying no to a woman."

"Shit," Carl said, almost shouting. "Are you saying he might have married her as well?"

"Maybe," Lott said, keeping his voice calm. "Not a word to anyone. Let us investigate because she might be our suspect."

Carl nodded.

"Can you get us her name and address?" Rogers asked.

"I know it very well," he said, shaking his head. "Her name is Kate McDonald. She's married to the governor of the state. The Governor's Mansion is down in the north end of town. Tough to miss."

All Lott could do was stare at Carl. He didn't have one thought in his head.

Finally he glanced back at Rogers, who was also just staring blankly at Carl.

Neither of them had a thing to say.

Stan's possible first wife, possible backer in his corporation, and possible suspect in his death was a governor's wife.

They were suddenly so far in over their heads, it wasn't funny.

CHAPTER NINETEEN

October 2014.
Foothills.
Boise, Idaho

JULIA SAT IN SILENCE as Lott drove them back off the twisting roads of the foothills and down into the tree-lined streets of the North End part of the city. She had never been in this part of the town before, and it was beautiful. Older homes tucked back from the street covered like a tunnel with branches of large oaks lining both sides.

It was shaded and cool and everything was bright green and the homes were older, but well-kept and clearly loved.

Finally she turned to Lott. "Sorry about not telling you about Jane. I'm very proud of her and can't imagine how I didn't blab about her all the time over the last week."

Lott laughed. "Shocked for a moment, but it's understandable. We've sort of been focused on figuring out who killed her father."

"But I am sorry," she said.

"Part of getting to know each other," he said, waving her apology away.

"I like getting to know you," she said, smiling at him, relieved he wasn't upset in any way. In fact, she felt more relieved than she wanted to admit. In a very short time she had really come to value and enjoy and trust Lott. And had hopes for a lot more time together if she didn't do something stupid to blow it all up.

"I like getting to know you as well," he said, giving her that smile she was really starting to love. "I have a hunch that by the time this is over, we're going to know each other a lot more."

"I hope so," she said, turning back to watch the beautiful streets and homes go past.

"I hope so as well," he said.

They rode in a comfortable and relieved silence for a few blocks down the beautiful shady streets.

"Got any ideas of what we should do next?" he asked.

"Find someplace to eat and call Andor and fill him in on all this," she said. "Before Carl calls the first wife."

"You think he might?" Lott asked.

"It's big money and politics," she said. "So come to think of it, let's do a surprise visit before she can lawyer up."

Lott glanced at her and then smiled. "That's totally crazy, but I like how you think, Detective."

It was totally crazy. She knew that, but it might be the only way they get any information at all from a governor's wife. If it wasn't already too late.

She sat back as Lott used the GPS feature in the car to direct them to the Governor's Mansion.

The big white mansion was two stories tall in this same area of town. It was tucked back in the trees with a large fence around it and surrounded by trees. It looked more like a southern home than one for Idaho.

The building didn't look much bigger than some of the other large homes nearby. But Julia could imagine back when it was first built, the mansion sat up on a slight hill looking at the valley. Now the huge old trees blocked any chance at a view.

They pulled into an area labeled guest parking just off the street and a good hundred yards from the main house across a tree-covered huge lawn. There were no other cars at this point in the early afternoon.

And no one in sight.

Julie glanced around, thinking that fact very odd.

She and Lott climbed out into the warm afternoon air and moved to the gate and the speaker there. The gate was black iron and decorative and wide enough for large trucks to pass. The rest of the fence looked about the same but was mostly covered in climbing vines. Julia could see a number of obvious security cameras and more than likely there were a few not so obvious.

One camera was mounted right over the speaker.

Lott pushed the button and a moment later a woman's voice said, "Yes."

"Las Vegas Detectives Lott and Rogers," Lott said, "to see Mrs. McDonald on a private matter."

"One moment," the voice said.

After about thirty seconds a man's voice came back. "Please show your badges to the camera."

They both did.

The gate clicked and opened. "Please come up the driveway to the security building on the left. Be prepared to leave your guns."

Lott nodded and Julia led the way through the gate. Then the two of them moved up the beautiful flower-lined driveway. She wasn't sure what the low gold and red flowers were, but they seemed to be doing fine in the early fall heat.

Everything about this city had a beauty about it. She had never seen a place like it before. Nevada cities like Reno and Las Vegas were stark and dry, and even though Reno had the mountains towering over it, the poverty that ran alongside the casino lights was always in sharp contrast.

Here, this town seemed like the poster city for middle and upper class blue-collar living. Everything seemed maintained and painted and in the city brown didn't seem to be a color that was allowed.

At the security building, they were met by a man with a badge and a gun on his hip. Clearly in shape and more than likely military of some sort, even though he was dressed in a black shirt and black slacks and black shoes.

He checked their badges again and asked them for their guns.

"You two are a way out of jurisdiction," he said. "And retired. May I ask your business with the governor's wife?"

Julia was surprised he had discovered they were retired, but a quick internet search of the Nevada police data base would show that clearly. But it would also show their special exemption to work.

"It's a private matter involving a friend from her college days," Lott said.

Julia had no doubt that the governor's wife was watching on one of the cameras. So she decided to put her at ease a little bit. "We are working a very cold case and could use some more background information, if she wouldn't mind. We won't be long."

"Follow me," the man said, nodding after a moment.

Julia knew that more than likely the governor's wife had told him to bring

them in. It was the correct political move. If she lawyered up now, it would just prove she had something to hide and that was the last thing she would want.

Their surprise visit was paying off in at least that little way. Now it would be interesting to see what kind of answers she gave them.

They were shown into a side door and into a large, high-ceiling parlor that was furnished with modern furniture. The walls were painted off-white and pictures of former governors covered two walls. Tall windows looking out over the lawn filled the other two walls.

As they entered, a woman dressed in jogging clothes and tennis shoes came in. "Sorry for the attire," she said, smiling. "You caught me in the exercise room."

She had her dark brown hair pulled back off her face and clearly she had spent time in the sun, as well as had a couple face-lifts that made her look both fake and younger at the same time.

"Very sorry to intrude," Lott said after introducing them both.

"Call me Kate, please," she said and indicated that they sit down on the couch and she sat facing them in a big chair.

"We're here in Boise investigating a cold case from Las Vegas," Julia said, starting off. "Stan Rocha was murdered in 1992 and his murder never solved."

Kate nodded. "I know," she said. "I'm glad you are opening it back up finally."

"How do you know about the murder?" Julia asked.

At the security building, they were met by a man with a badge and a gun on his hip.

"Stan was my first husband," Kate said, looking Julia right in the eye.

Julia nodded. So they had been right after all.

"When Stan didn't come home," Kate said, "I sent investigators to find him. About six months after his death they discovered he had been shot in Las Vegas. It barely even made the papers at the time since there were no leads and so many other more important things happening in Las Vegas at the time."

"Is that when you discovered your first husband's habits with other women?" Lott said.

Kate didn't even bat an eye. "No, actually. Stan told me about all of his other wives in 1989, after he had married them all, including you, Detective Rogers."

Julia sat back. This was not going the way she had expected. Not at all.

"So you were angry?" Lott asked.

Kate actually laughed. "Not in the slightest. I forced him into marrying me after all. Poor Stan could never say no to a woman on anything."

Then Kate turned. "He liked you the most of all of them," she said.

Julie had no idea at all how to answer that, so she only nodded.

"Did you know about his three children?" Lott asked.

"Five children," she said. "I had two children with him as well. Both now grown and married and doing well."

"So your past with Stan is known?" Julia asked, trying to ignore for the moment the thought of now telling Jane she had four half-brothers and sisters.

Kate actually laughed at that. "Of course. You don't be married to a man running for any political office and try to hide things like this. The press knows I was married before Madison and had two children and that my first husband was killed in Las Vegas. And that his murder is unsolved."

Kate took a deep breath, clearly lost in memory. "Madison stepped in and helped when Stan vanished and did a great job being a father to my two children after we learned of Stan's death. The children were both so young, they don't remember their real father at all."

"He knew you before Stan was killed?" Lott asked.

Kate smiled. "There were five of us who hung around together in college. Me and Stan and Madison and Carla and Danny. Great friends."

Julia nodded. Clearly Stan's brother didn't know about any of this with his younger brother, including the two kids, so this kind of thing wasn't in the news much. Although from what she could tell of Stan's older brother, he didn't pay much attention to anything but his parents and his family money.

"One more question if you don't mind," Lott asked.

Kate waved her hand. "Glad to help, detectives, if it solves Stan's murder. And besides, you are helping me avoid a long half hour on the StairMaster."

"Did you know about his corporation?" Lott asked.

Julia was watching Kate closely when he asked that question and she was honestly shocked.

"What corporation?" Kate asked, leaning forward. "Stan had no money, which is why he married in every town, to have a place to stay while he searched for his lost treasures. I wouldn't give him any of my trust fund's money. I told him that was for the kids and to buy us all a house when he got done with his treasure quest, since he wasn't actually working.

And my parents were disgusted I had married him and wouldn't talk with me for years, even after Stan's death became known."

Lott shook his head and Julia did the same.

"What corporation?" Kate asked again, this time in a powerful, demanding voice that Julia instantly understood why Stan couldn't say no to her.

"Stan was the president and CEO and only officer of record in a Nevada Corporation called Breyfogle Incorporated," Lott said, "named after a lost mine to the west of Las Vegas."

"It was founded in 1989," Julia said, "and had property, mineral rights, and water rights all over the state, mostly corresponding with the areas of old lost mines and treasures. We only just learned about it."

"And it owned almost a dozen major warehouses," Lott said, including the one where his body was found. We just learned that as well."

Kate looked like she had lost most of her dark tan as she sat back in the big chair. "That's not possible."

"What's not possible," Julia said.

"Stan called me all excited one day that he had found one of his lost mines," Kate said. "He had done that maybe a dozen times before, usually to beg me to send him some money. I always refused and just ignored him on that call. But that time he didn't ask for money, and since I was pregnant with our second child, I didn't think much about it."

Lott glanced at Julia, then leaned forward. "Are you saying you think he might have actually found one of the lost treasures and not told you?"

Kate took a deep breath and leaned forward, clearly gathering herself. She looked at Julia. "You were married to him, Detective. Could he have kept that from you?"

"I didn't even know he was searching for treasure," Julia said, smiling. "Stan was the most tightlipped person I have ever met and the deeper I get into this investigation, the more I understand I knew nothing about the man I married and had a child with."

"Well," Kate said, sitting back and closing her eyes. "It seems that makes two of us."

CHAPTER TWENTY

October 2014.
Downtown.
Boise, Idaho

LOTT DROVE IN SILENCE through the beautiful, oak-covered streets of the North End of Boise, Idaho, heading back toward the center part of town. He knew where there was a decent restaurant down near the city parks on the river where they could have a late lunch. He was starving.

"It's been a long time since crawling out of bed this morning in Las Vegas," Rogers said, smiling at him. "I feel sort of shell-shocked to be honest."

"Food will help," Lott said.

"Soon, I hope," Rogers said.

"As fast as I can get us there without getting arrested."

She laughed.

They rode in silence for a few more blocks, then Rogers said, "We have five wives, five kids, a brother who is as much in the dark as anyone, and a lost corporation. That guy I married was a real piece of work, wasn't he?"

"He had his issues," Lott said, smiling at Rogers. "But if he did find that lost gold mine, how he dealt with it was far from stupid. He kept it out of the papers and kept the money to himself."

Suddenly Rogers turned toward him. "Gold mine," she said. "If he did find a gold mine, someone would have to work it. Right?"

Lott nodded, starting to see where she was headed.

"The ore would have to be processed and sold," she said, "and there would be records of all that in the state records. Right?"

"I know nothing about gold mining," Lott said, "but I'm betting you are on the money about that."

"We get to the restaurant," she said, "we have to call Andor and fill him in on all this."

"And we need to get Annie and Doc and their people looking into the mining of the Breyfogle as well," Lott said.

"Every time we hit a dead end on this, another five leads spring up," Rogers said.

"It certainly is keeping it interesting," Lott said, feeling both frustrated and challenged. It really felt good to be working on a case like this. His retirement had been clouded with Connie's sickness and death. He knew he hadn't been ready to retire and now it felt great to be back.

"If I don't get some food pretty soon," Rogers said, smiling at him, "I might make this case even more interesting by passing out on you."

"Six blocks," Lott said, turning on Capital Boulevard toward the old Union Pacific Historical Train Station on the hill. The place was the subject of just about half the postcards that came out of Boise.

And he had to admit, driving toward it, the big clock tower and sprawling grounds around the building on the hill did make it look like a postcard.

The restaurant he was aiming for was in a building just over the bridge and close to the edge of Boise State University. A steakhouse with huge sandwiches and perfect iced tea. Annie and Doc had brought him here on his only visit up to see them and he had wanted to go back ever since.

He pulled into the mostly empty parking lot and they headed through the warm afternoon air toward the front door of the red-brick exterior tucked in under some tall pine and fir trees. There was a smell of freshly-mowed grass combining with the smell of cooking steak. Just about perfect for an early fall afternoon.

Inside, the steak smell got stronger and Lott could feel his stomach starting to really rumble and his mouth watering. A waitress with brown hair and a matching brown uniform with tan blouse and brown slacks and shoes got them seated at a big wooden table with soft booth seats around it. The seats were made out of some fake leather but were amazingly comfortable.

"Do you have some sort of bread we could snack on while we look at the menu?" Lott asked.

"Crazy hungry," Rogers said, smiling at the waitress who smiled back and promised to bring their classic butter rolls with their two iced teas.

Lot glanced at her. "You get Andor, I'll call Annie and get her started on the research on the mine."

"You got it," she said.

They were both talking when the waitress got back with the drinks and bread. And they both stopped the conversation long enough to take a large bite of the butter roll. It tasted like heaven as far as he was concerned.

Across the table, Rogers rolled her eyes in pleasure as she bit into the roll and all he could do was laugh. He was really enjoying his time with her. He had to trust that if they did solve this case, their time together would continue.

For some reason, he had just thought himself too old to get romantically involved again. And too set in his ways, as Connie had often said of him.

But it seems Rogers wasn't giving him much choice in the matter. If she just wasn't so damn good-looking and funny and smart and fun to be with, he might be able to stop the feelings.

But she was all of those things and he was going to have to relax and just go with it.

Far, far easier said than done.

CHAPTER TWENTY-ONE

October 2014.
Downtown.
Boise, Idaho

LOTT EXPLAINED to his daughter, Annie, what had happened with the brother and then at the Governor's Mansion. Annie had been flat stunned that they had had the courage to just go investigate the governor's wife.

Lott mentioned that if Annie had people doing research, it would be helpful to see if there were any articles on the governor's wife's first marriage when he was running for office.

And articles about the two kids.

Annie said she was excited to be involved and said she would get people

on that, on the mining output, and permits and everything. So far they had found no further trace of what happened to who controlled the corporation after Rocha was killed.

Rogers finished her conversation with Andor just slightly before Lott hung up with his daughter.

"He thinks we were nuts," she said, smiling as she took out another roll.

"Annie thought the same thing. But I have her investigating the governor's wife's story. And her kids."

"Good," Rogers said. "And you have her going on the mineral sales from a mine like the Breyfogle."

"I do," Lott said.

"Andor's still searching for the Impala," Rogers said. "Trying to figure out who owned it. He checked if Rocha had registered it in Idaho, but he hadn't. Andor will look into the chance that the governor's wife had owned it."

"Oh, great thinking," he said as the waitress came with her order pad and another basket of hot butter rolls that seemed to melt in his mouth.

They both ordered steaks and baked potatoes. He ordered a rib-eye and she ordered a top sirloin, both medium rare.

Then as the waitress left, they both grabbed a hot roll. The food was helping him, and from what he could tell, Rogers was feeling better as well.

"So what's next on our plan?"

She opened her notebook and looked at her notes. "We've talked to the brother and he didn't even know his brother was ever in town or about his first wife."

"And the first wife was shocked by the news of the corporation and possible mine," Lott said.

"She was," Rogers said, nodding and staring at her notebook.

Lott watched her, trying to figure out what was bothering him. Something pretty major, but he just couldn't put his finger on it.

"We need to investigate the two friends the governor's wife mentioned," Rogers said after a moment.

Rogers nodded and then what had been bothering him suddenly snapped into place. "Who would have the power to hide a corporation and even help Stan set it up?"

"Someone with money," Rogers said, frowning.

"Exactly," Lott said. "We need to have a look at the governor's early days. Did he have money? Was he the backer behind his friend's crazy searches?"

"Love triangle," Rogers said, nodding. "I'll bet he was in love with Kate and helped Stan leave to search for treasure to try to work his way into Kate's life."

"It makes as much sense as anything we've come up with so far," Lott said. "I'll call Annie and get her researching into McDonald's past as well."

Rogers nodded and looked at her notes again. "We're still missing one major thing we came looking for. Where did he keep his extra stuff, his driver's licenses, corporate records, things like that?"

Lott finished off the last of the roll as he thought about that. She was right. Rocha's mother didn't have any of it. The governor's wife clearly didn't have it since, if she had, she would have known about the corporation.

"So we have a missing corporation and a missing stash of personal papers," Lott said. "Wouldn't surprise me that McDonald had it all."

"It would make sense," Rogers said. "But it made sense his mother had it all."

"True," Lott said. So far this case was just one crazy twist and turn and dead-end road after another.

"We're also missing a car," Rogers said.

"Seems that while everyone is digging into the past, we need to talk to the other two wives. Maybe he confided in one of them."

Rogers nodded and put her notebook away as the waitress brought their food. "I was afraid you were going to say that."

"You want me to go?" Lott asked, studying her.

She shook her head. "I've met two of them. I can manage the other two. And we're making a great team talking with them."

He smiled. "That we are."

Then, before he dug into his wonderful-smelling steak and baked potato, he called Annie back.

After he quickly told her what they thought might have happened with the love triangle and the governor, all she said was, "What a hornet's nest."

"Just have your investigator be very careful," Lott said.

Annie actually laughed at that. "Oh, trust me, no trace. Our people are that good. Just you two don't kick the thing anymore."

"I promise," he said.

His daughter just laughed at him, knowing that he was just joking.

He hung up and dug into his steak. Across the table Rogers was already halfway done with hers.

And smiling with every bite.

CHAPTER TWENTY-TWO

October 2014.
Boise Airport.
Boise, Idaho

JULIA STOOD JUST INSIDE the air-conditioned private building that served as the office and waiting room for Doc Hill's private jet. The room was carpeted and had three expensive couches and a couple of magazines on a coffee table. Against one wall was a coffee and tea bar and some fresh doughnuts filled a plate there as well.

If she hadn't been so full from the wonderful steak dinner, she would have taken one.

The ground crew had just finished up a flight check and now they were all waiting for a copilot to arrive. Then she and Lott would be headed out.

She couldn't believe, and never would have believed, that on any case as a detective, she would be flying in such comfort and style.

Yet here she stood, waiting a few minutes for people to service a private jet just for her and Lott to fly to Winnemucca and then on to Salt Lake so they could talk to her former husband's other wives.

Actually, she more than likely should stop thinking of Stan as her former husband. Their marriage had never been valid, since he had already been married before her to at least one other woman. It had been a sham from moment one.

She still couldn't believe that she had missed the signs that Stan wasn't what he seemed. As a detective, she had always prided herself in catching the smallest details in a case. She had always

figured that Stan might have a girlfriend somewhere, but since she didn't really even know what he did when he left and couldn't get him to talk about it at all, she clearly hadn't cared that much.

Something about that bothered her as well. Maybe she knew, deep down, that she was only a rest stop for Stan to drop by at times and have sex and eat and sleep. And the marriage had just made it seem right to her for a time.

Looking back, she didn't think she much cared at all until she got pregnant with Jane.

Julia shook that thought away. Once they found Stan's killer, she was going to search out a counselor and get some help putting all this in perspective. Just so she could safely trust herself with another relationship.

She glanced back at the small waiting area. Lott was pacing in front of one couch, talking with his daughter. Maybe Annie and her research team had found something.

She hoped so.

It had been a very long day since she and Lott had climbed on that plane in Las Vegas a little before eight in the morning. Now it was going on six in the evening Boise time. Once they were in the air, they would be in Winnemucca in thirty minutes. They hoped to talk with the wife there and be back in the air and on the way to Salt Lake in an hour.

Through the big window, Julia could see a man dressed like a pilot walk toward the plane and climb on board. Looks like they were about ready.

"Talk to you after we talk with the Winnemucca wife," Lott said to his daughter and clicked off the phone.

"Any luck," Julia asked as he came over to stand beside her.

"The Breyfogle Company and the sole stock owner were extremely rich," Lott said. "Annie thinks they are getting closer to digging out who that person might be."

"Mining money?" Julia asked.

"Gold and silver," Lott said. "Plus plowing the money into more land and water rights and mineral rights made them even richer very quickly. Annie and her people are finding that information out easily enough, just not who was running the place."

"How about employee names," Julia asked.

Lott nodded. "They've got about fifty higher level manager's names, some of which were vice presidents. If we need to, we can interview them."

Julia knew that would be a lot of work, but if they hit solid dead-ends from here, they would do just that.

"Governor was broke as a college student," Lott said. "He had no real money until he married Kate. It seemed her family approved of him."

"Any chance Kate's family might have a hand in Stan's murder?" Julia asked.

"A logical motive," Lott said. "Annie and her people are digging into them all. Bound to be some ugly rat's nests back in those lives somewhere."

"You mean more ugly than a governor's wife being married to a bigamist before she married the governor?"

Lott laughed. "Seems that detail never hit any papers."

"Yet," Julia said.

From the door of the jet, Julia saw the pilot wave for them to come out.

"Well, you ready to go talk with one of your husband's other wives?" Lott asked as they headed out the door and into the warm evening air and the rumbling noises of the airport around them.

"You sure know how to make a trip sound exciting," Julia said.

"Better than Disneyland," Lott said.

"Wifeland?" Julia asked. "We find many more wives and it just might be enough for a theme park."

Lott laughed. "And all the kids could run it."

Julia really laughed. "Got that right. I'm not looking forward to telling Jane she has four half-brothers and sisters."

"Don't blame you there at all," Lott said, now suddenly serious as they neared the plane. "Might want to talk with Annie about that problem before you talk to Jane. Get a younger person's perspective on how to approach it."

Lott stopped at the bottom of the stairs leading up into the jet and looked at her directly, those wonderful dark eyes of his clearly worried about her.

"I will," she said, smiling at him. "Thanks. And thanks for the great dinner."

And then she did something that surprised even herself.

She kissed him lightly on the lips before starting up the stairs. Sort of a thank-you kiss and a promise of the future kiss.

And it was nice. Really nice, especially the totally surprised look on his face as she turned away.

CHAPTER TWENTY-THREE

October 2014.
Winnemucca, Nevada

FROM THE AIR, as the jet turned to make an approach to the runway, Winnemucca wasn't much more than a wide area of buildings and some casino signs stretching along the old highway beside the freeway between Reno and Salt Lake. The town had been there long before the freeway, and parts of it showed, even from a couple thousand feet in the air.

The town had spread out some with some classic subdivisions and mobile home parks on the road toward Boise. The desert around it was brown and there weren't many patches of green showing at all. Very, very different from the city of Boise, where everything seemed green and covered by lush trees.

Somehow, Annie had arranged for them to have a car waiting. Lott was pretty convinced that Doc had called in a favor from a local casino owner who had sent a minion to rent a car and wait at the airport.

They weren't going to have the car more than an hour if everything went as planned.

He and Julia had talked about the case on the way down, both puzzling about how Stan had managed to start the corporation and keep it secret from all his wives.

Not a word was said about the kiss getting into the plane. Lott had been shocked. He had to admit that. But not upset. He hoped at some point to be kissing-close to Julia and it appeared she hoped the same thing about him.

They had called ahead from Boise to the Winnemucca wife whose actual name was Stephanie Benz. She was a bookkeeper and her husband owned a small restaurant near one end of town that geared mostly to the locals instead of the tourists coming through.

She had agreed to talk with them when she learned it was about Stan

Rocha. She said her husband was at work and it would be better if they could meet her at her office in the back of a service station and repair shop.

Lott had little doubt that the woman would add anything to the picture they were building, but they didn't dare not talk with her and let her know what was happening. And that her daughter had grandparents in Boise that were very rich.

Since Stan's brother had known about the kids and done nothing to help in their support, Lott was hoping that some of the wives just might go after the family. He knew Rogers never would, and he knew Kate, the wife of the governor, didn't need to. But the other three certainly could make Carl pay a little for his cold heartedness over the years in not helping out with his brother's children.

Stephanie turned out to be another thin, blonde, smoker, with a smoker's cough and rough voice. She sort of reminded Lott of Denise Miller in Las Vegas.

Stephanie's office was stacked high with files and a full ashtray the size of a dinner plate dominated one corner of her desk.

"Can we talk outside?" Lott asked, after they were introduced. He had no desire to smell like a dead ashtray all the way to Salt Lake.

"Thank you," Rogers whispered to him as she went past him back out into the fresh, desert air that smelled of hot sagebrush instead of a full ashtray.

Stephanie didn't seem to mind and as soon as they were outside on the parking area in the shade of the building, she lit up another Camel.

"So what did you find out about Stan?" she asked after blowing the smoke up into the warm evening air.

"He was killed in Las Vegas in 1992," Lott said, letting Rogers just take notes.

"Figured something like that happened to him," she said. "He learned I was pregnant and just vanished into thin air. I got the marriage annulled three years later and married Burt. We had two more kids and he treated Stan's kid like his own."

"Nice of him," Rogers said, writing on her notepad while talking.

"So why are you here after all these years?" Stephanie asked.

"We're trying to find out who killed him," Rogers said. "You have any idea who might have wanted him dead?"

Stephanie laughed and then coughed. "Stan was a mooch, but a nice guy. Can't imagine why anyone would want him dead."

"You know what he did for a living?" Lott asked.

"Some sort of traveling salesman I figured," she said. "He never told me. Then she looked puzzled. "When did you say he was killed?"

"May 1992," Lott said, glancing at Rogers who had a puzzled look on her face.

"Weird," Stephanie said, blowing smoke out her nose as she said that. "He must have joined Elvis and his crew."

"What do you mean?" Rogers asked.

"Oh, people around town said they spotted him at times over the next ten years, mostly out along the highway headed south. I just figured they were either imagining things, or Stan didn't want to see me anymore because I had a kid. I was always pissed at him for not stopping and seeing his kid."

She laughed again. "Guess he couldn't do that, being dead and all."

"Yeah, kind of tough," Lott said, shaking his head.

Rogers smiled at him and they asked Stephanie a few more basic questions, then gave her Carl's address in Boise and headed back for the airport.

"You doing okay?" Lott asked Rogers. He was really worried about her and this entire task of telling Stan's other wives what had happened.

"Actually doing fine," Rogers said, smiling at him with that wonderful smile of hers. "And thanks for getting us out of that office."

"I think we lost some years off our lives just stepping in there," Lott said.

"I still think that once we are back at the plane I'm going to change clothes."

Lott nodded to that. They had both brought along overnight bags just in case they were forced to stay in Boise. But now it was possible they could talk to the Salt Lake wife and be home for a late meal at the Bellagio and then a regular night's sleep. They might as well get out of the smoke residue for the next part of the trip.

"So what did you think of that?" Lott asked her as they pulled in near the plane at the small airport runway. They had only been away from the plane for less than thirty minutes.

"I liked that she thought Stan joined Elvis," Rogers said, shaking her head.

Lott laughed, but he suddenly had an idea that none of them had yet considered.

As Rogers was in the back private area of the plane changing clothes, he called Annie.

"Did Rocha's company have any mining operations to the south of Winnemucca?"

"Hang on," she said and he could hear some rustling of papers.

"Yeah, he did," she said. "An old lost silver mine about thirty miles south.

Company bought the land in 1993 and opened up a mine there in 1995. Why?"

"Because the Winnemucca wife said there were sightings of Stan like Elvis years after he was killed. All south of town."

"Now that's weird," Annie said. "You sure that was Rocha's body you found?"

"We were at the time," Lott said. "Thanks, I'll call Andor and get him on it first thing in the morning."

"I'll keep that angle in mind as well."

He had just got Andor to pick up the phone when Rogers came out of the back wearing a clean white blouse and tan slacks. Her hair was brushed back and tied and her face looked like it was freshly washed.

She was amazingly attractive.

"You remember," Lott said to Andor, "how we confirmed the identity of the body?"

Across from him Rogers' eyes got huge.

"Clothes, driver's license on the body was about it if I remember right."

"That's what I remember as well," Lott said.

"You saying that might have been someone else?"

"This case is so strange, I don't think we can rule out anything."

"I agree," Andor said.

Lott looked at Rogers. "You up for taking a look at the scene pictures and autopsy pictures?"

"Not a problem," she said.

"Can you have the pictures waiting for us at the airport in Salt Lake in about thirty minutes?"

"I can't," Andor said, laughing. "But I'll bet your daughter can get them right out of the computer file and fire them to you. Want me to call her?"

"Would you?" Lott asked. "We're going to be in the air shortly and she knows my suspicion."

"Where did this come from?" Andor asked.

"Elvis," Lott said, laughing. "I'll explain later. Just get that information on the way."

"Autopsy results as well," Rogers said loud enough for Andor to hear.

As Lott hung up and put his phone away, he looked at Rogers puzzled.

"He had a tattoo on his left leg. Always wondered what it meant."

"What was it?" Lott asked.

"The letters KM in bright red and blue on his hip where no one would see them unless he was naked."

Lott felt even more puzzled. "KM?"

"Kate McDonald," Rogers said. "His only real wife. I just now put that together."

"Sorry," Lott said.

She waved him off. "Just go get changed so we can get this flight in the air."

He nodded. She was as tough a detective as they came, he had no doubt about that. But he had no idea how she was standing up to all this. He doubted he'd be able to.

CHAPTER TWENTY-FOUR

October 2014.
Salt Lake City International Airport.
Salt Lake, Utah

IT WAS AFTER EIGHT in the evening Salt Lake time, seven Las Vegas time. Lott and Rogers sat on Doc Hill's private jet, comparing notes, trying to figure out exactly where they should go next. April had brought them both glasses of iced tea and it tasted wonderful to Lott.

It had been a long day for both of them, and Lott's feeling was that they should head back to Las Vegas as planned and get some sleep.

But they had decided to take thirty minutes and make sure of that decision before telling the pilots to go.

Plus, they were waiting for the files with the pictures from the autopsy and the warehouse to come in to make sure they were chasing the right murder.

Ruby Rocha, Stan's Salt Lake wife, turned out to be deep in her faith when she married Stan for life and into the next life and forever, as her church believed. When he left, she had just waited for him to return.

That simple.

She had waited for twenty-two years.

She had done nothing else with her life, it seemed.

Tragic, very tragic as far as Lott was concerned. And he caught himself thinking that and wondering a little if he hadn't been doing the same thing with how he felt about Connie. More than likely, he had.

Maybe it really was time, as Annie kept telling him, to move on. He could wait until the day he died and Connie would never return. He had to finally admit that. He didn't want to, but he had to.

That fact was really hard to see when inside the feelings. Not so hard to see when looking at Ruby Rocha lying in a huge Hospice Care bed. She now weighed almost four hundred pounds and was being chewed up by all the problems associated with not taking care of herself medically at that weight. Plus she had a couple forms of cancer that had gone untreated.

They found her in an assisted living home and the nurse on duty had warned them to not upset her. She had very little time left to live. Maybe less than a month.

So they had decided to just not talk with her. There seemed to be no point. Stan Rocha, by marrying her, had killed Ruby just as effectively as putting a bullet in her brain.

So they had headed back to the airport, riding in silence in the cab they had decided to take to see Ruby. It seemed neither of them wanted to talk about her. Lott knew he sure didn't.

There just wasn't much to talk about.

By the time they got back in the plane, the files had not yet arrived from Annie with Stan's autopsy pictures. So they sat across from each other in big leather chairs, their notebooks in hand, iced teas beside them, going back over everything from the day.

Lott had no idea how much this jet cost Doc, but Lott sure liked the comfort of it.

They had just finished when the pilot, a smiling young man by the name of Lawrence, wearing dark slacks and a white dress shirt with his sleeves rolled up, came back into the cabin and said, "Detectives, the information you are waiting for from Annie is coming through now."

He pointed to a desk in the rear of the main cabin, tucked off to the right side. He went to it and pushed a couple of buttons and a monitor rose from the desk and a keyboard swung out.

Lott just shook his head. Of course a private plane like this would have a desk to work at, just as it had a bedroom in the back to sleep in.

Lawrence got the computer up and running for them with a couple more buttons and then said, "Let me know when you are ready to go. And to where."

"Thanks," Lott said. "Really appreciate it."

The pilot nodded. "Glad to help out." He then headed back toward the front as Julia sat down at the screen and pulled up the images.

Lott stood over her right shoulder so he could see the screen as well. He hoped this was a good idea. He knew Rogers was a good detective and had seen her share of death scenes, but seeing her own husband the way they had found him wasn't going to be easy.

The first one was of the warehouse scene and it made Julia sit back slightly.

It actually surprised Lott a little as well. He hadn't looked at those pictures for a long time. There was a bloated man's body in pants and a ripped-open shirt lying face-up on the floor, dead eyes staring at the ceiling.

The image brought back the incredible memories of that case for Lott, mostly attached to the smell of that body being in a hot warehouse and on the floor for seven days before being found.

It was not a smell he ever wanted to remember. No human death smell ever was. It was the kind of cloying, thick smell that ate at you and got into every pore of your skin and clothes.

Connie hadn't let him anywhere near the insides of the house when he got home that day. She had forced him to take his clothes off in the garage and then run for the shower while she opened windows.

It had taken a week for the smell to be completely out of his car after the short ride home. He had finally had to take the car in and have it detailed out to get rid of the last of it.

And Connie did something with his clothes that involved a long stick and a big black garbage bag.

The body in the image was even more bloated than Lott remembered it being. Lott now understood why they had just assumed the wallet with the victim was the right one. They had tested the fingerprints as well, but Stan Rocha's prints had not been in the system.

"Can't tell," Julia said, shaking her head as she clicked through the five or six angles of photos of the body. "Looks like him in general. Same basic size and shape."

Then she brought up the first autopsy photo and gasped.

It was of the same bloated body, only now naked, the clothes cut away, the body lying on the morgue table.

"You all right?" he asked, putting his hand gently on her shoulder. He liked the feel of her strong muscles under his touch and he let his hand rest there only a moment before pulling it away.

"I am," she said. "But your hunch was right. That's not Stan Rocha."

Now it was Lott's turn to jerk. He had suggested that because of the Winnemucca wife's comment. He really didn't expect to be right.

"How can you be so sure?" he asked, staring at the bloated body on the table.

"He's missing the KM tattoo on his side," she said, pointing.

Lott nodded.

She clicked to the image of the other hip.

Nothing there either.

"And Stan was circumcised," Rogers said, pointing at the body's private parts.

It was very clear to Lott this man had not been circumcised in any fashion.

"I'll be go to hell," Lott said, standing and stepping back as Rogers quickly moved through the rest of the photos, then clicked off the computer and turned to him.

"So who the hell is our murder victim?" Lott asked, feeling more stunned than he wanted to admit.

"And where did Stan disappear to?" Rogers asked.

"And did he kill that man to stage his own disappearance?" Lott asked.

They both remained in silence for a moment before Lott finally broke it. "I think we need to head back to Vegas."

Julia nodded. "I agree. Stan is wrapped up in this completely, since his identity was on the body. He staged this I'm betting anything. But we need to go back and start over, look at everything again."

"Do you really think that the man you knew could execute someone to stage his own death?" Lott asked.

"Honestly," Rogers said, "I can't imagine Stan hurting a fly. But I can imagine him staging all this. He hid a lot from me, and his other wives, and his family. This kind of deception is right up his alley."

With that, Lott nodded and turned to the front of the plane to tell the pilots to take them home.

After that he turned back to see Julia watching him. He smiled at her. "Looks like Elvis hasn't left the building just yet."

She actually laughed.

He sat down and buckled in across from her and for the entire short flight to Las Vegas, all he could think about was how he mis-identified the victim in his very first case as a detective.

PART THREE

CHAPTER TWENTY-FIVE

October 2014.
Las Vegas International Airport.
Las Vegas, Nevada

JULIA WAS GLAD that Lott hadn't wanted to talk much on the trip back to Vegas. The flight had only taken less than forty minutes and the entire time she just kept going over and over what they had discovered.

The real stunner was that Stan might still be alive. How he had remained hidden for twenty-two years was beyond her, but if he was alive, he had done just that.

She had spent over two decades knowing he was dead. And Jane had always thought her father murdered. How was she going to react to all this?

Julia decided that she would wait until they had all this solved before even thinking of talking with Jane.

Also, there was something about that body in the warehouse that seemed familiar. And it wasn't because it had a general similarity to Stan. For some reason that body and how it had been shot rang bells for her. She just couldn't, for the life of her, remember from what.

After they landed and the jet was moving toward the private hangar areas, she looked at Lott. "We got to tell Andor and Annie about this."

Lott nodded. "Thinking the same thing. Got any ideas after that?"

She shook her head. "That body looks vaguely familiar somehow, but darned if I can place it."

"It does?" Lott asked, looking puzzled. "And not because it looks like Stan?

She shook her head. "There's something else. The bullet pattern for one. Was his shirt closed or open when he was shot?"

Lott frowned. "Open. No holes in the shirt at all, and the bullets didn't go through, so no holes in the back either."

'So the body might have been dressed in Stan's clothes after it was shot."

"Likely," Lott said. "I remember that we were very frustrated because the body had been cleaned before it was dumped. No trace evidence at all except for the residue that Annie traced in her investigation."

"Weird, just damn weird," Annie said, shaking her head. There wasn't a

damn thing about this case that had been straightforward.

"We'll run the prints," Lott said. "I'll have Andor do that quickly. It's only a bit after eight here."

"Feels a lot later than that," she said. "Long day."

"A productive one, though," Lott said. "You hungry?"

"I will be after a shower and a change of clothes," she said, smiling at him.

"Me too," Lott said, nodding as the plane eased to a stop. "I'll call Annie, tell her what we discovered, and see if she can meet us at the Café Bellagio a little after nine."

"I'll call Andor," she said. "I'll get him on the fingerprints and have him meet us as well."

"We have a plan," Lott said, smiling.

Julia felt glad for at least that much.

But deep down inside, she was feeling shocked that Stan might still be alive. And that if he was alive, he had let her raise Jane alone and never helped in the slightest.

And that just pissed her off.

CHAPTER TWENTY-SIX

October 2014.
Café Bellagio.
Las Vegas, Nevada

JULIA FELT A LOT BETTER once she had gotten home, taken a quick shower, and gotten into some fresh clothes. She needed to be comfortable tonight, so she went with a tan blouse, dark slacks, and comfortable low-heeled shoes. She pulled her hair back off her face and left it down long.

It was still a warm evening outside, but she grabbed a light jacket just in case she would need it later, and then headed for her car.

After just this one day, it was amazing how much more she knew about her former husband. Far more than she ever imagined knowing. Certainly a lot more than she knew about him when they were married.

There was a large part of her that was angry at herself. How could she not know all this back when they were together. Stan had been a master of hiding things, and she had been a master of denial. In a marriage, it always took two.

It was still going to take some time for her to forgive herself for not knowing at least some of this.

One thing for certain, as the day had gone on, she had gotten angrier and angrier at Stan. And now that she had a hunch he staged his own death, her anger was boiling. Especially after seeing what he had done to Ruby in Salt Lake. She had played the part of the dutiful wife, waiting for the missing husband to return.

And if he was alive, he had just let her.

And now that devotion was going to kill Rub in a very ugly fashion.

Maybe, just maybe, Julia knew she might have been doing the same thing, avoiding relationships, never remarrying. And she had at least thought Stan was dead.

Why hadn't she moved on as well?

That was going to be a topic she and a counselor were going to work out as soon as they had some more answers as to what really happened to Stan.

By the time she made it to the Café Bellagio, Lott was already sitting with his daughter at a table tucked off to one side.

Annie got up, smiling and hugged Julia.

"Thank Doc for the use of his plane," Julia said as they sat down. "It was a joy to be in and allowed a lot of this to happen today."

"That it did," Lott said, nodding.

"Doc said he was just glad he could help," Annie said. "He'll join us as soon as he's done with the tournament."

Julia nodded. The daily tournaments at the Bellagio often attracted some of the top players in the world. She had stood on the rail and watched many hours of those tournaments. At some point, she hoped to have enough courage and money to sit down in one. But for the moment, when she got back to playing poker, she would keep herself satisfied playing with the tourists in some of the other rooms with buy-ins under a hundred bucks instead of north of a thousand.

"I'm dying to hear what you two found today," Annie said. "From the tidbits Dad has been giving me along the way, it was amazing amounts."

Lott smiled at his daughter. "Soon as Andor gets here, we'll lay it all out."

"He's on his way," Julia said, pointing in the direction of Andor coming in the door.

As he came up to the table, he dropped a manilla file folder in front of Julia.

He nodded to everyone and then sat down.

After the day, Julia was almost afraid to pick up the folder and see what was in it.

"Rogers, you said you thought the body looked familiar," Andor said, smiling at her. "More than just a passing resemblance to your ex-husband."

"I did," Julia said. "Can't seem to get a grasp on from where though."

Andor pointed at the file. "You two just solved one of Reno's most famous missing body cases."

Suddenly she knew exactly where she recognized the body.

"The fingerprints match the Stanton Case?" she asked, staring at Andor. Was that even possible?

Andor grinned. "Spot on the money."

"I'll be go to hell," she said, opening the file to stare at naked pictures of Benny Stanton. The same guy, the same bullet patterns, only he was not bloated at all. The photo she had in front of her was taken just before an autopsy was supposed to have taken place on the body.

And just before the body vanished without a trace from the MEs basement office.

The guy who had executed Benny Stanton had already confessed, and they had the pictures and crime scene photos, so the body vanishing had just been an annoyance and a headline grabber in the papers. She remembered it well as a city cop, not yet a detective. It was the topic of a lot of conversations for months after it happened.

She couldn't remember the name of the family member who had shot Benny, but the last Julia had heard, he had died in prison a few years back. That body going missing had caused a real stir in Reno.

No one seemed to have a motive for taking it, and there were no suspects at all. It just wasn't often a body was stolen like that.

From that point forward, for years, it had always been sort of a standard joke among detectives to try to not pull "a Stanton" when they were dealing with a body.

"Someone want to fill all of us in?" Annie asked.

She turned the folder around so Lott and his daughter could see them. "We don't have a murder."

Lott looked at her, clearly puzzled.

"That's Benny Stanton," Julia said, feeling amazingly light and happy at the moment. "He was shot and killed by a family member in a fight over a car twenty-two years ago. The family member confessed and died in prison. Benny's body was stolen from the ME's office right before the autopsy was to be performed. No trace, no motive, nothing."

"So you're telling us that Stan Rocha wasn't killed back then?" Annie asked, looking up at her.

"That's right," Julia said. "My gut tells me that Stan stole Benny's body, dressed it in his clothes, left his wallet with it, and then put it in a warehouse where eventually someone would find it."

"And he would be declared dead," Lott said.

"Exactly," Julia said.

"And what happened to Stan?" Andor asked. "With five wives and five kids, I can sort of see why he would want to vanish. But where'd he go?"

Julie looked over at Annie, who was smiling at that question. Julia had a hunch Annie knew the answer, but she wanted to let Annie confirm it.

"He just kept running his company," Annie said. "He never went anywhere. A man by the name of David Buel, ran the companies. It wasn't until we went back into the history of the Lost Breyfogle Mine legend that we ran across the name of David Buel. Breyfogle worked for a David Buel back in the 1870s."

"You're kidding me?" Andor asked.

"Nope," Annie said.

Julia nodded. "The minute I realized he wasn't killed, I knew he had to have kept working, chasing his lost mines. Tell me, did that company of his have any money?"

"Not a penny," Annie said, taking a file from the floor beside her chair and sliding it over to Julia. "Every dollar it earned it sank back into buying more property and land and mining rights. Land rich, cash very poor. In fact, it had no employees, even though we thought it did at first. That's why it was so hard to track. Buel was the only name associated with the company at all."

"So the son-of-a-bitch really was broke when we were together," Julia said, nodding. "Did he make any money on the sale?"

"From what my people can find," Annie said, "he made a lot. But it was structured to pay out over a ten-year period, the last year being next year."

Julia looked at Lott, then at Andor, who was looking as puzzled as she felt. So she just went ahead and asked, even though she was very, very afraid of the answer.

"So, you are telling me you know where this David Buel is?"

Annie smiled and nodded. "He lives about a mile from here."

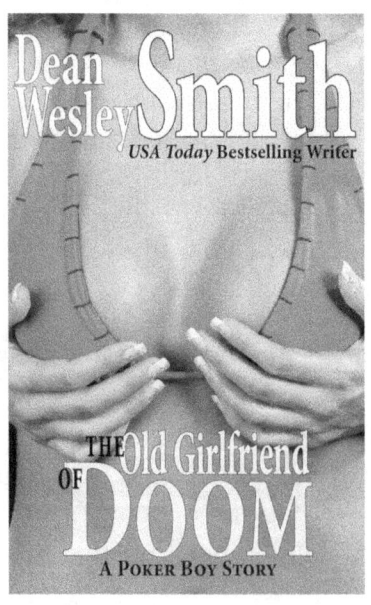

Julia felt stunned, more so than with any other bit of news that kept slamming at her in this case.

Stan was alive and if Annie was right, living just a mile from where they were sitting.

"Let's go arrest that bastard," Andor said, pushing his chair back.

"On what charge, Detective?" Annie asked. "You have no murder, you have adult children, he stole only a body twenty-two years ago, and he married five times without a divorce. I'm pretty sure the statute of limitations has passed on the theft. Not so sure about the bigamy charges. We'd have to talk with a prosecutor to figure out if being declared dead changes that."

Suddenly the four former detectives sitting around the table had nothing to say.

And all Julia could do was take slow, deep breaths, and try to make some sense out of all of this.

An impossible task.

CHAPTER TWENTY-SEVEN

October 2014.
Pleasant Hills.
Las Vegas, Nevada

LOTT SAT ALONE at his kitchen table, working at a bowl of shredded wheat covered in milk, trying to get enough energy to just go to bed. In one day they had been in three states and discovered more about Stan Rocha and his life from twenty years ago than Lott ever wanted to know about another person.

A bunch of what they discovered wasn't pretty, right down to the point where the guy had stolen a body in Reno and faked his own death.

And by doing so left five wives and five children without a husband or a father.

He was some kind of creep, of that there was no doubt. A selfish, pathetic one as far as Lott was concerned.

One thing good had come of the day. The Cold Poker Gang had cleared another cold case, one that Lott had given them no chance to clear when they started. That felt good.

The poker game this week was going to be fun.

And the Chief of Police was happy about it when Andor called him from the Bellagio.

Lott and Andor and Julia and Annie, along with the Chief of Police, had an appointment tomorrow morning at eleven to talk with the prosecuting attorney, Hanson Evans, about the possible charges against Rocha. Lott had a gut feeling there just wasn't going to be much Evans was going to be able to do.

Bigamy was a felony, but it was rarely prosecuted and now that Rocha was found alive, all the wives would have to do was file for an annulment or a divorce under Nevada law and the bigamy charges would be moot. And four of the wives hadn't even actually been legally married to Rocha, since he had first married Kate McDonald a few years earlier.

Plus the statute of limitations had passed on the body theft.

But there were still a few things that really nagged Lott about all this. And his tired mind just wouldn't let the worry go.

Lott had little doubt that Stan Rocha was devious enough to fake his own death. And enough of an ass to walk away from five wives and his kids. But he wouldn't have been able to do the actual theft

4

alone. He had to have help, real money help, to do such a thing, and Rocha just didn't have the funds to do that.

And who could he have trusted to do such a thing and stay quiet for twenty-two years?

So who helped him? And why?

Suddenly the image of Kate McDonald being shocked about Stan's corporation flared into his memory. The governor's wife was actually very upset about that, more so than she should have been after all the years. She said she knew that Stan had been killed, so why be shocked at the corporation?

Was it possible that to clear out Stan from her life, maybe so she could get on with an affair with the future governor, Kate and the future governor had helped Stan fake his own death?

Having Stan suddenly die made sense for the future governor's wife. It solved the problem of her husband, the bigamist. It solved the problem of her moving on with her two kids, and having a regular relationship with someone her parents approved of.

And from the sounds of it, it also allowed Stan to just keep on with his search for lost treasures.

Lott got up and started pacing. Connie had hated it when he paced in the kitchen late at night, worrying about a case. But it helped him think.

He glanced at the clock over the stove. It was only a little before eleven in the evening. It felt more like three in the morning.

Annie would still be awake. More than likely this case was still bothering her as well.

A few seconds later Annie answered her cell phone. Lott could hear the sounds of a poker room in the background. More than likely she had joined a cash game at the Bellagio while waiting for Doc to get finished in the tournament.

"Sorry to bother you," he said.

She laughed. "Can't let this one go yet, huh Dad?"

"Exactly," he said. "Did your people do research into the governor and Stan's first wife?"

"They sure did," Annie said. "Hang on, let me get my bag from the desk here where I have all the files and then find a quieter place to talk."

He held on, still pacing the kitchen, as she asked for her bag, then ducked off to an area of the poker room with empty tables.

"Got it all right here," she said after a moment.

"When were Kate and the governor married?"

"Almost one year after Stan's fake death," she said. "You think she had a hand in helping him take the body?"

"I'm betting that she and the future governor both did," Lott said. "Only thing that makes sense. But I'm also betting, since she knew that Stan was still alive, she would have filed for divorce from Stan quietly at some point, just to get it on the record in case he suddenly came back to life or the actual identity of the body was discovered. Did you look for a divorce by Kate from Stan?"

"Shit," Annie said. "Of course she would have done exactly that. I'll get someone searching both Idaho and Nevada and we'll have the information before tomorrow morning."

Lott laughed. "We let that become public, we cause Kate and the governor no amount of political trouble."

"If they actually did help Stan fake his death," Annie said. "They deserve every problem that can be shoveled at them."

"Oh, I like your attitude, dear daughter," Lott said.

"So," Annie said, "is Julia there with you right now?"

"No, why?" Lott asked.

"Bummer," Annie said. "See you tomorrow morning."

Lott stopped pacing and hung up, staring at the phone for a moment. Sometimes his daughter just had a way of making herself very clear without actually saying anything on topic.

He took a deep breath and quickly dialed Rogers' number before he got cold feet.

She answered with a quick "Hi."

"Just wanted to say that it was great working and traveling and being with you today."

"Thank you," she said. "I wouldn't have managed to get through it all without you there."

"So get some sleep and I'll see you in the morning," Lott said.

"Thanks, I will," Julia said. "And thanks for the call. It made me smile."

"Night," he said.

"Night," she said in return.

And then he hung up.

He sat back down at the kitchen table to finish his now soggy shredded wheat.

That had felt right.

And she wasn't the only one smiling.

CHAPTER TWENTY-EIGHT

October 2014.
Café Bellagio
Las Vegas, Nevada

LOTT WAS THE ONLY ONE in the Café Bellagio when Julia got there. Somehow he had again beaten her there after their meeting with the Prosecuting Attorney this morning. Andor should be right behind her somewhere. They all had their own cars.

She walked up to Lott, who smiled up at her from a table tucked against some plants to the right of the main door.

She went around to his side of the table and kissed him on the cheek, then sat down next to him.

She smiled at his shocked, but pleased look.

"That was for being such a nice guy and that wonderful phone call last night. I needed someone right at that moment to tell me they cared."

"I very much care," he said, looking her right in the eyes with those fantastic, dark eyes of his. She couldn't imagine ever growing tired of looking into those eyes.

"I know," she said, keeping her gaze locked with his. "And I care as well. And once we get through this mess, I'd love to find out where this feeling between us might lead."

"Now that's a great plan, detective," he said, smiling.

Right at that moment all she wanted to do was lean over and kiss him completely. But out of the corner of her eye she could see Andor striding toward the table.

"Well, that meeting was a bust," Andor said as he grabbed a menu and dropped into a chair across from them. "We can't even arrest that bastard."

"We knew that going in," Lott said. "But we can cause a lot more grief than simply arresting him."

"Oh, oh, folks, Lott has that devious look on his face."

"I like it," Julia said, winking at him.

He kept smiling but blushed a little, which she found even more charming.

"Oh trust me," Andor said, "that look has gotten us into more trouble over the years than I want to think about."

"Not thinking of doing anything rash," Lott said. "Just this."

He pointed to where Annie was coming toward them with a young guy who looked to be in his late twenties. The guy had long brown hair, a short-sleeved blue dress shirt tucked into jeans, and he carried a backpack slung over one shoulder.

He was looking around as if he had never been in the place before.

Julia had no idea what Lott and Annie were up to, but after the surprise this morning about Kate McDonald getting a divorce from Stan after she knew he was supposedly dead, Julia had a hunch this punishment for Stan and Kate and the governor of Idaho was going to be pretty nasty.

And she liked that.

Since there wasn't a thing the prosecuting attorney could do that would be worth the state's time and money, revenge was just about the only card left to deal Stan and Kate and the governor for what they did to so many people.

Annie and her guest stopped at the table and Annie introduced the three of them, using the word detective in front of each of their names. Then she turned to the young man with her.

"Detectives, I'd like you to meet Robert Austin, the political reporter for the *Idaho Statesman* newspaper and a freelance journalist for the *Associated Press.*"

Julia was stunned. And pleased beyond words.

Annie got herself and Robert seated, then said, "Doc sent his plane this morning to bring Robert here. I gave him all the information I had to read on the way down. Now it's up to you three to explain how all this came about and what you know.

"Over lunch, right?" Andor asked as a waitress approached.

"Over lunch," Annie said, laughing.

Julia reached over and touched Lott's arm. "Was this your idea?" she whispered.

"It was if you like it," he said. "Otherwise I'm blaming my daughter."

"I like it a lot," Julia said, laughing. "Far better than putting the bunch of them in jail."

And now, for the first time since she learned Stan was alive, she was looking forward to seeing his face. And the shock on it when he discovered that he and Kate and the governor's scheme was blown.

CHAPTER TWENTY-NINE

October 2014.
Café Bellagio
Las Vegas, Nevada

THEY SPENT AN HOUR briefing the reporter on the story and all the poor kid did was get more and more excited. For a moment, Lott thought he just might start drooling.

"This story has everything," Austin said after they had filled him in on all the sordid details. "Politics, scandal with a sitting governor, bigamy, lost treasures, stolen bodies, and corporation underhandedness. This will hit the national nightly news, it's so strange."

"Perfect," Julia said.

"Can't thank you enough for calling me in," Austin said. "And that fantastic plane ride."

Coming Next Issue in Smith's Monthly
The first ever Poker Boy novel
and the origin of Poker Boy's team.

"Our pleasure," Annie said. "Just make sure every fact you publish is backed up, so this guy and the governor can't snake their way out of this."

"Oh, trust me," he said. "Both the AP and the Statesman check everything I do carefully. And I make sure it's accurate before I give it to them."

The kid sounded perfect to Lott. This case was going to make his career, of that there was no doubt. And from the looks of it, he already had a pretty good career.

"Have you got a lawyer looking into how much Rocha is going to owe each of his remaining four wives from his sale of the business?" Austin asked. "I'm pretty sure they should have gotten some of it under the laws of most states."

Lott sort of jerked and Julia sat beside him looking stunned. The question felt like it had almost quieted down the entire casino.

Lott couldn't believe he hadn't thought of that at all, and Julia suddenly seemed to lose focus in her eyes on just thinking about the idea.

"Hadn't even thought of that, huh?" Austin said, smiling, looking around at the stunned group of detectives. "And I am pretty sure that the IRS and Nevada State Tax Commission need to be informed on all this as well, since I'm betting there was a lot of hidden income over the years, fraudulently withheld from taxes."

"Oh, shit," Andor said. "This is getting better by the minute. Kid, I like you."

"Thanks, Detective," the kid said, smiling. "I'm sure I'll think of a few more nasty grenades to toss at this jerk before it's all over."

"Just keep lobbing, kid," Andor said, laughing. "Keep lobbing."

"And there's a lot of money there," Annie said. "All the property, water rights, mineral rights and such added up to millions and millions in the sale. I'll get our financial people on it, see what stones they can turn over."

"Thanks," Lott said.

"Yes, thanks," Julia said. And then she turned to Austin. "I'll give you any interview you want as long as you leave my daughter out of all this."

"Deal," Austin said. "I can't see bringing in the kids on this at all. So thank you, Detective."

At that point Andor picked up his cell phone and called the department. All of them watched as he nodded, then said, "We're on our way."

"What was that?" Annie asked.

Andor smiled. "The Chief of Police isn't happy we can't arrest this guy either, so he offered to put a car watching the house until we got there. Rocha is still inside. So what say we go jerk this guy's chain a little?"

Lott liked that idea a lot.

And beside him, Julia nodded and smiled. Then she said simply, "It will be my pleasure."

CHAPTER THIRTY

October 2014.
Near the University of Nevada Campus
Las Vegas, Nevada

JULIA SAT BESIDE LOTT in his Cadillac SUV and stared at the home tucked back under some trees in an older subdivision. Stan had ended up living a lot nicer than she and Jane had ever lived. And that made her angry as well.

Andor pulled in behind Lott and behind him Annie and the reporter arrived. Their plan was simple. Andor and Lott would go up to the door and introduce themselves. She would stay off to one side until the moment was right to step forward.

A television crew would be filming the entire thing from a hidden van across the street and a freelance photographer had joined Austin and would be taking pictures, for a time without Rocha even knowing about it.

Also, both Lott and Andor were wired for sound, so everyone in all the cars could hear the conversation.

"You ready for this?" Lott glanced over at her, clearly worried.

"If I hadn't discovered all the really shitty things this guy did to a lot of people, I wouldn't be. Now I'm just angry and want to bring him to justice, even if that justice is to take all his money and turn him over to the IRS."

"So that means you're ready?" Lott asked, smiling.

"I'm twenty-two years of ready," she said, smiling back at him.

With that they both stepped out into the warm afternoon air. It wasn't hot and a soft breeze blew the leaves in the trees.

"Nice place," Andor said, joining the two of them as they headed across the street.

"Better than any of the four wives he cheated got to live in," she said.

"Just don't shoot the bastard, Detective," Andor said. "Even though I doubt a jury in the world would convict you."

Julia laughed. "Oh trust me, we're not letting him off that easily."

The house was a two-story Tudor-style building with high-pitched roof and a front door that was up four steps off the sidewalk. The lawn was well-cared-for and very green, considering how hot the summer had been.

Julia stepped off to one side so when Rocha opened the door, he wouldn't see her.

Lott and Andor went up to the door and Lott turned to the cars across the street and signaled they should start.

Then Andor banged on the door.

A moment later Julia heard the door open and a man say, "Yes?"

"Detectives Lott and Williams," Andor said. "Are you David Buel?"

"I am," the man said, and that time the memory of Stan's voice came back strong.

"AKA Stan Rocha?" Lott said.

"Excuse me?" the man asked.

Julia stepped away from the side of the building and walked up the four steps until she was face-to-face with her husband. He had aged and his skin had weathered in twenty-two years. He now wore a moustache and beard. His hairline had receded and his hair had gone to salt and pepper. He had on brown slacks and a brown dress shirt and looked like any fifty-some-year-old executive home on a warm afternoon.

He looked at her puzzled for a moment until she said, "Hi, Stan. Nice seeing you so healthy after all these years of being dead."

He hesitated, his eyes growing wide as he recognized her. "Julia?"

"Detective Rogers to you," she said, her voice as cold as she could make it. "When you and your first wife and her boyfriend hatched the scheme to help you escape from your children and your mistakes, you lost all right to call me anything but Detective."

"So," Andor said, his voice low and mean, "We need you to step out of the house, sir, so we can talk with you."

Andor had his hand on his gun when he made that request, and Julia saw Stan swallow hard and nod.

Julia stepped down onto the sidewalk and Lott followed her.

Andor flanked Stan and they moved so that Stan was facing the television van and cameras.

"First off, Mr. Rocha, why did you fake your own death?" Andor asked.

Stan looked slightly panicked. "Kate wanted out and she and McDonald were afraid that if I got caught with so many wives, it would look poorly on them."

"So you stole a body from Reno?" Lott said as Julia stood there, staring at her husband.

He kept glancing at her and then his eyes would dart away.

"No, I didn't take the body. Kate and McDonald did that in his van. It made me sick to have to help them dress the body in my clothes when they got down here."

Julia just shook her head at the excuse of a man she had married. The poor bastard had just cost the governor of Idaho his job.

"And when exactly did you find the lost Breyfogle Mine? And start the Breyfogle Corporation?" Lott asked, setting Stan up to lose all his money.

"Early 1989," Stan said, actually acting proud for a moment.

"And you didn't keep track of your other four wives?" Andor said. "Or any of your five kids?"

Stan shook his head and actually hung his head a little. "Kate said I didn't dare, being dead and all." Then he looked up, surprised. "Five?"

Julia didn't give him the courtesy of telling him about Jane. He didn't deserve to know. It would be up to Jane later on to decide if she wanted her father to know about her.

"So you left them for single mothers to raise?" Lott asked. "Most of your wives, you know, never heard about your fake death. They just thought you walked out on them."

"Oh," Stan said, his face going whiter than it had been before. "That's not what I wanted."

"And you left your mother and father wondering when you would come home," Andor said. "They didn't hear about your little scheme either."

Stan just shook his head, staring at the ground in front of him.

"Aren't you even a little bit sorry?" Julia asked, her voice far, far colder than she intended it to be.

"Every day," Stan said. "Four years after we staged my death, I told Kate I couldn't stand it anymore and wanted to see my children. But she said they would kill me if I ever opened my mouth or showed my face.

At that, Andor coughed, turning away slightly, trying to cover a laugh.

All Julia could do was shake her head.

"So did you find other lost treasures?" Lott asked.

Stan nodded, his face brightening again. "I did. And I'm still looking for the Lost Dutchman Mine."

"Well, I doubt you are going to be doing much of that from where you are going," Andor said.

Stan just looked puzzled.

Julia stared at the man she had let trick her for years. What had she ever seen in such a worthless piece of human trash?

Julia turned her back on her husband and waved for the reporter and camera crew in the van to come on over.

Stan's eyes got huge as he saw them come out of the van and another car.

"We expect you to answer every question they have for you honestly," Andor said, his hand back on his gun. He had moved between Stan and the door of his home. "I'll be right here making sure."

Lott and Julia started to walk away together when Stan called out to her. "Julia?"

She spun and walked back to him, getting right up into his face. "My name is Detective Rogers to you, asshole," she said, almost spitting at him. "And if you don't answer every question these reporters have for you completely and honestly, you will see me and my gun and my handcuffs once again and it won't be pleasant. Do you understand?"

Stan swallowed and then nodded.

"Do we have an agreement?" she demanded, inches from his face.

"Yes," he said softly.

"Yes what?" she shouted back at him.

"Yes, Detective," he said.

"That's better. Now make sure you answer everything truthfully. Trust me, you never want to see me again."

He nodded and she spun and strode back toward Lott.

Then she winked at him and she could tell that he barely got turned away from

Stan before breaking into a smile and choking down the laughter.

Damned if that hadn't felt good. For the first time in a lot of years she felt free.

CHAPTER THIRTY-ONE

October 2014.
Near the University of Nevada Campus
Las Vegas, Nevada

THEY CLIMBED back in the car and Julia looked over at the handsome man sitting beside her.

"Thank you," she said, smiling at him. She really had fallen for this man and she knew he had fallen for her. They both had a distance to go to get healthy and learn about each other, but she knew that would be part of the fun.

"I think that was all my pleasure," Lott said, giving her that grin she loved so much. "After all these years, it's great to put that case away for good."

"And that husband as well," she said.

Lott laughed at that and then asked, "So where next? Detective?"

She looked into his eyes and smiled. "I've got a daughter who lives about five blocks from here. I think it's about time I tell her about her father, don't you?"

"Before she sees it on the news," Lott said, indicating the camera and reporter on the front lawn across the street.

"Yeah, better from me than that way. I'll give you the directions."

He glanced at her, a line of worry crossing his face. "You want me along?"

"Damn right I do," Julia said. "You two better get used to each other, since I plan on hanging around you for some time to come."

"I like the sounds of that," he said, breaking back into a wide smile and pulling the car away from the curb.

She reached over and rested her hand gently on his leg and said simply, "So do I, Detective. So do I."

~

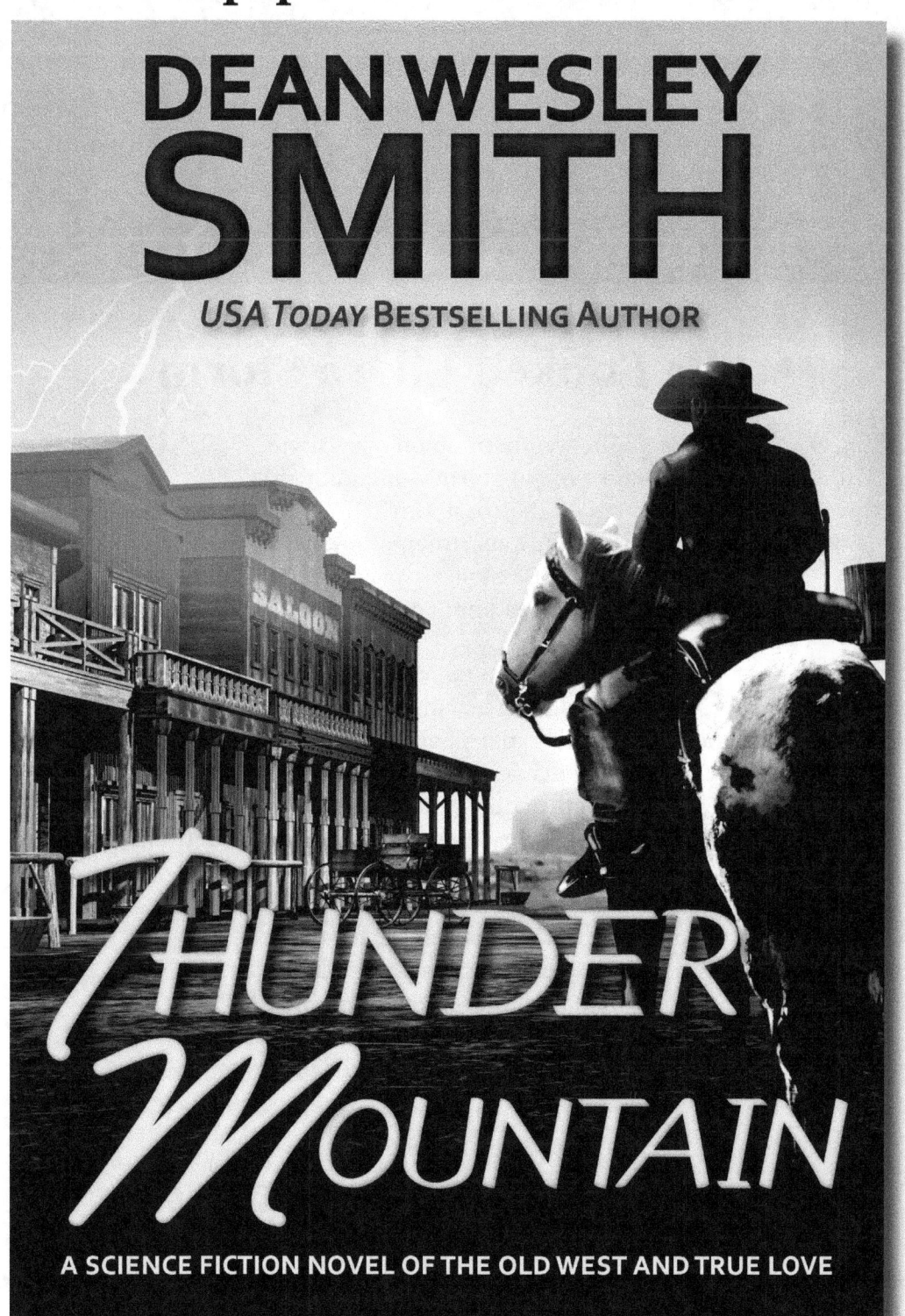

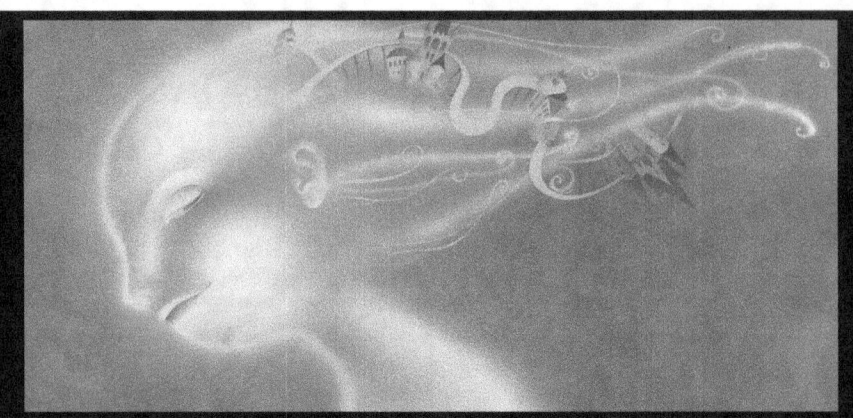

Poems by DEAN WESLEY SMITH

She Looked Like a Storm

The weatherman on television
said a major storm was coming in.
It was still a ways off the coast, threatening on the horizon.
She came into my apartment, took her coat off,
leaving jeans, a white blouse and assorted underwear
still on, threatening on the horizon.

The weatherman on television said the storm
would arrive within the hour
and showed cool radar images of how close it was.
We had drinks, dinner, more drinks,
then we sat on the couch, the lights low, and kissed.
I kept checking how close I was to getting to the buttons.

The weatherman said the storm was on top of the city,
that it was snowing in even the lower elevations,
the streets getting slippery and dangerous.
She had her blouse, jeans, and bra off.
Inside her lace panties a storm approached,
my future getting slippery and dangerous.

www.ingramcontent.com/pod-product-compliance
Lightning Source LLC
Chambersburg PA
CBHW081151170626
46813CB00009B/3158